WINTERING

ALSO BY KRISSY KNEEN

Affection: a memoir of love, sex and intimacy
Triptych
Steeplechase
The Adventures of Holly White and the Incredible Sex Machine
An Uncertain Grace

Krissy Kneen is a Brisbane writer. Her last novel, *An Uncertain Grace*, was shortlisted for the 2018 Stella Prize. In 2014 she won the Thomas Shapcott Poetry Prize for *Eating My Grandmother*.
krissykneen.com
@krissykneen

WINTERING
KRISSY KNEEN

t

TEXT PUBLISHING MELBOURNE AUSTRALIA

textpublishing.com.au

The Text Publishing Company
Swann House
22 William Street
Melbourne Victoria 3000
Australia

Copyright © Krissy Kneen, 2018

The moral right of Krissy Kneen to be identified as the author of this work has been asserted.

All rights reserved. Without limiting the rights under copyright above, no part of this publication shall be reproduced, stored in or introduced into a retrieval system, or transmitted in any form or by any means (electronic, mechanical, photocopying, recording or otherwise), without the prior permission of both the copyright owner and the publisher of this book.

Published by The Text Publishing Company, 2018

Book design by Imogen Stubbs
Cover photograph by Cosma Andrei/Stocksy
Typeset in Bembo 12.5/17.5 by J&M Typesetting

Printed and bound in Australia by Griffin Press, an accredited ISO/NZS 14001:2004 Environmental Management System printer

ISBN: 9781925603880 (paperback)
ISBN: 9781925626858 (ebook)

A catalogue record for this book is available from the National Library of Australia

This book is printed on paper certified against the Forest Stewardship Council® Standards. Griffin Press holds FSC chain-of-custody certification SGS-COC-005088. FSC promotes environmentally responsible, socially beneficial and economically viable management of the world's forests.

*For my father, Barry Elphick,
my heart in the deep south*

Jessica liked the torchlight. She liked the way her footsteps seemed to echo louder in the surrounding dark, the way the torch bounced off the stalactites, the mineral glitter. This was how a show cave should be: quiet, black, infused with a wintery chill. She could taste the morning and the cave's acidity in the air. She bent to lift a scrap of paper off the floor, stashed it in the plastic bag. It already contained a crazy assortment of human detritus: a tissue, a receipt; a dropped cotton bud, of all things.

She was thinking of the unseen waste that would have entered the fragile ecosystem of the cave with this litter. Skin cells, hair, mud dragged in from God knows where and all the micro-organisms that would be squelching through it. Hastings Cave was constantly contaminated, a dirty cave. This is what would happen to Winter Cave, her cave, the cave where she had carefully gathered her research. It would be a tragedy if it was ever opened up for public display. She felt the hairs on her arms rise imagining it. The torchlight fell on the little cluster of stalagmites that the guides called Titania's Garden.

A flash of red. What was that?

Entrails. A little pile of animal viscera strewn along the rock.

Jessica ducked under the chain-link barrier. This particular part of the cave system had a very thin floor, seemingly carved out by a relentless current—little waves and eddies etched into the surface, glistening pools. She knew that the river had flooded the cavern at one time or another. Just thinking about it made her uneasy as she placed a tentative foot on the flowstone. The water rising fast in the cramped space, the huge teeth of the rock formation closing on you from above as you struggled against the tide.

She had anticipated skulls. She sometimes imagined whole skeletons lurking beneath the solidified sediment; thought one day a stalactite would snap off and the grinning jaw of a human skull would emerge, screaming like something from a horror film. She had heard things at night too. Odd cracks and clicks when she was locking up and her imagination conjured spirits of the dead. The ghosts of massacred Aborigines rising up, serial killers hiding among the shadows. But this actual gore was unanticipated. Shocking. There should not be any kind of animal down here in the depths of the earth, let alone a dead and disembowelled one.

She shuffled out onto the shelf, paused. One careful step after another.

It was a possum, a large one, bristling black and mean-mouthed. The face had been gnawed into. The eyes were gone, sucked from the skull. The stomach had been ripped open and, when she bent to take a leg in one hand and dragged it to one side, she could see that it had been gutted—the organs the most succulent parts. The carcass, speared onto the rod of a stalagmite, must have been shoved down with extraordinary force. The blunt-ended rock pushed through the creature's flesh. A thousand years of rock growth damaged in an instant.

Jessica thought briefly about taping off the area, setting it up like a crime scene. Photographing the corpse and bringing in the team of investigators to unravel the mystery. It was quite possible the possum had crept into the cave just before closing time, when the great iron doors were swung shut and double bolted—but what sort of predator could possibly creep in to kill it in such a brutal way? And then sneak out again past a locked gate?

No, the killer must have come up via the river caverns. Something sure-footed: able to manage the treacherous climb and somehow find its way back out again.

Unless it was still lurking here somewhere.

Jessica felt a shiver creep along her shoulders and swung her torch sharply into the corners of the chamber. There was no time for a *CSI*-style investigation; the first group of tourists would be assembling in an hour. She grimaced as she lifted the carcass, stone cold but still oozing blood. She popped it into her plastic bag, along with the cotton bud and the Band-Aid and the ticket stub. The guts dragged behind, slapping against the edge of the bag. Jessica pursed her lips and made a small sound in the back of her throat as she picked up the flaccid trail with her fingers and secured it inside the plastic.

The stalagmite, coated in thick red slop, would certainly be damaged by this. Normal skin acids from hands reaching out to grab a column did enough harm. There was a slippery patch of ground and a formation stretching from floor to ceiling at the bottom of the incline where people would reach out to the cold damp pillar to steady themselves. She didn't blame them. They slipped in their useless city soles. One old man had fallen on her tour and she had wondered about fractured hips and winches before he heaved himself up off the floor of the cavern, refusing any help, limping on his way.

A woman died once. Not in the cave, but that was where she

collapsed. It was on Jessica's day off; she heard about it later—the defib machine barking orders in its mechanical American accent, the struggle to get the woman back up the two hundred and fifty stairs. She died in the ambulance, but it was clear that the caves had claimed her, and the next morning, on Jessica's regular dawn litter round, there were signs of death: coins spilled and left to bleed their metals into the acidic damp; the instruction sheet from the defibrillator trampled and dampening at the edge of a stair; a single glove. She'd picked it up and turned it in her hand and wondered if perhaps it was her glove, the woman's, dropped while she was still living. Jessica had held it to her nose and gasped at the scent of violets.

As she neared the entrance of the cave she was breathing more deeply. All those stairs and now the air rushing in to meet her with the sun. It always snapped a little colder at dawn and Jessica shrugged her parka more firmly onto her shoulders. She would have pulled her hood up if it wasn't for the blood on both hands.

A clang. Metal against metal. She stopped, rested her elbow on her raised knee, caught between steps as she listened to the rattling from above. And what if someone were to lock that gate while she was here in the dark? What if, more likely, the dog or fox or whatever it was that killed the possum was there at the top of the stairs, leaning against the heavy metal door? She listened. More clanging and, yes, the sound of footsteps. Human: boots, stomping across the wooden platform. Jessica hurried up the last twisting flight.

'Gus?'

Gus turned, tucking his brown shirt into his trousers. He was wearing a ludicrous beanie with floppy woollen lappets falling over his ears. Each one was finished off with a plait and a pompom: he looked like a schoolgirl interrupted while dressing for a sports carnival. He swept the beanie off his head when he saw Jessica, lifted his fingers to tousle his thick dark hair. Stopped when he saw the gory bag.

'What the fuck?' he said.

She nodded. 'What indeed.'

'What is…A cat? Dog?'

'Possum.'

'Seriously.'

She nodded. 'There's a bit of it left in Titania's Palace.'

'Where did it come from?'

'Crawled in? I don't know.'

Gus walked to the edge of the stairs and looked down.

'Like a satanic ritual or something?' Gus asked.

'Oh God, I hadn't even thought of that. The organs were gone. I thought maybe a dog.'

He reached over to the light switches and flicked them, waited for the loud hum as the whole system turned on. 'Did you go all the way through?'

'Just to Titania's Palace.'

'I'll get a bucket.'

'And gloves. Thick gloves.'

'Did you bring your gun?' Half a smile.

She shook her head as if this might be a serious question. He was joking, but, not for the first time, she wished she had never told him about the gun. It seemed to have become a recurring motif.

'It won't still be in there, right? The dog or whatever?' He checked his watch. 'Half an hour till the first group gets here.'

'Better get that bucket.' She waited, nervously, peering down into the cavern as he disappeared into the workers' room.

By noon the possum was all but forgotten. The temperature was bitter and there was no whiff of dead smell near the bin where Jessica had dumped it. The corpse might well have frozen solid if not for the heater that the staff crowded around between tours.

In the afternoon she was on her fifth tour when she looked up to the ceiling of Titania's Palace, and her train of thought reminded her. She was thinking terrible things about a young boy on the tour, all grabbing hands and stomping boots. Jessica hovered near him, wary. He was only small, his head no higher than her waist, and yet he seemed to suck up a disproportionate amount of energy. She was wound up, cranky. She looked up to the long thin formations on the roof that were called straws, and imagined snapping one off and stabbing the boy in the eye with it, and that gave her the jolt to remember the disembowelled corpse.

The boy's mother was a broken shell of a creature, wrapped in layers of fabric. Thermal underwear, jumpers, a scarf and a puffy jacket. Jessica watched her shivering despite the swaddling. She had arrived with the boy tugging on one of her hands—a tow-rope for a stalling vehicle—a man in a red beanie barrelling up the track in front of them. Jessica watched him stop at the stump of an old-growth tree, wider than the girth of five large men. The rest of the tree had cracked and tumbled to the ground beside it, a creep of green blanketing the damp trunk, which crumbled off into the forest. The man in the red beanie had assumed a fake martial-arts pose, kicking at the trunk, saying *Take my picture, take my picture* as the child leapt up to kick at the tree with his father. Not a posed kick, but a genuine bark-destroying thump. The mother reached wearily into her handbag for a camera as the son whinged at her to hurry up and *take our picture now. Now!*

Now those same boots were stomping too close to the stalagmites. Jessica manoeuvred herself between the child and the delicate rock formations. She imagined picking the kid up and bringing him down hard on the particular stalagmite that had already proven itself so apt for homicide.

'Look!' The boy was yelling so loud that they could probably hear him back at the guides' room. 'That one's as tall as me! Look! Take a photo.'

Jessica dropped to a crouch beside the child and pointed to the little patch of stalagmites, Titania's Garden.

'See in there?'

The boy nodded, mercifully quiet for the first time in forty-five minutes.

'See that big fat one there?' she whispered.

The child nodded again. He was already bored with listening. He shifted his weight from foot to foot as if he needed to pee.

'Something was killed this morning.'

'For real?'

'Yep. A possum. A big possum. Almost as big as you. Something lifted it and crashed it down onto that big fat one there. It ripped through his body like he was made of jelly.'

'Mum—' he began to yell in his renewed excitement, but Jessica held his arm tight and shushed him quickly.

'That thing that killed him? It might still be in here. It might be waiting in the darkness there at the end of the chamber. It might be waiting for the noisiest little boy to come along. They like the noisy ones, these apex predators. Have you heard of that? Apex predator?'

The boy, quiet now, nodded gently.

'Well, they like the smallest and the noisiest ones. So I am just wondering if it is safe for you to be yelling like you did? Or to be kicking at the stalagmites or touching the columns, leaving the scent of your hands and feet for the apex predator?' The boy stared, silent and wide-eyed.

'Not saying that's how it is going to happen. I just think it's possible. Don't you?'

The child had turned to stone. He tucked his hands behind his back and crept away from Jessica quietly, tiptoeing towards his mother.

'Okay. Titania's Palace.' Jessica stood and swept her hand around. 'That's what we call this chamber. And you know we are so far down in the cave system by now that it is almost totally dark in here without the lights. Do you want to see that? Have you ever been in a cave where they turn the lights out?'

A few people nodded. A few said yes. Jessica stepped towards the light box mounted on the wall. 'Okay,' she said. I want you to be really quiet. Super quiet, or the cave beasts might start to pay a bit too much attention.'

Laughter, shuffling. The boy turned his face into his mother's hip.

'Let's find us some cave beasts,' the boy's father said, guffawing. And Jessica wondered if she should spin the man the same story she had frightened the boy with. It might take more than a retelling of events. She could take him upstairs and lift the lid on the metal bin and show him the possum corpse.

She hit the light switch. The group fell silent. She saw the memory of light at the corners of her eyes and heard the people breathing, the sound of her own heartbeat pumping blood through her ears. A shuffling. People, probably, but she was quick to flick the light back on. Too early. She usually waited up to five minutes in the pitch black.

Relief flooded over her with the light. Nothing there in the cave with them, just people, scuffing their feet in the dark. She looked over to the child, who had turned very pale. He lifted his face, pleading with his mother. 'I don't feel well.'

In winter the sun rises at eight and sets at five. Barely nine hours of light. By four it was time for Jessica to heft the complicated metal lock and turn the key till it clicked in place. She had checked all the chambers and rooms, every corner of darkness on the stairs. She usually liked to do her last check in the dark with a torch. Communing with the dark, she called it. Today she left the main lights on. There were cave crickets clustering on the ceiling. Dark spiders beginning to emerge from their hides among the straws and stalactites in the dark corners of the rock face above. No sign of anything but arthropods. She heard the bolt click with something like relief.

'We've got to lug this bloody thing back now.' Gus was huffing as if he had been running. It was the cold getting into his lungs.

'We could just go into the forest a bit and ditch it there.'

'Wouldn't that encourage whatever it is to just hang around the caves?'

Jessica shrugged. 'There's nowhere to bury it down at the shack.'

'Can't we put it in with the rubbish?'

They both stood looking down into the metal bin.

'Okay,' Gus said eventually. 'You take your side…'

It still didn't smell bad. It wouldn't start to for days—a week, or longer. The sun barely touched ground in the forest. Everything damp and icy, the ground frozen to the core. The roadkill on the roadsides stiff, locked into their final moments.

'What do you think did it?' Jessica asked as she hefted her side of the bin.

'Aren't you the scientist?'

She narrowed her eyes, made a thin line of her mouth. 'After—what? Eight years' study?—I can be pretty sure it wasn't slaughtered by a glow-worm.'

'Ha, ha. I don't know. Dog? Feral cat? Probably a dog.'

'Yeah. I guess it must have come up from the creek somehow.'

'Does it creep you out to think of all the parts of the cave we haven't explored?'

She looked at him. 'Are you going to pick your end up?'

Gus actually giggled. 'Thought you'd never ask.'

They hefted. Gus grunted. They shuffled together, the dead weight swinging between them.

'On three,' said Gus.

'Just lift it.'

It landed with a metallic thud in the bin.

'Hey, Jess? I'm having a thing this Friday.'

'A thing?'

'Gathering. Small gathering.'

'Is it your birthday?'

'Something like that. And I wondered if you wanted to, you know. I'd like you to—just pizza, but my flatmate's making the bases from scratch and Lidia's coming and some people from here...'

Jessica frowned. She liked Gus. She liked Lidia. She liked pizza.

'Bring Matthew, of course.'

Matthew hated Gus. Matthew hated Lidia. He would be furious if she went alone. She remembered that one time she stayed back drinking with them after work. She frowned. Backed away from the memory cautiously. They were in a good place now, she and Matthew. They had come to a beautiful balance. She tried to imagine his arm around her. His breath on her neck, kissing her gently the way she liked it.

'Oh, Gus, I would love to, but Matthew's got this—'

'No worries. Just wanted to say you're welcome. Any time. We catch up most Fridays, you know. And other nights. Just saying if you want to hang out...'

'I'd like that. I will. Another time.'

But she wouldn't. Her smile felt fake now. It felt like it belonged somewhere else. Beneath it there was just a blank stretch of mouthless skin.

'Soon,' she said with her fake mouth. 'I promise.'

Jessica shifted on the damp bench and her raincoat creaked under her. She pulled the zip up higher around her neck. Two weeks till the solstice and how could it get colder? Her hair was damp already but she pulled her hood up against the rain. Looked at her phone. No bars at all—just an *SOS ONLY* in the corner of the screen. It dropped out entirely when she shuffled to her left. A dog, even a feral one, would not attack an adult human. She shifted back to her right. She could call triple zero if she saw it, and an hour later the police might arrive. She thrust her hands into her empty pockets and thought again about her gun. She didn't usually carry it; hadn't held it since they bought the thing. Matthew insisted that she buy it, living so far south, down at the end of the world. It had seemed an unnecessary extravagance—dangerous, ridiculous. Less so at this moment, though.

Matthew should have been here by now. Even if he stopped in Geeveston for petrol he'd still have plenty of time to make it down to Hastings Cave by eight o'clock. It was tempting to go through the rigmarole of unlocking the building and turning the alarm off just to sit inside, out of the cold. There was a landline in there and she could call him. She drifted between anxiety and anger. He should be here by now. He should know to be here by now.

She needed a puffy down jacket. They were expensive, but it was just one of those things, like her boots, like her boat. Just an essential part of living down here. She would get one in Hobart when she went back to see David, her supervisor. She'd have to plan for it, take the money out in stages. If she took it all at once Matthew would get funny about it. They were pretty expensive. It was an indulgence, really. Maybe she could find something on eBay.

Finally, shivering, she stood and began to walk down the concrete ramp towards the front door of the gift shop.

The sound of tyres on gravel, the slush of mud spraying up the side of the car. The swing of headlights on high beam. He was driving too fast and for once she didn't mind. She really didn't want to be left here in the cold dark. He could do a hundred and twenty in the mud for all she cared.

He beeped, as if she wouldn't hear him slam the brakes on and skid to a halt. Beeped again, and she raised a hand. Of course she had heard him. She was already hurrying back up the ramp.

'You were ages,' she snapped as she pulled her muddy feet into the car.

'Yeah. Sorry, hon. Seals in the pens.'

'Did you have to dynamite them again?'

'You don't want to know. Carnage, that's all I'll say.'

She slammed the door and turned the heat up to full. 'Dead possum in the cave this morning.'

'Really?'

'Do you remember that feral cat on the track two years ago?'

'Ha. Yeah. Size of a dog.'

'Small dog,' she said.

'Big enough. You going to go out hunting this one?'

'I reported it to Parks.'

'I'll ask around. See if anyone's lost pets or stock.'

She leaned over and kissed him on the cheek and there was that smile she loved as he swung the car around, skidding, fishtailing. She would pick up her car tomorrow; not a day too soon.

Riding with Matthew she could see the teenage boy she never knew. The roo shooter, the drunk driver who lost his first licence at seventeen, the smart teenager who hadn't had the opportunity to go past Year 10. He was a different man now, but sometimes she caught a glimpse of that boy behind the wheel.

She closed her eyes.

'God, it's a long day,' she murmured, winding the passenger seat back so she could recline a little.

'Tell me about it.'

Jessica was on a boat. But no. The slow rocking from side to side was not the gentle rise and fall of the tide. She was in a car. Matthew's car. He was driving her home from work. She opened her eyes to a world dark as nightmare. Tried to sit up, struggling against her seatbelt. She could see nothing.

Suddenly the tall trees appeared, highlighted in the headlights where there had only been darkness before. The car adjusted to this new view of the road. She must be sleeping. She blinked, blinked again and the world disappeared. One minute there were the thin, tight pickets of tall trees, lined up so close you could never hope to push between them, then they were gone. Snap to black.

This was the southern forest, a packed mass of eucalypts. Sometimes she peered at the ranks of trees and wondered about the first settlers, how they managed to push their way into the forest, felling one huge trunk at a time. Before this, before the saws and scythes of the white folk, how did the Aboriginal Australians do it? Leave it be, avoid the thickest parts, probably. Live with it.

She must be dreaming these trees, popping into focus and then blacked out as if the moon was suddenly turned off.

Not the moon. The headlights, the headlights of the car. She could feel the forward motion, the curve of the tyres on the dark road. She could feel the potholes under the bouncing car. And then the forest blazed to vibrant life again. Two little eyes on the side of the road, glowing red. A wallaby, standing still in a ditch, staring at the car, surprised, just as she was surprised by the way the headlights suddenly appeared out of the blackness, pulling the metal bulk of the car with them.

'What the fuck!' she snapped.

Fucking Matthew playing chicken with the headlights. Again. While she was asleep and unsuspecting.

'Matthew. What the fuck?'

'What?'

'Did you have the headlights off?'

'What?' All mock hurt, falsely accused, for a moment. Then he slapped the wheel and laughed. 'Just for a second. Only a second, honestly. I didn't think you'd wake up.'

'Fuck you! Didn't think I'd wake up? Get *fucked*.' She ratcheted the seat to upright.

'Hey,' he said. 'Hey, hey. No harm done.'

She tried to calm herself but she could feel her chest catch, her shoulders huffing up and down with her wet breath.

'Hey.' He reached over to touch her knee. 'Hey. Hey.'

'I've told you not to…You could have…We could…' Her voice caught and hiccuped as she spoke. She was beginning to sob.

'Oh, baby.' He was patting her knee as if she really were a baby, patting her to make her stop crying.

She took a deep and halting breath. Steadied herself.

'I still have to finish the revisions to the introduction when I get home.'

'I'll make dinner, I'll make us tuna and rice, okay?'

She nodded. Her breath shuddered.

'You like that? Tuna and rice?'

'It's just,' she blew her nose. 'Oh God, I'll never finish.'

'Yeah you will. No need to rush it. You've been working on it for years. Stupid supervisor can wait.'

'He can't…'

'You're so smart, baby.' He reached over and mussed up her hair. 'Look at you. My girlfriend the doctor. Doctor Weir. Doctor Jessica Weir!'

He beeped the horn once, a long excited drone.

She slapped him on the arm. 'Stop doing that. And don't fuck around with the lights ever again. I've told you.'

'Okay.'

'So fucking stupid.'

'Okay, doctor,' he said. 'Okay,' and he grinned so wide she couldn't stay mad at him. She leaned over and kissed his shoulder and he smelled warm and earthy and safe.

She opened her eyes. She was always so tired in the morning, but today she felt like her arms were leaden. Her head throbbed. Her eyes felt puffy. She had been crying. She remembered. Blinked the memory away.

Stupid fight, anyway.

Flower. A gorgeous bright circle of yellow on Matthew's pillow, staring at her, wide-eyed. She dragged herself up to a sitting position and reached over for the flower.

Her head was pounding. Stupid, stupid fight.

But here was a flower and the sun already up outside the window and a bright patch of yellow shining through the curtain and falling onto her feet under the blanket.

Gorgeous sunshiny day.

She slipped her feet onto the floor, breathing in the smell of bacon. He was cooking breakfast.

'Matthew?'

Bacon and eggs.

She slipped her feet into her ugg boots and pulled a jumper on over her pyjamas. It was still cold but the light from the window warmed her spirits.

She bent down and picked up another flower from the floor. A daisy chain looped around the doorhandle. She slipped it over her wrist and opened the door. Classical music on the record player. Bach. She felt her love for Matthew flood into her chest along with the waft of bacon and the sad, slow gathering of the notes.

More flowers, laid in a deliberate line. Like her mother's Easter egg trail, a line of little chocolate eggs leading to a chocolate bunny hidden somewhere in the compound. She remembered the hunts they set for the kids every year, her excitement, waking to it. She bent, plucked, bent, plucked. It was as if the music was perfectly timed to her footsteps. The cello swelled upward and she turned the corner and there was the dining-room table draped in paper daisies, a huge bunch of red roses in the centre. Boiled eggs, toast soldiers, fresh baked bread. He must have started before dawn. Had he picked the flowers?

She stood with a bunch of yellow in her fist and watched him emerge from the kitchen with cultured butter on a plate. He had made butter too.

He stopped when he saw her. He smiled and she watched as his eyes filled up and a single tear spilled over and traced a line down his cheek.

'I'm so sorry, Jessica. I love you so much.'

The fight. She glanced over to where her laptop was resting on her desk. It was fine. No damage. Nothing broken. She felt her own eyes swelling with tears and wiped them away with the back of her hand.

'Forgive me. Please.'

'You baked bread.' She heard her voice waver. She swallowed.

'I just wanted...' He put the butter dish down beside her plate.

The music ushered her to her seat. She sank into it. The light from the window warmed her face as she glanced out to where the ocean lapped at the sand. The sea was so calm today. She watched a shell roll onto the shore and then slip back into the ocean again.

She buttered the slice of bread on her plate and raised it to her lips. Still warm, the butter melting into it. She took a bite and felt her breath catch in her throat. She heard a sobbing sound. It was coming from her own mouth. She tried to swallow it.

'I love you,' she said. 'I love you, just…Don't leave me.'

'What?' He stepped towards her, wrapped his hands around her shoulders. 'I'd never leave you. I was frightened…'

'I…'

'You'll be finished study soon. You'll be a doctor. You could go anywhere. Why would you stay with me? You're so smart. You could do anything. Go anywhere. I'm a dumb nothing.'

She sank into the hug. Clung to his arms. Stupid fight. She could barely remember…

'You'll leave me,' he said.

'I won't.' She turned towards him, pulled his face towards her. There was butter on her fingers and she kissed a trail of it off his cheeks.

'But I'm just a dumb fuck from the bush. I'm just a hick.'

'Don't say that. You're the smartest man I know. You're the only man I know who's read Kant and Foucault, and Deleuze and all of Hemingway…'

She kissed him again, gently. He kissed her back.

'It's not about a doctorate, high school, that's just…nothing… stupid. Look at this?' Jessica nodded to the table. 'Look at what you have to teach me. I'd be lost without you. You know that.'

'You're not leaving?'

'Of course not.'
'But you said—'
'Stupid fight. I'm an idiot! I'm so sorry. I'm just—'
'Stressed.'
'Yeah.'
'I know. I wish it hadn't—'
'It's gone. It never happened.'
'Really?'
'I swear.'
'You swear by your *Arachnocampas*?'
'I swear by my colony: we never had that fight. Today is going to be the best day ever.'

He smiled. He took his seat at the table next to her. 'I've packed a picnic basket. The weather's amazing. Let's go—'

'To Winter Cave?'
'That's the plan.'
'Aren't you supposed to go in to work?'
'I called in sick already.'
'I love you, Matthew.'
'I love you too, Jessica.'

She grinned. The record ended and the needle arm lifted, made a slow journey back to the edge of the record, and then lowered itself delicately into the groove. The music began, stern yet gentle. Jessica lifted the freshly baked bread to her lips. Her wrist was a little sore. There was a darkening of the skin there, barely noticeable. It would fade quickly. She bit down into the warm bread. This was exactly what her love tasted like, sounded like. It was going to be a wonderful day.

That one sunny day.

A brief thaw and then winter crashed over them again, settling into her bones.

She stamped sand from her boots and shrugged the heavy coat from her shoulders, unwinding the thick woollen snake from her neck. Her mother had given her the scarf, but Jessica wore it anyway, the only thing she owned that could battle the deep chill of the winters here. Still, when she unwrapped it and hung it on the hook by the door she breathed easier, as if she'd removed the hands of her mother from her throat.

'Hey,' she said into the dark emptiness of the cottage. The sea hushed back at her. Matthew wasn't home. Of course. She checked her watch. He would just be finishing his shift, then the long drive. The flowers were still bright in their vases, but the roses were fully blown now, a few petals resting on the tabletop. She picked one up and nestled it against her upper lip. It felt like velvet; it smelled rich and thick as honey. A warm scent, even in the bone-chill of the cabin.

Her laptop was still on the coffee table. She hadn't booted it up since…that night. It felt like years ago now, but she still had to finish formatting the bibliography. She would have to face it sooner or later.

Jessica bent to the fireplace. Twigs, torn paper, a little bundle of kindling. She built the wood up as Matthew had taught her. A log on either side, one balanced neatly on top. Her hands were still shaking with cold; she laced them together in her lap. Watched the fire catch. Their lives had been rendered down to this. Everything was all about the fireplace now, they tended it like a child. The first responsibility in the morning, the last thing to feed before bed. Is the wood chopped? Is enough of it dry? Have we got kindling? She sat back on her heels and watched the flames as they grew fat and red and sucked all the minutes out of her evening.

The fridge was full of fish. A cray in the freezer that she had pulled out of the pot yesterday morning, salmon cheap or 'borrowed' from the fish farm. Half-a-dozen filleted flathead that she had pulled into the boat with her own hands. She should be sick of fish but she wasn't. Down the road at Cockle Creek there was a woman who put a boat out every day. Matthew had told her about it. Ninety years old, and still setting out with her net and line. Jessica wondered if that would be her one day, old and hunched and gutting her catch right here on the ocean.

The phone buzzed.

Just leaving now x.

She responded with an x of her own and turned to the freezer. Fish stew—there were always little plastic containers in the freezer. Stew and soup and pie and lasagne. She felt loved whenever she peered into the fridge.

Matthew would be home soon, smelling of brine, hungry and cold to the bone. She put one more log on the fire, opened the flue all the way, listened to the roar and crackle. Outside the wind dropped to a low whistle. The ocean breathed.

★

She woke, hungry. She checked her watch. Maybe he had been called back at the last minute, someone late for their shift, some accident at the pens and all hands needed. Where had she put the phone? She searched blearily on the couch for it. Maybe it had slipped under a cushion.

It was cold. The fire was dying.

She lurched sleepily towards it and added a handful of sticks, a couple of logs. That should be enough to get them through till morning. It wasn't the first time Matthew had been late. She shuffled into the kitchen. The stew was defrosted but it was too late for dinner now. She ate a little of the salmon that Matthew had smoked under the house.

Teeth, pyjamas, bed.

He would find his meal in the fridge when he returned, although by now he must have eaten at work, especially if he was on overtime. These small domestic details, the comfort of them.

She opened the door to the bathroom and the cold met her. Like someone had died in there—a thing her mother used to say. She turned on the hot tap and dipped her toothbrush under the stream, dreading the shock of cold water on her teeth. All these things that she had learnt since leaving Queensland, coming as far south as you could go before you hit the icy deserts of Antarctica. As far away from her childhood life as was physically possible without shifting to a different continent.

Footsteps in the front room. A rattling nail-click on the floor-boards. Jessica sat upright in bed. She reached out for Matthew. She could smell him breathing beside her but when her hand touched the pillow it was cold, with the faint reek of old sweat.

She should change the sheets. She blinked. The book he had been reading was facedown on the bedside table. She hated the way he did that, cracking the spine.

Footsteps. A soft pad-pad-padding. There was a dog in the shack. A dog in their lounge room and, as well as that, the door was open to the beach. She was sure of it. She could feel the ice chill creeping in under the bedroom door, the sound of the ocean too loud. King tide and the water licking the lip of the rock wall.

She slipped her feet over the edge of the bed. Hissed at the icy shock of the floorboards.

Why was the bedroom door closed? Jessica never closed it. They left it open to channel the heat from the fireplace down the corridor and into the bedroom. Tonight in particular she had made sure it was open. She was waiting for Matthew; wanted to hear him open the front door. The animal was moving around in the kitchen, searching for scraps, she supposed. Jessica could smell it, a strong wild smell like you get near a tree full of fruit bats.

What if the animal was sick, rabid? It was her mother in her head again, with the fables and bogeymen. An animal in the house, and immediately it has to be rabid.

Rabies, though. At university she had read about the symptoms. Insatiable thirst and yet at the same time a terrible fear of water; spasms, raging—the stuff of nightmares. She knew full well that on this continent only bats carried the lyssavirus; nonetheless she took the key from the bedside table and unlocked the drawer where they kept the gun.

There was dust on the barrel. She wiped it down with the palm of her hand. Thinking, as she always did, what a ridiculous thing it had been to buy. She usually walked alone on the tracks around here and had never thought to bring the weapon. She checked the chamber, fumbled in the box for bullets. Her fingers slipped the heavy metal nuggets into the chamber. It felt comfortable in the palm of her hand, an old memory. Her mother—*don't ever, ever point that thing at anyone ever. Not even when it isn't loaded.* How easily the weight of it nestled in her palm: the feeling of something she was good at. Blue ribbons every year in the church competition, and her brother's perpetual envy. Jessica was flooded now with that old mix of pride and shame. *We don't need a gun, Matthew. Do you know that statistically most guns are only ever used to harm a member of your own family?*

She was glad of it now, though. The feral smell drifted in under the door, strong and sharp. She heard something shift in the kitchen, a clatter as something metal—a bowl? A knife?—fell to the floor. More scrabbling of claws on floorboards, something leaping out of the way.

Jessica opened the door. The corridor was dark but for a vague glow from the last coals in the fireplace at the end. She stepped into the narrow space. She felt the wind gusting, heard the ocean too close and again the tick of the claws. She edged forward.

The phone rang.

Christ. She dropped the gun, which landed hard on her toe. If not for the safety, she would have shot her own foot off. This was the first lesson her mother had given her: the cardinal sin of dropping the weapon.

She bent to pick it up. Heard, simultaneously, the gallop of soft feet, a scramble as the creature slipped on the boards and raced out onto the balcony, taking the stairs at a great leap. She ran to the lounge room and flicked the light on, blinking in the sudden glare, but there was no sign of an animal. The light spilled down onto the sparse garden, the coffin-shaped plot of dirt and young acacias planted over the septic system. Beyond this the rocks paced down to the thin line of sand. The water eased in, slapping against the boulders before dragging more of the beach out to sea.

The phone was still ringing.

Matthew.

The phone, the shrill tone and the sound of it buzzing against a hard surface. She pushed her papers aside; a stack of journals cascaded onto the floor and she bent to snatch the phone up just as it went silent. A number she didn't recognise.

Jessica called Matthew's phone again and listened to the desolate beeping. Then there was the sound of another call coming through. The unknown number again.

'Hello?' she said.

'Who am I speaking to?'

'Who's this?'

'I'm a police officer, miss.' He gave a name she didn't catch.

She looked around the cold lounge room. The fire was almost out. The pot was resting clean and unused on the stove, the stew still in its container in the fridge. She looked at the gun in her hand, at the fruit bowl that had tumbled onto the floor, lemons cowering under it, half-hidden by the silver lip.

Matthew. The silence on the phone caught in her lungs.

'Where is he?' Her voice sounded thin. There was no breath behind it.

'Who is this, please?'

'Jessica. Jessica Weir.'

'I'm sorry, miss, but this was the last number—'

'Matthew's on his way home. From work. He's late. He should be home soon.'

And only the ocean breathing into the silence as if her own chest were rising and falling without fail. As if his heart were still beating. As if nothing in the world had changed. When they were all dead and buried the ocean would still rise and fall and none of it would matter at all.

'We've found a car, miss, but there's no sign of a driver. I'm going to need your address. You might, ah…you might want to file a missing persons report.'

And the ocean coming in with a whisper, out with a rush. Always and forever.

Jessica had forgotten the scarf. It was the adrenaline, she supposed, that surge of panic and, oddly, a growing sense of anger. She was angry to have fallen asleep when she should have been out looking for him, angry that the policeman on the phone could not share her overwhelming sense of dread. She took the corners too fast, forced herself to slow down, easing her foot off the throttle.

She swerved, accelerated into the corner, swung too wide, felt the tyres skid off the edge and slip in the mud of the verge before she could angle the car back on course. Matthew was out there. Matthew was waiting for her. She hit the thick patch of forest and glanced at the passenger seat where her phone sat, reduced to a simple camera. No internet, no network. Not even SOS only. She was holding her breath again. She forced herself to breathe.

The lights flashing blue red blue. Yellow tape, the kind you saw on crime shows. Had Matthew committed a crime? She didn't understand. Was he sitting, cuffed, in one of the police cars? She counted five of them and an ambulance as she eased the car to a stop at the edge of the taped-off area.

An officer moved towards her window. He was saying something, she saw his mouth move but couldn't hear him. He turned his finger in a clockwise motion. The symbol for crazy. She was going mad. She was insane. Parts of the forest lit up with the reflection of torchlight. The Pajero was right there. His car. Their car.

She turned towards the policeman. No, not the crazy sign—he wanted her to wind the window down. She pressed the button and a blast of icy air rushed into the cabin.

'Won't be long, miss. We'll let you go by in a minute.'

She shook her head.

'Are you…Is there anything I can help you with?'

'That's our car.'

'I'm sorry—'

'That's our car.'

She pointed. Her breath came out of her mouth, puffs of smoke. She wasn't cold. She was burning up. Here was the evidence, steaming up her windscreen and erasing the image of their four-wheel drive.

'That's my car.' She said again. 'That's my partner. Matthew. My partner. *Matthew!*' she was shouting now, leaning her head out the window and screaming. The cold air scraped her lungs on her in-breath. 'Matthew!'

The officer was holding his hand out as if to stop the sound but it was loud and sure and echoing. Other officers were walking towards her car, and she was still shouting his name. Over and over, the repetition leaching the meaning from the word. Matthewmatthewmatthew just a jumble of syllables, piercing the night like the light from the torches. Policemen surrounded her car.

'Miss. Miss. All right, miss.'

And when she stopped giving voice to the meaningless word she could still hear the note of panic, high and shrill at the edge of the silent forest.

They shook their heads as she pulled in to the carpark. She could see they had already called in an extra person to cover her shift.

'What are you doing here?' It was Lidia.

Jessica genuinely considered the question. Her eyes were red, she knew, and the skin under them was bruised from staring at the ceiling.

'Go home,' said Lidia. 'We've got you covered. You can't be at work with...with all this going on.'

They had all heard, of course. Someone told someone told someone and the whole south was ringing with the news. Bloke missing, distraught girlfriend. They had replaced her now and they were already counting the shifts till she would give her notice. She might not even stay around for her own graduation. What was the point? She didn't really have any friends at uni. Or in Tasmania at all.

Jessica still stubbornly sprayed herself with perfume bought from fancy city shops. She put soy milk in her coffee and the look they gave her cup spoke volumes. She made herself a soy macchiato on her lunch break, for godsake. People who drank any kind of macchiato did not belong around here. They were counting the days all right, and when the counting was done she would go home to wherever it was. Brisbane? Maybe Townsville, wasn't that where her mother lived? Somewhere that didn't have a winter.

Jessica turned the car around in the muddy carpark. She drove back to the shack and her stomach groaned with sickness and with hunger all at once. She had made a breakfast and watched the eggs go cold on the plate. The flowers were dead now but she refused to throw the shrivelled stems away, the smell of the water in the vase turned her stomach, the eggs were rank with death. She had felt ravenous after a night without sleep and yet, when she picked up her fork, there was nothing she wanted less than food.

She wanted something, though. The wanting was eating out her chest, and she drove home too fast, chasing the idea of whatever it was. The sun was coming up and there would be a search on. Or maybe not. She glanced at the impenetrable wall of tree trunks. He couldn't have walked out into the forest. There was no path for anything bigger than a wallaby. She tried to keep her eyes on the road but her gaze kept straying into the darkness. The forest pushing in against the sides of the car till she felt the breath pressed right out of her and even if she wanted to she wouldn't be able to draw in enough air to scream.

At home the ocean breathed for her. As long as it inhaled, sucking the bulk out of the ocean, then exhaled, pushing itself up higher onto the beach, as long as the sound of it mimicked the rise and fall of her chest, she would know she was alive.

She let her coat fall to the floor. She hadn't swept. Her coat lay in the sand and dust and mud. She kicked her shoes off by the dead fire and let them sit where they fell.

She shivered, staring at her laptop. She hadn't opened the laptop since…

Why had they fought? She could barely remember it now. She remembered what came after. Bacon and bread fresh from his hands and a picnic basket shushing against long grass. Spreading a blanket out under the wakeful glimmer of the glow-worms. The taste of smoked salmon on her tongue, champagne washing it down, a kiss, and the chill of the cave floor against her naked back as she rolled under him. So cold, and when she bit into his shoulder she tasted it, the damp cave. His chest hot against her bare breasts.

She picked up her laptop. The blue case she had clipped onto it was askew and when she eased it back onto the metal, sand fell off onto the coffee table. She brushed it away.

There. Gone.

As if none of it had happened. She hugged the laptop to her chest.

There was something she needed to do, some deadline. She barely knew what day it was. It was as if the world had restarted in the middle of the night and this was the first day. She was still learning how to live in this brand-new and desolate world.

When she opened the computer it started up, the familiar chime and whirr. Relief washed over her. Of course her computer still worked. She realised only now how scared she had been that it might be permanently damaged. She was startled by the flat beep of a reminder window popping up on her screen: *file essay*. She opened her word document: *Glass Sponges Thrive as Antarctic Temperatures Rise*.

She sat hesitantly at her desk. Next week there would be another deadline, then another. She had once considered this her real work, more important than the cave tours, less important than her PhD. Everything arse up. There was no money in the PhD. Hardly any money in the science writing. The rent she paid to Matthew's mother was serviced by the three days a week at the caves. But the science was always more important to her. He teased her. *So much work for your beer money.* Matthew wasn't here to rib her about it but *Scienceweekly.com* would still trudge ahead, one deadline after another.

She was about to look over the sponges article, but she hesitated. Some other deadline. She struggled to remember what had been happening in her life.

Her PhD. She had been finishing the referencing. Had finished, in fact. And here it was, all of it, the PDF files nestled in her documents folder. She had started writing the email that would end it: eight years of her life. All she needed to do was press send.

Her finger hovered. *Are you sure you've done the best you can?* Matthew's words.

No. She wasn't sure.

Never would be, but she was done with it now.

She did it: hit send. Waited for some sign to mark the end of those long years of hard work.

Just a sinking feeling. And this numbness, unbroken.

She went back to the *Scienceweekly* file. All her research about glass sponges was surprisingly still there in the document, a relic from the before time. She pulled on her fingerless gloves, her writing gloves.

And looked up two hours later, surprised by the passing of time. It didn't feel right. It wasn't real. She'd walk into the kitchen and Matthew would be there scooping bolognese into freezer containers. She checked. He wasn't.

She thought: *I'll have to call his mother and, oh God, his brother.* She would have to tell her own mother at some point—and a whole community would be gathering to pray, as if this constituted some kind of valuable addition to the police search. She would have to report him missing to the handful of other people who would care. But for now she had a deadline and a colony of Antarctic glass sponges that suddenly seemed more important than anything in the empty despair of the real world.

She went back to the story and when it was done and filed she quickly googled 'hunt for giant octopus' before the reality of her life could take hold of her once more. If only *Scienceweekly* could become *Sciencedaily* she might never have to acknowledge Matthew's disappearance at all.

She could go back to the caves. All the people there that Matthew used to sneer at. Do-gooders, tree-huggers, university-educated greenie snobs. Gus and Lidia and Paul. The people at uni, her supervisor, David, the other PhD students, elite narcissists. Of whom she was one: Matthew was right about that.

Without Matthew, who would cook? Who would tidy? Who would stoke the fire obsessively as if it was the only thing keeping you alive? Jessica looked into the fireplace. The coals were greying, a chill had settled over the room. Matthew was out there in the cold. A fire *was* the only thing keeping her alive. She shivered and put another log on.

There were three knocks, a pause and then three more. It was mid-morning or maybe the day had slipped seamlessly into afternoon. Jessica had let the fire go out again. The shack was as cold as it had ever been; she could barely stretch out her fingers.

She reassembled herself, placing her feet deliberately on the unwelcoming floor, forcing the disparate parts of her body to follow. She swayed and thought she might collapse, but managed to stretch over to the curtain and lift it. A cruel shaft of sunlight slapped at her face.

His car was outside.

The flood of relief was heavy in her limbs. She felt her face grow hot, her lips stretch up into a grin. She laughed but it was a strange choked sound that was more like a sob.

Three knocks on the door. Why would Matthew knock? The sob turned into a high nervous laugh. Of course it wasn't Matthew. Just his car. The weight of relief dissipated and she was able to get herself down the corridor to the front door, her hand up to tame the wild tangle of her hair.

There was a man in uniform at the door. She wondered if he had been there at the crime scene. She wondered if he would see that she hadn't changed her clothes since then. Matthew's car was parked neatly. This police officer had brought it to her like a trophy: the blood-stained head of a stag.

Blood on the fender. He had hit something. She felt a jar as if her own body had thudded into a wallaby. She was losing track of the edges of things. She couldn't count the number of hours that had passed.

He had hit something. He had stopped the car. The door opened. He stepped out. She felt it in her body as if all this had happened to her. Then he vanished.

And here she was, a ghost in the world.

The story played in her memory as if she had been there. The police at the scene had told her the car door was open. Blood on the fender. He'd hit something on the road, only there was no sign of it now, no roadkill. Maybe it was only slightly injured. It picked itself up, hopped into the forest. That's what happened. Matthew just hopped off into the forest.

She stepped past the policeman, touched the side of Matthew's car as if to comfort it. The door was closed. Why did they tell her the door was left open when here it was, closed now? Who closed his car door?

There, there, home now. She touched the door.

'Miss?' The policeman was talking. 'Do you have anyone who can stay with you?'

Jessica shook her head.

'Family, friends?'

No.

'Is there anywhere you can go—'

'No.' It sounded sharp and angry, she tried to soften her voice. 'I'm staying here. If he comes home I want to be here.'

'We're continuing the search. Helicopters. We've got some help from the local fishermen. Got boats out on the bay. If we find anything, we'll contact you.' He looked dubious. He looked as if he didn't expect Matthew to be found. He looked as if he thought she should give up hope. Grieve, leave, move on.

'I have a boat. I can search.'

'We'll let you know if we find anything.'

She resisted the urge to push him back off her front path. 'I know,' she said. 'Stop saying that. You told me that last night.' Surely it wasn't just last night. How many days had passed? And was it this policeman or someone else? All the faces blurring into this one here. He seemed sweet, this young officer. His left eye struggling to stick with her face, sliding a little to one side. Lazy eye. She shouldn't take it out on him. It wasn't his fault.

'Thank you,' she said. 'I want to search too. Take the boat out.'

'You should contact your people. His people. His family.'

She felt the blood running away from her face. Maybe she was bleeding out. She'd fall to the ground right here.

She saw his police car then, parked a little further up the road, keeping a respectful distance. Someone in the driver's seat, just waiting for his partner to finish up.

'Here.' Lazy Eye held something out to her. She took it, feeling the cold weight of Matthew's phone settle in her hand. 'He left this in the car.' He would never go anywhere without his phone. The fact that she was holding it in her hand meant something was terribly wrong. 'We'll be in touch. You should call someone. Get someone out here.'

Someone.

She nodded. Tried to smile. Waited till Lazy Eye found his way to the police car, opened the passenger door and eased himself inside. She watched him indicate and slip onto the road. When the car was out of sight she opened the door of the Pajero, hefted herself up into the cab. She sat behind the wheel.

He had been sitting here. How many hours ago now? Only last night. He had turned the key that was still in the ignition. He had listened to—what? She turned the key and the CD blared: Björk, *Debut*. One of her favourites. She was surprised to know he was listening to her music in the car. Perhaps it was a message. She turned the ignition off. She was sounding just like her mother: signs, portents, signals from the grave. All the God stuff.

She locked the car and climbed the stairs. Inside the cabin it was as cold as outside. She should be wearing a jumper. At the very least she should attend to the fire. She put the phone carefully down at the table in front of the seat he always settled into.

She knelt at the fireplace.

I am man! I make fire! The ghost of his voice still joking with her, his caveman routine. Jessica stacked the kindling, tore paper and crumpled it into balls. She lit the little tepee of sticks and watched the flames lick at the wood. When it had taken hold she put a heavier log in. She sat back on her heels, mesmerised by the glow and crackle. The warmth settled on her like a hug.

There was toast on her plate. She wondered how it had got there. She didn't remember taking it out of the toaster or spreading the butter. She didn't remember taking a packet of smoked salmon out of the fridge or cutting the cryovac seal. Matthew was so proud of his cryovac machine. He vacuum-sealed everything he could. She could smell the woody scent of this salmon. A hint of the rosemary that grew beside the back door. Rosemary, chilli, cedarwood; each batch of salmon smoked in a different flavour. He had the same method with his beer, adding just a hint of herb or ginger or changing the amount of hops. He made notes in a set of books he kept on the shelf in the kitchen. Beer tests, smoke tests, marinades, each one carefully notated. It was her job to taste and rate: a sliding scale, one to ten. He trusted her taste implicitly, but refused to let her touch the smoker. This was his business. He took such pride and pleasure in it. *Man smoke fish! Woman eat fish!*

Jessica lifted a slice of salmon out of the packet with her knife. The smell of him everywhere. Laid the flesh on her toast. She was far from hungry but she picked it up, put it in her mouth.

Chewing was harder than she expected.

She picked up his phone and tapped the message symbol, flicked back through the texts.

Do we need milk?
Turn the radio on now
Salmon breakout
Get the net out
Coming home
Coming home now
Just heading back
Be home soon
x

She laid more wood on the fire. She put Matthew's phone down and opened the sliding glass door to the beach. The water and the fish inside it, the currents, the barbed rocks, the oysters clinging sharply to those rocks, the gulls straight as arrows, their beaks like knives. She stepped down onto the short strand and there was the soft sand and the hard sand beyond it and although she was not wearing shoes the winter could not penetrate her flesh.

Water lapped at her toes. Water sucked at her ankles. Water to her knees. She felt nothing. When the water lapped at her crotch she remembered. A sudden pain in her gut and she felt the heat of it like blood on her thighs. She looked down, expecting to see her stomach torn open.

She had pissed herself, still warm at her crotch but invisible against the dark stain of salt water slapping up to her waist. If she kept walking the water would be up to her heart. Then she would just need to stand for a few minutes and she would sleep, slipping under, sleeping and sleeping and sleeping for the longest ever time. And she was so tired.

Jessica turned, with an effort, and walked back to shore, peeling her wet jeans off and letting them trail in the sand.

She dropped them on the steps. Maybe her neighbours, the few buildings that were still occupied through winter, would see her hauling herself bare-legged up the steps and back into her shack. They would say nothing. Southport was that kind of town.

I'll pick up bread on the way home. Just leaving work now. Shall I order for you? Where are you?

All the questions he had for her. All the answers she had given. They were all still here. She went over and over them. Searching for some clue.

She picked up her own phone. *Where are you?* And his phone beeped as if he were still alive somewhere and could answer it. *Where are you?* She held her own phone in her hand. She closed her eyes. She wanted his answer. Even if it was a terrible thing, an answer plucked from the grave and thrown at her from the horror of her empty future. She wanted God. She wanted the devil. Just like her mother, when the chips were down she wanted a miracle.

She pulled on some tracksuit pants and sandshoes. Cold to the bone. Unlocked his car. *The door was found open.* She sat inside behind the wheel. He had hit something. An animal.

Back inside she warmed her hands on his phone. There were photos of her, photos of them together. His phone could never forget how happy they were. She tapped the camera icon.

A video. The last thing his phone had stored. She pressed play.

Headlights, the reflection of light in the straight poles of trees. A thick white stripe down the centre of the road. The picture snapped to black but the camera was still recording. She turned the sound up. She could hear the tyres on the road even under the sound of Björk singing. Light snapping on.

Bastard! He was playing chicken. She hated that he was playing chicken and filming it and that people would say it served him right that he was gone. She would have said it herself if he'd been here for her to yell at him.

On the video, trees were passing, passing…black again. The sound of tyres shushing to the rhythm of the music, and a laugh as he snapped the lights back on and him laughing at the sight of something in the road. Something, a shape of fur and the lighter lines broken across its side, ribs exposed to the glare of headlights. A starved dog? But striped? The footage was too blurred, the scale uncertain, but the thing leaping or standing up on its back legs looked like a begging dog or…like a person.

Surely a person, a man rearing up from a crouch to standing as the car bore down on it. A thud and a shiver of blurred image, chaos as the camera slid from where it must have been sitting on the dashboard. Then the filming stopped.

That was the last thing on the camera.

She played it again.

The stupidity of his acceleration through darkness, the danger of it, then the dog. A dog…or then maybe…maybe a thin man? Was that the stretch of a jaw opening? Too wide. Wide like a crocodile. Impossible to tell if these were ribs rubbed raw of flesh or the pale gaps between dark markings on the flank of the animal.

Jessica was holding her breath as she did every time she hit that stretch of road.

She breathed in. Listened to the ocean and made herself breathe to the rhythm of its lapping. She played the clip again. It seemed even less clear on the second and then third viewing, as if each time she pressed play a little bit of the resolution was worn away.

Some animal, some person. It, or he, rose up or reared or stood. It was not an answer but a series of questions. The video fell to blackness. She played it again.

'Hey.'

He was holding a basket of produce. Baby carrots, honey, chocolate, cheeses, whisky. She noticed with just a tingling of interest a small wooden box stamped with the word *truffle*. It was only seeing the box and remembering her first taste of Matthew's fresh truffled risotto that reminded her she was hungry. Glen looked a little like Matthew, but he was thicker around the face, heavier in the shoulders. He was taller, too, and when he hugged her she felt like she was suffocating against his chest. He smelled faintly of diesel with a cloying top note of cheap soap. She tried not to push him away, struggling to delicately free herself from his arms.

Behind Glen, Matthew's mother and father (Gina and Matt; it was important that she remember their names this time) stood arm in arm looking tired and sullen. She knew Rhianna would be with them and followed the cloud of smoke to where she was puffing furiously on a cigarette, leaning on a hire car. She was peering angrily at the flat expanse of ocean visible between two of the cottages.

'We thought you might have forgotten to feed yourself,' said Glen.

'No, that's not it at all.' Gina might have been scolding him. Jessica remembered that Gina always sounded like she was scolding someone. 'It's just that the markets were on at Salamanca on the way through and we never get down to the city, so we thought…'

'It's lovely. Thank you.' Jessica took the basket, which was heavier than she had expected. Fudge, apple paste, spiced cherries. In her first weeks down here she'd eaten so many spiced cherries. 'You should come in.'

She shuffled back, holding the door open with her foot until all three of them had squeezed past. She stared out towards Rhianna, who held up the cigarette and shrugged.

Jessica let the door slap loudly closed behind her. The house was a mess. She wasn't expecting them. Had they answered her email? She really couldn't remember. Maybe they had said they were coming. Where would they stay?

'I hadn't—I didn't…'

'Hey, we should have called from Huonville. Let you know.' Glen was looking around the lounge room, the plates piled up on the table, the clothes that she had just dropped to the floor. Jessica noticed a pair of her underwear spread out gusset-up on top of the jeans she had stepped out of last night, crotch gaping towards the ceiling. She kicked at the pile on the way past, covering the underwear with a T-shirt. She rested the basket on the kitchen bench. The gun was lying there on the bench, just where she had left it. She picked it up and slipped it carefully into the cutlery drawer.

'We're just here to help.'

Gina's face collapsed in on itself. The smile turned down, her forehead became a tangle of wrinkles, her eyes leaked water.

'Ginny,' Matt whispered, 'don't start that again. Not helping.

Just not helping.'

Gina pursed her lips and returned to smiling but there was nothing real in it.

'Well, I...'

Glen rested a hand on Jessica's shoulder and she noticed the tension in her neck. 'We're staying at a rental in Dover.' They wouldn't be expecting her to put them up, which was a relief.

Jessica realised she was still carrying her keys. She'd been about to get in the car. She wanted to drive back there, as she had three times already since sunrise. Two nights in the cold. They burned in her mind like notches scratched into a prison cell wall. How many nights could he survive? She wanted to stand at the place where they'd found the car, listening to the helicopters hovering overhead, watching the police talk purposefully into their handsets, watching the bars on her phone dwindle to nothing and the words *SOS only* take their place in the corner of the screen.

Yes, she thought every time she saw the words illuminated there, yes, that was an appropriate assessment of her current situation.

'Anyway, we just thought we would say hello, see how you're going. You have my number?'

Jessica nodded, even though she didn't know. Matthew's things were all around her. His table, his chairs, his beer kit downstairs, his guitar, his taxidermised salmon above the television, DVDs. Did it all belong to them now? There was nothing of her in the place except her computer and some journals and papers and books.

'We want you to come over for dinner. At the rental place. Here.' Glen typed something into his phone and in a second her own phone beeped and her heart leapt in her chest. For a moment she thought it was the police, some new development in the search, *we have found his body.* But when she looked, the message said Glen Masterton. He had sent her his address.

'Don't bring wine. Don't bring anything. Just come. Or call. I can pick you up. Will you come?'

She nodded. She didn't want to go anywhere. She didn't want to leave the house unless it was to stand there in the road where he was lost. He would come back to her either here or there. He didn't know the address in Dover; he would never find her there.

'I'll pick you up, actually. Don't drive. I don't want you driving.'

Why was she nodding?

He turned her towards him and pressed her into his chest. There was something wrong with the way he smelled.

She had met the family twice. Two interminable Christmases. Each time she had smelled this same thing, stale beer, nervous sweat, an underlying unpleasantness working hard against his winning smile. She pulled away as quickly as she could without appearing rude. She looked out past the sliding door, past the porch and out over the ocean. Clear sky, no chance of rain.

He cupped her chin as Matthew always did. 'I'll pick you up. Just be here after sunset. Can you be here?'

She was nodding, mutely, like an idiot. Nod, nod, nod.

And then, suddenly it seemed, she was standing at the door, staring out to where Rhianna dropped the butt of her cigarette on the ground and stepped on it with her thick hiking boot. Rhianna held up her hand as if to press it against a window. She didn't wave, just held it there and Jessica held up her own hand, pressing the air, feeling suddenly more lonely than she had ever felt.

She watched as Rhianna gathered her thin and gently twitching limbs together and folded herself into the back seat of the car next to her brother. She slammed the door shut. Their father backed out too sharply, skidding the wheels on the loose gravel at the edge of the road. They seemed to belong here. Their great-great-grandparents had joined the killing lines, hunting out the real locals, and killing everyone in their path. She imagined them walking through the same forests now, searching for one of their own, closing ranks. The acidic hug of Matthew's brother dragging her into their fold.

She shivered. Closed the door of the shack behind her.

In the basket she found a jar of anchovy paste, which she hated but Matthew loved. She lifted it and placed it carefully on the shelf, for when he came home. She lifted her hand to her face and covered her eyes.

Pressing against tears with the palm of her empty hand.

'And how's your mother, then?'

Jessica had enjoyed the relative silence of the car ride. Glen driving steadily, slowing only once when a wallaby hopped out in front of the car. At the place where Matthew had disappeared Glen reached over and held her thigh as if perhaps to restrain her from leaping out of the car and breaking through the crime-scene tape. It was only after they rounded the bend and Glen put his hand back on the wheel that Jessica wondered if the gesture was vaguely sexual.

She'd shifted a little towards the passenger side.

'My mother?' They had never met her mother. Jessica wondered what Matthew might have told them.

Gina handed her a glass of white wine and Jessica took a big gulp. 'I think she's okay.'

'Oh. Don't you keep in touch?'

'Mother.' Rhianna rolled her eyes. She was wearing a short-sleeved T-shirt. Must have a fast metabolism. She was always twitching and shifting from foot to foot. Thin as a stick, and her skin looked dry and sallow.

'What?'

Rhianna rolled her eyes again and pursed her lips. It was easy to imagine her as an old woman, a husk of flesh with those same narrow, angry eyes and smoker's lines around her disappointed mouth.

'I told her about Matthew, I emailed her.' Jessica realised she sounded defensive. She took another big sip of wine.

'Here.' Gina took hold of her coat and Jessica shrugged it off.

She let Matthew's mother lead her to the dinner table, an ugly rectangle of opaque glass held up by black metal tubes. Nothing in the rental house matched. There was a print of dolphins in fluorescent blues above an avocado velour couch, and a painting of a ship on a rough sea that seemed like a consolation prize for the view over the RSL carpark. She could still hear the ocean but all she could see through the window was a line of industrial bins.

They sat nervously across from each other. They had never been in a room together without Matthew mediating. *Don't talk about politics, don't talk about race, don't talk about religion.* He had counted out the dangerous topics on his thick, callused fingers. *Well, what is it safe to talk about?* And he said, *Weather's always a goodie.*

Rhianna tapped her knife on the glass tabletop and Jessica

could see the yellowed marks on her fingers, could smell it on her clothes.

'Gosh,' Jessica blurted, 'the winter's cold this year.'

'Can't get the wood dry for burning.' Matt shook his head. 'Do you find that? Or do you buy it in, like?'

'We buy most of it.'

'Well. You haven't got the acreage.'

'She's got that whole forest down there, Dad. You'd get some in the forest, Jess, right?'

'No. That's national park.'

Matt shook his head. 'Time we claimed it back off the parks. Open it up. Bloody waste to lock all that good wood up like that.'

Matthew would have jumped in here to rescue her. A joke, something charming said with a nudge and a wink. She found she had nothing but her own truth. The forest needed some protection. It wasn't going to fight back and protect itself.

'We might have to agree to disagree,' was all she could manage.

'You staying on now?' Gina interjected.

Rhianna stared sharply at her mother. 'Give it a rest. He's not even definitely dead yet. It's only been a couple of days.'

'I wasn't...' Gina's eyes flooded with tears and she stood, moving towards the kitchen, 'I just meant now she's finished at the university. You've finished there, right?' Gina thrust her hands into flowered kitchen gloves, lifted a steaming pot off the stove and lugged it to the table.

'Just got to submit. Then the corrections, if I pass...'

'See? So I was just asking—'

'I'm not sure if I'll stay. I haven't...I didn't get time to think about it.'

'Your mother will probably be glad to see you go home, right?'

'I imagine so,' Jessica said.

'Do you want us to say grace?'

Jessica looked up. She had no idea what Gina could mean. She didn't know what the answer should be. They were waiting for her to speak.

'If you want to.'

'Only for you,' Gina said. 'If you need that. With your mum…'

'Oh.' Jessica shook her head. 'Oh, then no.'

'So.' Glen scooped a ladleful of stew onto his plate. 'You work up them caves, right?'

'Yeah, I'm there three days a week. Cave tours, mostly; a bit in the hot springs and the cafe. Cleaning.'

'Do they get dirty much?' said Glen.

'Worms,' Jessica said. 'And leaves. But lots of earthworms coming in after the rain. And kids dropping things in the change rooms.'

They all nodded. There was nothing really to follow with. She stared down at the meat on her plate and all she could smell was that reek of feral animal, the scent that had woken her on the night he disappeared. A dog in the house and her hands slipping easily around the grip of the gun.

'What do you say to a girl with a PhD in Hobart?' asked Rhianna.

'Can I have fries with that?' Jessica nodded. She had heard it before.

Rhianna snorted. Jessica half-smiled. She liked Matthew's sister. Maybe they could be friends.

She cleared her throat. Find something to fill the silence. 'Do you do much fishing up at Bay of Fires?'

'Nah. Can't stand boats,' said Matt. 'Bloody money wasters. Got to clean all the parts out every time, flush the motor, scrape them back. Bloody useless things.'

Glen shovelled food into his mouth and spoke through it. 'You go out, don't you? Matthew said you like to put a net out.'

'Yeah. Now and then.' It suddenly seemed excessive to tell them that she went out on the water every day.

'What you bring in? Cray?'

'Sometimes, yeah. Trumpeter. Pull in some flathead in the bay.'

'Bony bloody things,' Matt said.

'You've got to know how to fillet it, I suppose.' Jessica bent to her food. She had nothing to talk to them about at all.

'They won't find him,' Gina said finally. 'You know they won't find him tomorrow or the next day. You should start thinking about that.'

Her husband thumped his palm against the table and Gina flinched as if she had been hit.

Jessica sucked her breath in. Did she look like that when Matthew flew off the handle? Did she look so…cowed? She hoped not.

'Well, where can he be?' Gina said. 'It's fucking minus two degrees out there of a night. Two nights, Matt.' She had her head ducked low to her shoulders as if she was anticipating a slap. When she picked up her glass it shook.

Jessica reached for her wine and clamped her fingers tightly onto the stem. It was what they were all thinking. Tomorrow the police and volunteers would pick up the search again, but it was what they would all be thinking. Minus two degrees of a night. And Matthew out there in it.

Jessica was nothing to them. She was living with their son and she wouldn't have been their first choice for him, either. She saw herself through their eyes. City girl, short, a little fat, her years in lecture theatres bleaching away any prettiness she might once have had. She had seen photographs of the girlfriends before her, blonde or red-headed, thin as his sister, flirting with the camera with their harsh practical eyes and lifted bosoms. One of them wearing a bikini underneath a down-filled jacket with desert boots and a beanie. Ridiculous. But she had noticed the way his family looked her up and down when they met her, their obvious surprise.

This meal was a kind of goodbye. A wake for him, but mostly for her.

'You know I'd better...' she began.

Rhianna tapped a cigarette out of the packet, slipped it between her lips, clicking her lighter on the table as if beating out Morse code.

'Write him off, Mum. Go on. You bloody know he could be anywhere? Have they followed up with all his bitches? Ouch.' She flinched. 'Don't frigging do that, Glen. She's smart, Miss PhD. She knows what he's like. Even bloody—the last one, what's her name, Sharon, was it? Even she picked it and she was dumb as fuck. We should be asking Jess for all their names and numbers. Did you check his phone already?'

Jessica found herself standing with her mouth agape.

'I don't think—'

'Jesus, Rhianna.' Glen pushed his plate away and stew slopped over onto the tablecloth.

'Well, what the fuck are we doing talking about fucking flathead or whatever when our fucking brother is gone? Our brother. And you know what he's like. If he's not dead already, he's gone into hiding somewhere. We all know he could've just ducked his head down, get the heat off.'

'Shut your fucking mouth, Rhianna!' Matt stood and Jessica noticed the way they all leaned away from him. Even Rhianna, who seemed unfazed by anything. This temper, Matthew's temper, running through the men in his family.

Matt picked up his dinner plate and for a moment it was held, suspended. All faces turned to watch as he carefully aimed his plate over the heads at the table and flung it towards the kitchen. The plate smashed. Runnels of gravy trickled down the side of the refrigerator.

'Take Jess home now, Glen.'

His voice was quiet and cold. It slid into Jessica's veins and stayed there.

She pushed her chair back from the table. 'Thanks, Mrs Masterton, for dinner.'

Gina didn't answer. Her eyes never strayed from her husband's stony face.

'I'll do it.' Rhianna hurried to get her coat.

'You've had three glasses—' Glen started, but his father tutted and he shut up.

'What? Cops going to pull me over?' Rhianna was pulling her boots on, lacing them. Jessica hurried to do the same.

In the car Rhianna offered the packet and Jessica hesitated, then took a cigarette. She wound down the window and it was like pressing a block of ice to her face. She was getting a headache just from breathing it.

'Arsehole,' Rhianna said, nodding her head back towards the rental house. 'They're all arseholes.'

Jessica leaned over to catch a light.

Matthew had broken a plate once. Jessica remembered, didn't want to remember. The same way his father did, no real rage in him, just a cold, calculated lift and throw. It must have been pesto. She remembered the green splatter she had to wipe off the wall. She remembered apologising—of course it had been her fault. She had been a constant provocation. Opinionated, snobbish, rude. She shuddered when she remembered how awful she had been when they first met, straight out of undergrad, knowing everything and nothing.

'No one's going to tell the cops where he is. Am I right?' Rhianna turned her head away from the road to stare at Jessica for an extended moment. Matthew's eyes. She began to feel nervous about the bend coming up.

'I really don't know what you mean.'

'Really?' Rhianna was mocking her accent, putting English plum into it. City accent.

'Seriously.'

Rhianna shrugged. Looked back to the road and adjusted the wheel. 'Okay.'

'Well?'

'What?'

'What do you mean?' asked Jessica.

'If you *really* don't know, I'm not going to tell you, am I?'

'But you think he's alive?'

She pursed her narrow lips. 'I'd give it fifty one way and sixty the other.' Which made no sense at all, but Jessica left it at that. She threw the butt of the cigarette out the window, wound it up and huddled the coat tighter around her shoulders.

'Fucking freezing,' she said.

'You're not wrong, doctor girlfriend,' said Rhianna. 'You are not wrong.'

She had been out in the boat. She still held the life jacket clutched to her chest like a baby. She preferred it out here with the fishermen. They were used to the silences. Ten of them on the water, checking the very edges of the land. The water so clear she could see straight to the coarse sand at the bottom. Clumps of kelp, flathead pretending to be rocks. The volunteers peered towards the bottom, reversed, moved on, peered again. Looking for a body. He would have had to push through five kilometres of thick forest before plunging to his death at the bottom of a cliff face, but she supposed it was possible.

She heard someone shout across the waves, saw a second boat churn towards the first. Both men peering into the water, both boats tilting to one side as they did so. She watched, heart racing, as one of the men leaned over and started to drag something into the boat. She thought it might be over right there. But then the boat swivelled. He was pulling a net and there were at least eight large salmon still twitching in it. A break-out from the fish pens. They would all be putting their nets out later. There'd be fish in hers too; she made a note to herself to take some over to his parents' place. To make up for last night.

She stood at the side of the road and hugged her life jacket as if she might drown without it. She had no idea how many men were out there. Mostly men—she had seen two women check in with the police and disappear into the forest together. A helicopter circled. It was pointless now. If he was out there they would be looking for a body.

She noticed how people avoided her. They looked down at their boots when they passed by, reporting directly to the police officer, giving her a wide berth. They all knew each other, stopped and enquired about wives and children and cousins. It seemed she was the only person who could not recall one name.

Eight years and she knew no one. *You wouldn't like them,* Matthew would tell her. *Just some locals. Just some do up the pub. Rednecks. Them up the road.*

She stared at strangers' heads adorned with leaves. It was like they were all wearing wreaths, participating in some rustic ceremony that she was excluded from. Then Glen emerged from the forest, one familiar face, and walked towards her. He was panting. A cut on his arm had begun to bleed.

'I don't know how you could find anything in there,' he said to her, leaning against her car. It was cold but he was sweating. She could smell the acrid scent off him: stress-sweat. Matthew would smell bad, too, when he was angry or upset. Most days. They seemed to have hit a patch of bad days. Always reeking of anger. Family trait, then. Odd. She had never noticed the similarities before. When Matthew and Glen were standing side by side she saw only their differences.

'Hey,' he said, 'do you mind if I ask you something?' They had not yet mentioned the night before but it was there, a cold dead place between them.

'Were you okay? I mean before…' He indicated the bush, tilting his chin. 'Were you guys solid?'

The police had asked about their relationship, their sex life, the intricacies of how they lived together. She had practised her answer and she gave it now, as if reciting a script.

'We have never been happier.'

'Okay, it's just that Matt—'

'What about Matthew?'

'Well, I know what he's like.'

'I don't know what you mean.'

'Come on, Jess. I'm on your side here.'

'I honestly don't know what you're talking about.'

He stepped away from her, looking closely at her face, examining it. Jessica felt exposed under his gaze. She looked away.

'All right.'

'He's not dead.' She sounded like Rhianna, the crazy edge to her voice, she knew it. Tomorrow they would call off the search. He was dead, or as good as dead. She had to start believing the evidence. She had to start coming to terms with it.

Glen shrugged. 'Maybe. Big country, isn't it?' He looked out at the tight bushland, the trees clinging to each other, separated only by prickly brush and tall grass. He pulled his cap off and rubbed his head. His eyes narrowed; he continued to rub the same spot. 'That's a fucking tick, isn't it? Is it?'

He had to bend down so she could confirm that, yes, he had picked up a fucking tick. He swore and threw his cap down on the ground.

'Here. I'll take you back to the shack. I've got some tweezers, I'll get it out.'

For a moment she thought he might refuse. He looked back towards the forest. It was so dense that they would miss him even if he were lying ten feet away from them. It was impossible. The search was impossible. Finding a body would be out of the question. The helicopter hovered low and close overhead. Jessica saw Glen duck involuntarily.

'Come on.'

After a moment's hesitation he opened the passenger door and climbed inside.

Rhianna was there, sitting on the balcony, dropping her ash over the edge into the septic garden below. She stood guiltily when they pulled the curtain and opened the door. Crushed the butt under her shoe and kicked it off the balcony.

'I got a tick,' said Glen.

'Fuck.' Rhianna pulled on her brother's shoulder till he dipped his head and let her search through the dark hair. 'Remember that New Year's Eve?'

Glen laughed. He pulled one of the dining-room chairs out and sat on it. 'God, Matt was a pussy, wasn't he? No headache yet. Just itching. Better get it out quick, though.' Jessica passed Rhianna a pair of tweezers and stepped back to let her concentrate on the inflamed patch of scalp.

'For a tough guy he was such a fag.' Rhianna leaned in with the tweezers and twisted, pulling at the same time. Her brother didn't even flinch.

'He was a dickhead, wasn't he?' he said.

Rhianna pulled a second time and Glen yelped, the smile suddenly gone as he pushed her firmly in the chest and sent her stumbling back against the couch.

'Fucking hurt.'

She recovered her balance and lunged at him, and he caught her by the wrist. Twisted it till she begged him to stop. Then he laughed.

'Fucking idiot.' Rhianna spat. Actually spat: Jessica stood in a corner of the room, staring in disbelief at the gob of spit on the floorboard.

'Slag,' her brother shouted after her as Rhianna stormed past him and out the door, cradling her hand.

She turned and spat again. This time she hit her target, landing the gob squarely on her brother's cheek. 'Fuck you.'

Glen watched as she thundered down the wooden stairs and stomped off along the high tide line. He licked the moisture that hung at the edge of his lip then rubbed it with his sleeve.

He turned to Jessica, as if finally remembering that she was there. 'Everyone's a fucking drama queen today, right?'

She said nothing.

'You should fuck off now too. I mean fuck off to the mainland or whatever. You can't stay here.'

'Why not?'

'Well…they know you're alone now.'

'Who?'

'The dogs.' He nodded with his chin back along the road to where the holiday shacks dotted the side of the road in pretty shades of pink, blue, lime green, yellow. 'Local fellas.'

'I'm not afraid of them,' she said.

'No?' He laughed. Cruel. She thought it sounded cruel. 'You should be.' The way he looked her up and down, she felt like her skin was crawling with lice. If he hadn't walked out then she would have asked him to leave.

Jessica shut the door behind him and locked it. Pulled the curtain across. She waited, listening to the sound of his car starting. When she heard it wheeze up the road she realised she was shivering. She opened the fireplace and laid another piece of wood across the coals.

There were no helicopters. There were no parked cars. A scrap of police tape still clung to one of the trees, trailing like a spent party popper.

She left the car idling and walked over to the flash of yellow. Tugged at the stubbornly knotted tape till it tore free. This was not a car accident. There would be no wreath taped to a pole. She stood there and tried to figure out what it was. Not an accident, not a heart attack, not even a murder, or at least there was no sign of a murder. What was it, then?

An act of God. Her mother's voice, so clear that she flinched, hunched her shoulders, ducked her head a little.

She was thirteen years old again and cowed. Eyes on the ground, trying not to look challenging, hoping not to catch the eye of Silas. Silas, standing at the front of the assembly, pontificating in that stupid accent; even now she could feel her lips curling back in a sneer at his Midwestern drawl. Silas pointing to one of the women, to her mother, a gesture for her to follow him, and then Jessica would curl up on her bunk wondering if one day he would point to her like that and she would have to follow him. To confession.

Jessica had been fiercely unpretty. She'd made herself so—the hunching of the shoulders, the gluttony that made her flesh pillowy, the shuffling of her feet against the cracked kitchen lino.

No. Matthew disappearing was not an act of God. This was why she hadn't called her mother. She had emailed, an old address, knowing that the congregation frowned on private emails. She didn't want her mother or the congregation to know about this at all, imposing their superstitious bullshit. There was an earthly explanation for this vanishing.

Jessica took his phone out of her jacket pocket where she had been carrying it since he vanished. She opened the text messages and scrolled through. His phone was full of strangers. Unlike her, Matthew was a social creature, always meeting someone after work or just ducking out to help someone with their splitter or to heft a boat up onto a trailer. *Should I come?* And of course his answer was the same every time: *God, no. You'd hate him.*

She knew a few people to chat with, up at the university. She didn't mind Gus, the other staff up at the caves. But she didn't know who Gary Grenhardt was, or EJ or Helmet or Jacker M. The messages themselves told her nothing. *See you there. I'm bringing a slab. Golum or cricket? Too much ginger makes it explode—fun.*

She found herself scrolling in earnest, searching for women. This was the kind of girlfriend she never wanted to be; but there was Rhianna, her cold flat stare, her contempt.

Cindy, Sharon, Carla, Maggie. He seemed to treat them all the same, a pleasant jokey style. *Gotta love them organics x. Too many shandys? x. How's the frostbite today? x.* Every text held an echo of his actual voice, his inflection, his easiness with everybody. He seemed to like everyone equally. There was no difference between a text to Cindy and one to her. He signed off with an x every time, but kisses were innocent enough. He always leaned in and kissed a lady on her upturned cheek. Jessica had stood beside him as he did this a hundred times at the food store. Matthew knew everyone. Matthew was friends with everyone.

Jessica stood and wandered into the kitchen. She opened the fridge. Maybe she was finally hungry. She pulled out instead the bottle of white wine Matthew's parents had brought. Opened her laptop.

She had just started a document on pyrosomes, unicorns of the sea. She sat staring at it until her head began to throb. She put her hands over her eyes and pressed hard. Now there were little flecks of light scattered across the dark of her eyelids. Illusions. Her mother used to say these flashes of light in the dark were angels watching over her.

The men out there searching had to give up eventually. Matthew, the flesh and blood of him, was gone. He had been real, but now he was just a phantom. There was no point hunting for him any longer. She had to believe he was gone. Going through his phone would not bring him back.

She opened a new Word document and wrote *MISSING* at the top of the page. She centred it, made the word bigger. A photo of his face, cheeky, handsome, smiling. Centred her name and number at the bottom of the page. Everyone in town knew he was missing. The flyers would be for the tourists. She pressed print. Watched a dozen iterations of Matthew's smile materialise on the printer.

She realised suddenly that she was lonely.

She turned to the fire now, nothing but coals, and fed it twigs and newspaper. Watched it blaze. Without a larger log it would be all light, no heat. A moment of incandescence, then the bone-deep cold of the southern shores.

She hefted a log onto the blaze and tried to remember who they bought the wood from. One of Matthew's friends, CJ or Jacker or Gary. She stared into the fire for a long time, then dragged herself to standing and picked up the phone again. Jessica plugged his phone into her laptop. *Always trust this computer?* Clicked *yes*. She watched as the images loaded down. When she clicked on the fragment of footage her throat clenched.

Light. Trees. Black. The sound of the car accelerating. Light again. The sound of his laugh. Dickhead. He was such a dickhead, just like his brother said. So much of his father in him. His brother's stupidity, *the blustering confidence of a fool*—her mother's words. She felt guilty for entertaining them. The lights snapping on to illuminate—she pressed the space bar to pause the image. Was it a dog? There was something around; whatever killed the possum in the caves would be roaming these woods. It had to be a dog. She pressed her finger against the screen, leaned closer. A striped dog? Or a starving, hungry dog, its ribs cruelly catching shadow? Play. Stop.

The creature's mouth opening. It was grainy, but that must be what that darkened line was, the glint of teeth. A grin too big for a dog's mouth. She knew what it looked like. A unicorn, a miracle, an act of God.

She left the image hanging on the screen and opened a new tab. *Dog, Southern Tasmania, striped.*

And the internet chugged through a billion possibilities and brought her some options. Thylacine. Tasmanian tiger. Extinct animals: thylacine.

She toggled back to the frozen image.

An imaginary creature, dead but not forgotten, a phantom. She moved the footage forward a little and the creature reared up. Thick, pale thighs like a man and the little smudge of shadow that must be a penis…She shook her head and moved forward to the point of impact, the blur as the phone slammed across the dashboard and perhaps a glimpse of Matthew's legs as it tumbled to the floor. It was impossible to be sure of anything. This was such a tiny fragment of nothing. This was less than an answer.

Would you like to delete original footage?

Sure. She had the information safe on her own laptop. She watched as the footage was moved from his phone into her possession. Photos of her smiling, photos of him laughing.

She was lonely. She could feel it in her bones, but there was something else. She was edgy, perhaps a little afraid. She didn't know her neighbours. She saw the man across the road, the one with the beagle, walk the dog along the shore every morning. That was it: a daily nod. It had been years and she knew no one.

She shut the laptop and tore the end off the loaf they'd brought her, still in the basket. She lifted the truffle box and put the little brown sphere gently on the middle shelf of the fridge. That would have cost them a fortune. They must know how much she loved truffles. Matthew must have told them. In three or four days it would be ripe, and by then she might be hungry enough to cook herself an omelette. She opened a packet of camembert and scooped some of it out with the wedge of bread. It was good sourdough, getting stale now. A few days since it was baked. More days since he had gone.

She fell into bed, still gnawing on the heel of bread. She would have to get up and clean her teeth. She would have to take off her bra and crawl into her pyjamas. Even these small tasks seemed impossible.

The sound of the acacia rubbing against the fibro wall, the wind howling against the corrugated roof. The space in the bed beside her, empty but still smelling of his sweat. She had put the gun back in the bedside drawer and she reached for it now. Checked it, and buried it under her pillow. She knew how to shoot a gun. She could hit a target at a distance. She had a good eye. It made her feel safe. Not safe, but safer. Perhaps with the awkward bulk of it under her head she would finally be able to sleep.

Matthew took her hand. She had put red cellophane over the end of a dolphin torch. He waved it wildly around, and the red light bounced off stalactites, stalagmites. He sang a stripper's bump-and-grind song, making circles with the red light.

'Shhhh.'

'What? Will I wake them? Are they asleep right now?'

'It's not—'

'Da!' he sang. 'Da-da! Boom Da-da! Boom, Dar-de-dar-da! Boom.' He turned the torch towards her and made red circles on her chest. She laughed despite herself.

'I've never taken anyone here before, Matthew.'

'I'm your first?'

'Stop it.'

'A virgin.'

'Matthew!'

'So why are you taking me to see the cave?'

She shrugged. 'Because it's my cave. I discovered this entrance, this network. It's connected to Exit and Mystery Cave, sure, but for now, until I publish my research, this cave is mine.'

'And...?'

She cocked her head to one side, a question.

'Because...you...love me! You love me! Admit it!'

She watched him as he swung the red light of the torch, making a red heart in the air.

'Yes,' she said. 'I do. I love you.'

'You love me!'

'All right. I said it already.'

And then they turned a tight corner and the cavern opened up before them and he fell suddenly silent, agape. They were looking up at the universe. Her universe.

'Welcome to Winter Cave.'

He said nothing. He turned silently towards her and then he held her and they kissed under a million winking lights.

'I love you so much, Jessica,' he said, when he came up for air.

She was awake now. She knew that this retelling was just a dream, a moment embedded in her subconscious, dragged up into REM sleep, a cruel reminder of what she had lost. She didn't want to open her eyes. She didn't want to remember. She heard a car rattle past the cabin, someone off to work, the early shift. She wanted to plunge into sleep but already the lights were winking out above her.

I love you, Jessica. But she was forcing it now. She was conjuring up his voice and it felt hollow, fake. It was too late to get the moment back. She was awake now, but she kept her eyes shut tight. She didn't want another day to dawn. She lay as still as she could while sleep receded like the tide.

The southernmost pub in Australia. Last watering hole, last convenience store, last petrol stop. The one time her mother came to visit, she called it *the end of the earth* and Jessica snapped back *the earth is round, if you haven't heard.* There is no end to the earth.

After years living five minutes' drive from the Southport pub, Jessica had never stepped inside. Of course she had often visited the shop attached to the building. It was the only place close by to get milk and bread and toilet paper, but for wine they would drive all the way to Dover. Half an hour, and a few dollars saved on the trip. Everything cost more at the local pub, even a takeaway bottle of riesling. She parked her car outside the building, in the muddy stretch of carpark. There were other cars here. Not many, but enough to know it was Friday night.

Three men were perched on high stools at the bar. Flannelette shirts, jeans, workboots. The youngest one was wearing a tan-coloured beanie. There was a woman, too. Jessica noticed her when she stepped up to the bar. She was holding an unlit cigarette between two fingers, as if she were smoking it, and staring up at the television in the corner. The sound was off, or so far down that it couldn't be heard over the country music coming from the speakers above the bar, but she watched as if she were following every word of the game show. Jessica and Matthew hadn't watched television much. Sometimes a DVD; mostly they just talked. She had often been out on the water or doing fieldwork in the caves or up in Hobart in the labs.

Still, she was drawn to the flicker of the screen. She stood in the middle of the room facing it till the woman with the cigarette turned to scowl at her, as if Jessica was reading a magazine over her shoulder.

She stepped up to the bar. The three men turned to stare at her. She pulled her jumper down over her hips, nodded to the woman at the bar. Jessica had seen her before, working in the convenience store on the other side of the building.

She leaned towards Jessica now. Grimaced. 'Sorry for your loss.'

One of the flannelette men shifted uncomfortably and turned back to his beer. The others continued to stare.

Jessica shrugged. 'I was hoping you would put up a flyer?' She handed the A4 page to the woman. Matthew grinning.

'Of course. Have you got a couple? We'll put one up in the shop for the campervanners. Grey nomads. There's a couple down there now.'

Jessica took another sheet out of her handbag. 'Thanks.'

'Stay for a drink, love.'

Jessica hesitated. She climbed up onto the barstool. 'Vodka soda, thanks.'

The woman poured her drink, waved her money away. 'I should have dropped a casserole down to you. I've been guilty, eh.'

'You know where I live?'

The woman snorted, smiled for the first time. 'You've got to get out more, darling, meet your neighbours. We all knew Matty.'

Matty. Jessica tried to fit the nickname to the man she knew.

Matty was the kind of bloke who played football and wore a flannie like the men at the bar. Any one of them could be a Matty. Certainly not her Matthew.

'He came in here?'

'He'd pop by sometimes after work. Showed off at the table.' She nodded to the deep green felt of a pool table, the rack of cues mounted on the wall beside a framed photograph of the Queen.

'I didn't know he played pool.'

'None of the locals'd play him. Took a bit of cash off any stray tourist that wandered in, though. Candy from babies. Never missed a pocket.'

Jessica took a gulp of her drink. She rested her elbows on the bar and looked around at the room. Matthew never mentioned the pub. She knew he sometimes stayed back at work for a drink with the boys. The braver ones accepted some of his home brew. They never took his smoked salmon. Sick of the sight of the damn fish, they told him. He laughed with her about it, but she knew he felt disappointed. He was a generous soul, made friends easily.

Jessica drank the rest of her vodka quickly and accepted another, pushing a ten-dollar bill forcefully across the counter.

'Will you be leaving, then?'

'Leaving?'

'Going back home.'

'This is my home.'

The woman pursed her lips. 'I didn't mean anything by it, love. But you're alone and everything.'

Jessica nodded. She stared across at the men, lifting their drinks, eyeing her warily.

'You're still hunting for him.'

She shrugged.

'You shouldn't be. He's gone, love. You've got a lot to think about now.'

Jessica said nothing.

'I'll drop that casserole up for you.'

'I'm fine.'

'Still. It's what we do.'

One of the flannelette men, the young one with the beanie, lifted his chin and the bartender moved away to pull a beer into a frosted glass, setting it in front of him.

'Thanks, Helen.'

She hadn't known the woman's name. She didn't know anyone's name. She wondered who Matthew knew, who he had played pool with, which of the locals he knew by name.

'No worries, Kev.'

Helen and Kev. How would she remember? She could barely remember the day of the week.

Jessica finished her drink. She shouldered her bag and pushed herself out into the night chill.

Running the gauntlet. That's what she was calling the drive up to Dover now. The place where she'd once hit a Tassie devil, the place where his car was found, the place where Rhianna told her not to trust Matthew. All the bad things were now signposted in her memory along this same road. It was a relief to come to the other side, where the road eased out into anonymous housing and she could breathe once more.

She slowed at Strathblane. The limit dropped to seventy anyway, but Jessica crawled past the township sign at under forty. There were police cars pulled up in a driveway and along the muddy verge, three of them. The cops were talking to a woman.

Jessica didn't want to be rude; a quick glance and she had to pick up speed again. A blonde woman, thin; ripped jeans. That was all the information she got as she moved past.

It was crazy to think that everything had something to do with Matthew, but she was becoming paranoid like that. Those men in the pub back at Southport, did they know anything? The bartender with her casserole—guilty conscience? She felt like everyone knew more about her boyfriend's disappearance than she did. She glanced in the rear-vision mirror but she couldn't quite see the woman on the front steps of her house, surrounded by police.

She pushed the tacks into the corkboard. Matthew smiled out at her. Beside him a photograph of a boat. Above him a kitten. Missing things, unwanted things, equipment, pets, boyfriends.

The Dover shop used to be well stocked. On Saturdays they'd come here to pick up treats. Local smoked trout, nice cheeses, wine. Matthew would eat a scallop pie from the bakery, sitting in the wan glare of the sun, and nag her to put sunscreen on. Looking up reports about ozone depletion on his iPhone, showing her horror photos of melanoma. He liked to protect her. It was almost like one of his hobbies.

Jessica let her fingers linger over tubes of sunscreen, cans of soup, dried noodles. Things had gone downhill in Dover. The food store changed hands, the pie shop closed—some awful personal tragedy. Matthew would have known all about it.

'Hey.'

She turned, startled. A man was towering over her—a giant. His face was hidden behind a full, scraggly beard; a dark knitted beanie was pulled low over severe eyebrows. He didn't meet her eyes, big hands rubbing nervously together. She noticed a hint of red flannel sticking up between his thick coat and his scarf and wondered if he was in logging. Was instantly ashamed of herself for the old cliché. City girl, judging the locals by their dress. Matthew would have teased her mercilessly on the way home.

'Sorry. I'm William. Will.'

The hand that he held out was worth three of hers. She felt strangely moved, as if this handshake was really a hug. She sank into it, letting herself relax a little, lingering in the warm embrace of the huge fingers.

'William?'

'Yeah. I used to work with Matty. I recognise you from your photo.'

'Photo?'

She watched his face fill up with red: a blush. Disarming. Shyness seemed out of place in such an imposing man.

'Oh. On his phone. In the lunch room, you know. Anyway. Sorry.'

She nodded.

'They're catching squid off the jetty here. Pulling them in. A whole bunch of them.'

She smiled. 'I love squid.'

'I know. Matty told me that. I said he should bring you along jigging with us but he never did. When I saw you just now I thought I could bring my jigs down Southport way. Tonight? Or tomorrow? We could catch enough in an hour for a couple of meals each. While the going's good, that is. Might all be over by the weekend and I'm back on nights then anyway.'

'Oh. I don't…Umm, sure. That would be great.'

He glanced up and she caught his eye for the first time. Another quick flush of blood across his cheeks. She felt certain that Will had been one of Matthew's close friends. Wondered why Matthew had never introduced them.

'Sun sets pretty early now,' he said, looking away again. 'Dusk any time from five, I suppose.'

'How about four-thirty, then?'

'Tonight, was it? I'll pick you up.'

'I suppose you know where we live. Everyone seems to.'

He shrugged, seemed embarrassed. 'You should wear a coat. You'll catch cold walking around like that. Wind's coming up off the icebergs, feels like. Eh?'

He reminded her of Matthew, a larger, shyer version of her boyfriend. It was her turn to feel the colour come into her cheeks.

'Thanks,' she said and turned back to the dusty tins of refried beans, worried that she might tear up and embarrass herself. She saw him leave out of the corner of her eye. Watched him squeeze into a car that would have been more comfortable for someone her size. His knees up around the steering wheel, the chassis scraping along the ground as he backed out over the gutter, awkward clashing of gears.

When he was well clear she stepped out into the wind. There really was ice in it. Her jumper was too thin, the cold cut right through it. She stared across at the pie shop—closed due to bereavement.

The pie shop, her boyfriend, the wind. Everything an omen.

She remembered walking up a hill, just outside the compound. How old would she have been? Thirteen? The congregation were all barefoot, some of the men carrying large wooden crosses. Her toe was bleeding. She was holding back tears, a sense of terror and of joy churning through her. The world was ending. In a few hours they would all be dead. They would ascend. They would be reborn.

She remembered her disappointment—everyone's disappointment—when dawn came and they were still alive. How could Silas get something like that so wrong? Her mother looked embarrassed on their descent.

How come he got it wrong, Mum? I mean, he's the mouthpiece of the Lord.

He wasn't wrong. The Lord pardoned us. A temporary pardon. See that bird? A butcherbird. It's a sign. The world will end soon, just not today.

She thought of her mother now. The feeling of dread so strong it was difficult to remain rational. Something terrible was happening, and not just to her: the world seemed to echo her loss. She was a scientist. She knew the earth had at least a few good decades left, but all the world was screaming out that she should carry those crosses up the hill right now. The End Times had finally arrived.

Police cars. Again. They were waiting at the house when she arrived.

She sat in the car for a moment, listening to the thud in her chest. If this was the moment it would stay with her forever. The sound of the ocean at high tide. The sky, dark-clouded and beginning to spit, spattering the windscreen. Was this how she would remember him? Raindrops on the windscreen?

She stepped out of the car. It was the same police officer, the one with the eye. It slid around to the left now as he tried to look at her. She found herself wondering if they let people into the police force with eye trouble, or if it was an accident on the job. He held his shoulders back, tough. Didn't look quite as young or sweet as he had a handful of days ago.

'Miss Weir.'

This wasn't it, then. If it was bad news he would be more contrite. And there were too many of them; she counted four on her front stairs alone. She could hear another two talking somewhere close, on the beach, perhaps. Under the house? She peered past Lazy Eye, trying to catch a glimpse of them.

'We just have to ask you a few questions about your, about Mr Masterton.'

'Yes?'

They had been under the house. She could see one of them

walking up the side stairs, brushing away cobwebs. She wasn't even sure if it was legal for them to be on her property. The shack was built on Crown land, she knew that—and even then, she was only renting from Matthew's mother. Did that affect her rights? She shut the car door firmly.

'Have you found him?' She knew they hadn't.

'Can we come in?'

She hesitated; nodded. 'Sure.' There really was nothing to hide, but she had an odd feeling of having done something wrong. It was her mother's old suspicion: gripping Jessica's hand tighter whenever a police officer passed them in the street.

She opened the front door. The place looked like someone had broken in and ransacked it. She was suddenly aware of her clothes, which seemed to be strewn from the front door right through into the kitchen.

She shrugged. They knew what had happened. They must know about the apathy that comes with grief.

There was nowhere to sit down. She pulled the chairs out from the table and tipped each of them sideways, spilling her papers. Her own copy of her bound thesis tumbled open onto the floor with a loud thud. She saw the pages turned over, bent, disfigured, torn. For a moment she almost felt a twinge of care.

She sat, and Lazy Eye perched awkwardly on the fold-out camp chair. They had never got around to buying proper furniture. Jessica had thought that her stay here would be temporary. Each passing year seemed like it might be her last. A permanent sense of temporality: years, poised to move on and yet never going anywhere at all.

'Your hus—Matthew. He liked to do a bit of home brewing?'

'You've been under the shack.'

'No—I—we just—everyone knows about that. He used to give it away at Christmas.'

She nodded. 'Is it illegal?'

'No. Nothing like that.'

'Did you see his smoker down there? He liked to smoke fish. Tried making cheese one time but we couldn't keep it warm enough for the culture to grow.'

'Miss Weir...'

She didn't like the way he said Miss, like he was making some comment about her relationship with Matthew. Passing judgment.

'What is this about?'

'Miss Weir.' Lazy Eye glanced back in the general direction of the two officers who were crowding the lounge room with their big shoulders and their tight blue trousers and gun belts. The room seemed even smaller with so many people in it. It was a tiny cottage, compact, self-contained. Big enough for the two of them but barely room for anyone else.

She wondered how the officers must see her now. Lost, probably. Defeated. She kicked at the fallen thesis, pushing it out from under her feet, crumpling the pages as she did it. She would never read the thing again. Eight years. The way she had looked forward to the title. Doctor.

'Did—Matthew have anything to do with drugs at all?'

Her brow furrowed. This was completely unexpected.

'What, home brew...?'

'No. Stronger drugs? Illegal drugs?'

'No.' There was no need to feel guarded about the question. This one was easy. 'No. Never.'

'Are you certain you never saw Mr Masterton high on drugs?'
'Never.'
'Consorting with anyone who was high on drugs?'
'Are you joking?'
'We just have to ask, Miss Weir.'

Dr Weir would be better: it said nothing about her relationship to Matthew. She would tick the 'Dr' box on every form from now on. She would introduce herself as Dr Weir whenever she took a tour through the caves.

'What's this about?'
'Was he friendly with anyone who deals or manufactures illegal drugs?'
'God, no. What? I don't know what you are talking about.'
He stood.
'What is this about?'
'We just have to follow every lead, Miss Weir.'
'Doctor.'
'What?'
'I just—it's—I'm Doctor Weir. Now.'
'Doctor Weir.'

She heard it and felt nothing. It didn't make a difference what they called her.

'We're sorry to bother you, Doctor Weir. We need more information…the investigation…Do you mind if we have a look in his room?'
'Our room.'

He waited. His eye slid away from her face. He wrestled it back. 'All right.'
'We're trying to find him, m—doctor.'

'His body.'

'We are just following up on a lead. I am really sorry to distress you, ma'am.'

He seemed like a nice enough person. He wasn't the enemy. She nodded, and waited quietly, hovering in the corridor as one of the police officers opened Matthew's bedroom drawers, and then hers. Lifted his magazines one by one off the bedside table. There was only room for one of them in the room; the others waited awkwardly by the front door.

The officer held up a notebook. It was the book Matthew kept his notes in, notes for brewing, notes for smoking, notes for preserving.

'Do you mind if we take this for a while?'

'I want it back.'

'Of course. Do you mind if we take his computer?'

'He didn't have a computer.'

'Really?'

'Yeah. The laptop's mine. He never touched it.'

'You still have his phone?'

She took it out of her pocket.

'Will this help you find him?'

Lazy Eye took it from her. Slipped it into a plastic bag. 'I hope so.'

She nodded. She noticed how the floor shook under their feet. Too many men crammed into too little space.

They stepped out into the icy midday sun and it felt like the air rushed back into the shack, filling it with emptiness. She touched her pocket and missed the weight of the phone.

In the lounge room she picked up the heavy bound book. Dr

Weir. She smoothed the cover down with the palm of her hand. *How Do Glow-worms Say Goodnight: The circadian rhythms of bioluminescence in the* Arachnocampa tasmaniensis *of Mystery and Exit caves and, in particular, Winter Cave.* The table was piled with books and papers. Jessica placed the thesis back on the chair.

She wrapped the scarf around her neck.

On the way to the car, she paused. Pushed past the overgrown fronds of the tree fern they had been meaning to cut back; ducked down the short flight of concrete steps. It was raining lightly and she tugged her hood up over her hair. The sound of the ocean hushed louder. High tide, and the water was already lapping against the rock wall.

It was dark under the house. When she switched the light on there was a scrabbling sound. Rats, perhaps, or a wallaby. Maybe even a devil, she'd heard of them making their nests underneath houses. She picked up a broom that was leaning against the wall. His crates of beer were just as he had left them. The plastic vat perched on a workbench, the bags of sawdust, the jars of herbs and spice. She took a step into the room and there was that sound again, a scuttling. She didn't want to have to face a rat. She backed away and left the broom near the entryway.

In the car she turned the heater on full and was blasted by cold air as she backed out onto the road. She shuddered and fiddled with the buttons, knowing the heater wouldn't warm up till the engine did.

The drive was automatic now. She didn't even remember indicating and turning onto the Ida Bay road. The forest swept by in thick clumps. The windscreen wipers cleared away the streaks of rain. She turned the music on. Bach. A sound from the before time. She glanced at the entry to Hastings and Newdegate caves. Next week perhaps she'd call them. Let them know she was ready to come back to work. She breathed out, felt her shoulders shift down: she hadn't realised that she was holding them so tight and high. She relaxed into the drive.

Jessica parked the car where she always parked it. She clicked the boot open, pulled her waders on. It was raining harder now but it didn't matter. There was a rain jacket in the back and she pulled it on over her coat. She always wore the jacket anyway but it was odd to start off on the walk without a backpack; it made her feel light, trudging along the muddy path. There was space to notice: the thick undergrowth, the thump of something hopping away, a bird screeching, a print in the mud—small, oddly shaped—with what might be a row of claws near the pad of the foot. An echidna, maybe? She didn't really know one print from another. She was always too absorbed in her own work to see anything outside of it.

The creek was flowing now; she'd have to watch that. There were times when she'd had to turn back, wait till the rain eased before making her way down to the cave again. The water came up quickly in the wet. Caverns flooded. She had heard about a school group trapped by a sudden downpour, the way back completely impassable. Two children swept away, along with a teacher who tried to rescue them. A second teacher claimed by the caves later when he took his own life, racked by guilt and grief. She had thought at the time how hard it must be for the one who survives.

Jessica picked an easy path across the creek, rock to slippery rock. Easier in the daytime, but she was glad of the gumboots.

She felt the calm of the cave as soon as she stepped through the unmarked entrance. The air was different in here. Colder, damper. Still. There was a silence as if she was holding a seashell up to each ear, a silence filled with the pulse of heart, the whoosh of blood.

She waited till her eyes adjusted. Closed them, counted to ten, lifted her chin and opened her eyes to the universe unfurled above. Her tiny, miraculous larval galaxy.

She knew everything that any human knew about these creatures. She knew that the glow occurred only in the larval stage. That it was used to attract prey, and that sometimes the prey was the adult incarnation of the glow-worm. Cannibalism—the children eating the adults. The children coming too close, eating the other children. She knew that now, in winter, all around her adult flies would be hatching out of the pupas, complete with sexual organs but without the ability to eat at all. They would fly and fuck and lay eggs and die. She had spent many hours contemplating the brutality of it. And yet, every time her eyes adjusted to the dark and she looked up at the little blue lights, she saw not a colony of worms but a whole universe—and her own self, so insignificant under the great sweep of the night sky.

The first cave was the largest. There was one of the biggest colonies of glow-worms in the world clustered here, dangling their sticky threads from the rocks above. She waited till the silence dissolved and the sounds of the world returned to her, the constant trickle of the creek, the drip of moisture. Her heart quietened.

She snapped her torch on and stepped carefully over rocks and mud towards the narrow passageway. There were three main paths into the cave system: Exit, Mystery and now, because of her own work, Winter Cave. She had spent eight years working in the caves—exploring, searching, questioning—and she had only scratched the surface.

There were mysteries here, rumours spread by speleologists, pictures on the rocks further north in the cave system, old pictures, sacred sites hidden away in the vast network of caves. She had never seen them, for all her exploration. The glow-worms lived closest to the entrance caves. No need to crawl through claustrophobic passages or dive through flooded caverns. She loved the caves, but they scared her too.

She squeezed through the narrow crevasse, feeling the walls push close around her. She ducked, turned side-on to negotiate a particularly narrow corridor. She remembered her first time in this passage. The terror that she would become trapped here, the rising panic. It had ebbed over the years, replaced by a sense of homecoming. Now it felt like a gentle cradling, a hug.

A cavern. Smaller than the entrance cave. The little lights on the ceiling and walls seemed to cluster in patches. There were areas of darkness like small islands between the glittering lights. She sat on her favourite rock, her chair, and folded her hands into her lap, letting the torchlight play around her feet.

For the first time since pushing through the narrow passageway into this chamber, she had nothing to learn from the place. She had no burning questions to be answered, no camera equipment to record the glow-worms' light emissions, no notebook to make notes about her work. She turned the torch off and sat in the dark, but it was not dark. There was always the half-light. Always the universe of larvae peering down at her.

She used to sit here and whisper to them. At first, she would ask them what her research question should be. After a year of study, they had answered her.

Do you sleep? she would ask, checking through the graphs mapped out by the raw data. Getting to know the universe, each individual star. *Do you sleep?* And they took a long, slow time to answer her, but when they replied their answer was as clear as if they had spoken.

Yes, they said. *We're sleeping now. Yes.*

Now her voice rang out, surprising her.

'Is Matthew dead?'

So this was why she had come here. This habit of sitting on the one rock and whispering her question to the universe. She pretended to be a woman of science but she was still her mother's daughter, looking for signs and miracles.

'Is Matthew really dead?'

No answer. Jessica took a deep breath. It was nine o'clock in the morning. She had waited seven years for the answer to her first question and she knew now that yes: at this time, her glow-worms would be sleeping.

William's car smelled masculine. Briny, with a hint of cheap aftershave. She looked down at her feet, expecting cans and chip packets, but the floor was meticulously clean and Jessica wondered if he had vacuumed it for her benefit.

William had known Matthew. She pulled the edge of her coat in and shut the car door. A shiver of relief. She could have driven down to the pier in her own car, but there was something chivalrous about the gesture of a lift. She was safe for now, in someone else's hands.

She watched them grip the wheel. Everything about William was too big for the car. What was it? A Hyundai of some kind, made for someone small and slight. His legs were like tree trunks forking up around the wheel; the handbrake was a toothpick in his fist.

He swung the car around and bumped across the pitted surface of the road. The cabins were all lined up along the beach, decorated in festive blue and yellow and orange. A few of them glowed warmly, lights blazing behind curtains. Most were dark.

There was a scent of burning wood in the air. Grey, wheezing breath coming from the chimneys of the occupied shacks.

'These would all be full in the summer?'

He framed it as a question and she nodded. He probably knew this area better than she did.

They pulled up alongside the pier and she opened her door, pushing it against the slap of the wind. Her hair was snatched back into a tangle—she would need a beanie and a thicker coat. She shrugged before he could say anything about it. 'I can't seem to organise myself,' she explained.

He reached into the back seat and emerged once more with a jacket. It hung down to her knees but it was lined in sheepskin and incredibly warm, and she was grateful.

He had the rods jigged up, four of them. The two shorter ones looked new. He took them and Jessica followed him, two steps for every stride down the wind-ravaged wood of the pier.

Three men were fishing, each holding their lines out under the spill of a light, pulling the lines backwards and forwards, bobbing them up and down, hoping to attract the squid. They walked past the first of the men and Jessica saw the patterns of dark ink sprayed out across the boards like bloodstains. As if there'd been a massacre here. She glanced into the man's bucket but it was impossible to see anything but a pool of black. Squid ink. They were biting, then.

Will stopped next to the pier light. Their shadows hung tight and squat beneath them.

'Have you used those jigs that flash?' he said.

'No. Never.'

'I seem to have more luck with them than anything.'

He held the rod over the edge of the pier and let the jig drop. No flashy casting out into the dark, just a simple flick and the lure plummeted. She watched it flare to life as it hit the water, the pulse of it jack-knifing down through the darkness. Matthew would have made more of a show of it. Matthew would have lifted and cast wide, attracting everyone's attention. He was like that: the happy clown. Performing for everyone, enjoying the attention, making everyone laugh at him; with him.

Jessica let her own jig follow Will's, a simple lift and drop. There wasn't really any need to cast out wide. The wind whipped and ran chill fingers through her hair. She reached round and found a lined hood and settled that on her head. She tugged a little on the line, pulled it gently to the left first and then to the right.

'The other day there was a bunch of them. All at once. Couldn't get the lines back in the water quick enough. I suppose they could have moved off by now, but can't hurt to get your other rod in, just in case.'

Jessica lowered the second lure. She didn't go in for these new gadgets but the flicker of light was pretty. It reminded her of her cave, the lights shining in the dark. She let it bob and play at the end of the jerking line.

'Matthew said you do some fishing.'

She shrugged. 'Some.'

'He made out like you were out there all the time.'

'I drop a net in. Put some pots out.'

'Up the Lune River?'

'No. Sand bars. Haven't worked out the way through up there.'

'Miserable things, sand bars…Oop.' He pulled on his line, reeled it in, a steady drag, and it was a squid, all right.

The creature seemed tiny, hanging on the line near his head. She dodged an arc of ink as he snapped it up in his giant's fist and it disappeared entirely. He turned to grin at her, a wide open face, childlike for a moment. Then, just as suddenly, the grin was gone and his eyes turned down and he was just a big hunch of a man, awkward, most of his head hidden under a knitted beanie and the tick of his collar. She tried to smile back but he was no longer looking in her direction.

'I—' A drag on the line stopped her. She reeled it in steadily, the bright flash of it. It swung over the rail of the pier and hung like a misshapen ghost, swaying; then a sucking gasp and she felt the force of the ink spit hard onto her cheek. She wiped her eyes on the sleeve of the jacket, his jacket.

'Damn.' She prodded at the stain with her fingertips.

'Nah, don't worry about that. Get it in the bucket.'

Jessica dangled it over the bucket, shook the line. The creature squirted more ink, rattling the plastic. She shook it again, legs stuck fast to the sharp spikes of the jig, and she pulled sharply. A section of the leg snapped off, writhing on the plastic.

'Better get it back in the water,' Will told her. He was already pulling up another squid. Her second line was tipping slowly and dragging against the rail. 'Here we go.'

One after another they pulled the beautiful primordial hunters shuddering from the water and eased them towards the bucket.

She pulled on a particularly heavy line and was surprised by a fat pop. Something bigger and rounder than the squid, all dark tentacles reaching up—as if to snap the line or perhaps scale it, climbing murderously towards her.

'Gonna eat that?'

She cleared the blade on her trousers and plunged it into the bulbous head of the octopus. 'Sure.'

'You'll have to show me how. Last time I tried it was like eating a boot.'

★

It wasn't alive. It was just the memory of life itching through the nervous system. Still, she felt unsettled, watching the octopus climb up the edge of her little metal sink. She lifted the legs one at a time and dropped them back in. They curled around the dead squid.

'I like this.'

She blinked. He was standing, peering at the wall: a watercolour of a boat on the beach. She had forgotten about him for a moment, looking at the octopus. These little moments of relief from knowing that she was in the world and Matthew was absent.

'It's a postcard.'

'Beautiful colours.'

'Yes.'

She uncurled the octopus leg and pulled the head free of the tube, that big silver eye staring up at her. The slippery layer of skin, so pale now, but in life an ever-changing show of colour and shape. Chromatophores, she remembered. Allowing them to hide in the weed, the sand, the shady bottom of the ocean.

Jessica stared through the window. Something had waved for her attention. A flash of moonlight on the crest of a wave?

'I was leaning towards cephalopods,' she said.

'Sorry?'

'Oh. In undergrad. When I had to specialise. I was interested in squid, mainly.'

'They are pretty great, aren't they?'

'I—' Yes. Something had moved out there in the dark. The night was alive.

'What?'

She felt the hairs at the base of her neck lifting. Something out there. People called this feeling intuition. Her mother would call it a whisper from the Lord. Science would say it was several pieces of sensory information linking up—rubbing against memory, past experiences—pricking her body towards flight or fighting. Something out there near the edge of the water.

'I—I don't remember what I was going to say.'

The octopus leg slapped her wrist, slippery, and she gasped. William was there in a second, towering over her, his head brushing the ceiling.

'It's like the undead. Look at it. All twitchy nerve endings.'

He lifted the tentacle off her wrist and shook it off his fingers, grimacing. 'Tough as a boot.'

'Not the way I cook it.'

'How's that?'

'Lemon juice,' she said. 'The enzymes start breaking down the meat before you cook it.' She placed her finger to the side of her nose then against her lips. He grinned. There was that childlike pleasure. This time she smiled back. It was nice to have someone in the house again, even just another body taking up some of the excess space.

She set the cast-iron pan on the stovetop and lit the gas. Salt and pepper squid to start. Octopus salad, and there was some chocolate at the back of the fridge somewhere. It was almost like a dinner party. Of course, there was also wine. She couldn't face the interminable nights without it.

Will stood at the glass door, peering out at the waves that always seemed close enough to lick at the foundations.

He slid the door open. The wind came in. He closed it.

'Sorry.'

A few of her papers gentled to the floor. She had tidied up a little but there was still a stack of her notes on the table.

He bent and picked the pages up. 'Matthew said you did a blog or something for like a science thing? Does it pay?'

'Science writing? A little. Beer money.' Matthew's words.

He nodded, smoothed out the top page. Notes for a feature on the impact of fish farming on the shark nursery area at Dover. She watched his eyes dart across the page. She could almost see them glaze over. This is why they never had guests to the cottage. Nobody wanted to know about the shark eggs or cephalopod chromatophores, particularly over dinner.

She fried the squid rings quickly, poured them out into a bowl. He sat at their table and the scene looked like something in a child's playhouse, his knees bent to one side as he hunched over the table to eat.

She was suddenly ravenous. She took two rings at once, stuffing them in with her fingers. She hadn't got the forks out. William ate with less ferocity, plucking the squid from the bowl almost daintily and chewing each ring for a long time.

'Did you play pool with Matthew?' She'd had no idea that she was about to ask this. He seemed as surprised by the question as she was. 'I hear he played pool,' she clarified.

'Did he?'

'After work.'

He looked away, out to the ocean. 'I wouldn't know about that.'

She picked up the empty bowl and put it in the sink.

'The trick is to cook it for the shortest time.'

'What?'

'The octopus.'

He stretched his legs out low, slipping them under the table with difficulty.

'Did...'

He smiled at her, angled his head to one side, waiting for her to find the words.

'Did you guys take stuff?'

'What, like steal?'

'No. I...Like, I don't know, speed? Ecstasy? Drugs.' She felt her cheeks growing hot. She was blushing. She held the back of her hand up to her face and felt the hot blood pooling there.

'Who?'

'You and Matthew. Matthew.'

'Do you think he took drugs?'

She caught another glimpse. Turned to the window to stare out into the dark.

William leaned forward to touch her shoulder. Then pulled his hand back sharply as if he was embarrassed to have touched her at all. 'I don't know anything about drugs,' he said. 'Why? Is there something...?'

'No. No. I never thought he took drugs. Till the police...But I didn't know he played pool. Why didn't I know he played pool?'

'Jessica—'

She looked over. He seemed cowed, head lowered, searching the backs of his hands as they fidgeted on the table. She tipped the pan on its side, scooped the sliced octopus into the salad bowl.

She knew what it was he was going to ask her. He wanted to ask her if she was okay. If she needed anything. If he could help. He was a nice man. She could see why Matthew liked him. A good, quiet, thoughtful person. She brought the salad bowl to the table. Warm octopus. She could smell the garlic steaming up from it.

'I fish every morning,' she said. 'I file my stories in the afternoon. There's food, shelter. The shack is cheap. My expenses are minimal. I go out for milk and bread, whatever, so I'm not housebound.'

'Sorry,' he said, and she imagined he was apologising for his presence at her table. He was no substitute for Matthew. He would know this.

He took a bite of octopus and glanced up at her, wide-eyed. 'Fuck, that's good.'

And then she grinned.

The ocean had provided another bounty.

Sometimes, before, she would haul the net out of the water, tricked into a false sense of hope by a tangle of weed or a young shark that she would have to pull free and throw back into the bay. The ocean was an unreliable provider and yet, since Matthew disappeared, she had pulled in a full net every morning. Crays in the pot, scrambling like cockroaches to get free. Her mother would say that the Lord was providing for her. A compassionate God, looking out for her in Matthew's absence.

Today five good-sized salmon slipped silvery onto the floor of the boat, a cod that would be good simmered with coconut milk and spices, three trumpeters. Her freezers would be close to full. She should stop fishing for a while, but the thought of it made her chest clench. That simple activity. Dawn and dusk, dragging the boat into the water, dropping the net. Moments of relief in her unbearable days.

She liked the way the boat pulled against her, the wrestle with the tide. The icy water that spilled over the top of her gumboots, freezing her toes. The sheer physical struggle a respite from the dead weight of loss. She waited for the tide and hauled at the crest of an incoming wave. The boat rose. She wrestled it close enough to tie the rope, then winched it out of the water. She gathered her catch in the large tub by the acacia tree before turning the dinghy upside down to let it drain. As she struggled the bucket of fish onto her shoulder and turned towards the shack, she saw there was a car out the front. A green utility, patched here and there and sealed with an ugly grey filler that covered half the door and a significant portion of the bonnet.

Jessica hefted the plastic container more solidly on her shoulder and felt a shift in the bucket, the death rattle of a fish tail slapping the plastic. She slid the door open and let the container thud heavily on the table.

Someone knocked at the front door.

The dinner plates were still there. Hers and William's. An empty bowl that had been full of octopus salad, the cushions displaced on the lounge chair where he had sat.

Before the disappearance there were never any visitors.

Another knock.

She stood in the corridor. The bright morning seeped in under the door, making the house seem darker. Her hands smelled of the ocean. When she reached for the doorhandle she noticed blood on her fingers. Jessica remembered the twitch of muscle as she slid the knife into the eye of a salmon, a slice to the belly. She had watched it bleed out into the boat.

She opened the door.

The woman was holding a casserole dish. White, dusted with blue flowers. She was wearing workboots, stained with mud and crusted with sand. Thick socks peeking out under the sad hang of a floral skirt, a thick knit jumper in pink and blue stripes, unravelling at one elbow. A scarf wrapped so many times around her neck that the bottom half of her face had disappeared entirely. She had wild white hair, thick clumps of it pulled carelessly up on top of her head, pinned there with an ugly metal clip. Her face was tired and folded in on itself, but the dark eyes set in deep above high cheekbones were sharp.

'For your loss,' she said, pushing the casserole towards Jessica. Her nails were cracked back, black with dirt. There was a sadness in this woman's face, a slackness in the skin under her eyes that felt familiar.

Jessica took the dish, warm as a child in her arms.

'I would have come earlier but I live down near Cockle Creek. News doesn't come as quick down there.'

Jessica nodded once more. She knew she should invite the woman inside but she remembered the two plates still sitting opposite each other on the dining-room table. She hesitated.

'Has anyone from Southport brought you food? Or from Dover?'

Jessica shook her head.

The woman's eyes narrowed, glistening like water. She seemed to roll an unspoken word around in her mouth and finally spat into the grass beside the landing.

'One of Matthew's friends took me squidding last night,' Jessica said, 'That was nice. I haven't…really made any friends here yet.'

'Cunts,' she said with unexpected violence. 'When my man was taken not one single person made the effort. I won't forget that and you shouldn't either.'

'I'm Jessica.'

'I know it. We all know everybody's business. Come down here for privacy and it's like hanging your knickers out on the grapevine.

'Will you come in for a coffee?'

'Yep.'

'Sorry, I didn't catch your name.'

'I didn't tell you. Thought you might have been warned about me.'

Jessica stood aside and let the woman shuffle inside. She didn't remove her boots, and sand and mud shook off them onto the floor.

'Sorry, we cooked some squid here last night. I haven't tidied up. When you're alone…'

The old woman peered at photographs lining the walls of the hall, fish skeletons, tumbledown barns, a fence almost consumed by sand. No photos of Matthew or her. Jessica hated the idea of putting your own face on the wall for everyone to see.

'Maude,' the woman said. It took Jessica a moment to realise she was offering her name.

'I have too many fish.' Jessica reached for the plastic bucket and pulled out the largest salmon. 'Will you take it?'

'Of course.'

'I'll wrap it for you.'

Jessica left the fish sitting on a stack of old newspapers.

'So…coffee?'

'Tea if you've got it.'

Jessica nodded and put the kettle on the stovetop. Tipped the old leaves from the teapot into the sink. She could see the mould growing through them, pressing the mulch together into a solid lump. She wondered when she had last used the pot and stopped herself from following the thread of memory that would run her back into that hard wall of grief. She searched in the basket on the counter for biscuits.

'You live in Cockle Creek?'

'Around there. Just out.' The woman pulled the stool out from the bench and lifted herself up onto it. She was small and thin, fingers brittle as twigs. She looked like a rag doll perched there. 'Not close enough to be one of the three. You know the sign? *Cockle Creek Population: 3.*'

Maude pursed her lips, considering. Jessica watched her come to a decision, cocking her head to one side. 'I live alone now so I'm not good at the social etiquette or whatever. I'll just come out and tell you right up front that my husband was taken too. Fifteen years ago.'

Jessica felt the blood draining from her face. She took a sharp breath, feeling as if she were still in her little boat out in the middle of the bay and the wind had suddenly turned.

'Taken?'

'By the tiger. We heard you got a photo of it, some video on his phone?'

'I—I don't...How do you know about that?'

The kettle screamed. It might have been air escaping from her own lungs.

Maude hopped off the stool and brushed past her to rescue the kettle. Jessica caught a whiff of stale damp fabric mixed with petrol fumes and tobacco as Maude poured the boiling water into the pot.

'Naomi says I can't just come out with it like that.'

Maude led Jessica towards the second stool at the kitchen bench, lowered her into it.

'You've got some video. The police looked on his phone. One of those policemen was talking about it. Said it was a dog.' She snorted. 'Everyone knows, so I don't know why I can't just talk to you about it.'

'You know about the phone?'

Maude shrugged. 'He was always wild, your man. Playing chicken on that bloody road. Used to do that when he was charged up in his teens. Could've killed people. Almost did.' She shook her head. 'Everyone knows everything about everyone. Even me, and I live way out of town. We know about your mum in that doomsday cult and we know your man plays a mean game of pool and we know—'

She paused, rubbed at her eyes with her wizened hand. 'Well,' she said. 'Just try keeping a secret around here.'

Jessica looked over at the discarded plates from last night's meal. Entertaining a man so soon after her husband goes missing. She supposed everyone would know that too. She let her shoulders slump and when Maude brought a cup of tea over she sipped greedily even though it was too pale and too sweet.

'There's twelve of us so far, so if you join us that's an unlucky number. Maybe a lucky one, we're divided on that score.'

'What do you mean twelve? Who are you talking about?'

The woman reached across the bench to pat her hand. It was a faint but awful smell, the smell that clings to the homeless and the very old, the smell of loneliness and neglect.

'Twelve widows,' she said, and squeezed Jessica's wrist uncomfortably hard. 'You are the thirteenth widow. We want you to join us. If you're ready.'

She was further down the road than she had ever been, past the turnoff to Hastings, past Ida Bay and her glow-worm caves. Wild country. Before the clear-felling the whole south end of the island must have looked like this.

Jessica tried to keep her eyes on the road but she kept glancing off into the bush. The forest disappeared into thick darkness just beyond the unsealed road, the sunlight unable to penetrate the wall of trees. The roadkill was phenomenal. She drove over a dead bird of some kind, a possum, big as a dog with ugly patchy fur, and the black hunched shape of a flattened devil. A wallaby sat bloating in the middle of the track and she swerved but not enough: she felt it bump under the tyres. A wave of death-scented air swept into the car. She wound up the windows.

Jessica was looking out for a branch in the road. She almost missed it, skidded to a stop and backed the car up to make the turn into the unsigned forestry track. This must be it, a cutting in the forest and the dirt road climbing up a gentle incline just as Maude had said. She bounced over corrugations, dipped and splashed into deep puddles. The forest closed in around the road: when it swung across to the left it was as if the forest had consumed it entirely.

Then she was looking at cars parked along a driveway. Old cars, plus a couple of newer four-wheel drives. Mostly speckled with bird shit and dead leaves, like her own car. She parked next to a Falcon. When she touched the side window, her fingers came away muddy.

The house was an old farmstead. Peeling wooden boards, holes in the veranda you could put a fist through. You couldn't hear the sea but you could see it in the rust on the curled metal railings. All the downfalls of coastal living without the benefits.

She pressed the buzzer beside the flyscreen. No sound. She knocked, an insipid rattle no one would hear. There was a peal of laughter, and she felt resentment roll through her. These people had lost loved ones too. Widows, Maude had called them. How could they laugh? She pushed the door open and heard it shudder closed behind her.

A coven of faces. All women, all weathered. Old, middle-aged, younger; one teenager among them, bent over and playing with a shoelace. When the girl sat up Jessica was shocked to see she was roundly pregnant. Maybe seventeen—eighteen at a stretch.

They were rough faces, the kind of people she and Matthew would sometimes stand next to at the liquor store. Joking about rednecks in the car on the way home, duelling banjos, *Deliverance*. These were the faces that used to stare at her suspiciously. City girl making a sea change. Before, in the better days, she would smile and pretend to be polite. All she had to do when she was out in public was hold on to Matthew's arm and let him talk. Now she felt lost.

'Jessica.' It was Maude. A familiar face, someone to cling to. 'Have a piece of apple cake.'

She moved towards the circle. There were so many of them. She counted ten. Maybe the other two couldn't make it this month. One of them made room on the couch and Jessica sat, the soggy couch rolling her closer to a thick damp thigh as a urinous fug of sweat and unwashed clothing swept over her. Someone pushed a plate of sliced cake at her face and she fended it off, taking a piece in her confusion, realising that now she would have to eat it.

'Welcome, darling.' An old, old woman, thin and wrinkled as a fallen apple.

Jessica blinked. Took a bite of the cake and felt it dry and thick in her mouth.

'Sorry about your husband, love.' This from a woman whose face seemed kinder.

'We weren't married,' she corrected.

The woman shrugged. There were long dark hairs growing out of her upper lip and her neck. She was wearing a brown shapeless dress, sweat-stained at the armpits. 'Married in the eyes of God. Law has nothing to do with it. Am I right?'

Jessica nodded tentatively.

'It's fucked that the tiger took him. No consolation. But it's totally fucked.'

Jessica tried to swallow the cake. It seemed to be swelling into her throat. She was choking on it. She was going to cough—she tensed and leaned forward—she couldn't breathe, she must be having a heart attack. She held her hand over her mouth and it stretched wide as a carnival clown behind the veil of her fingers. Cake sputtered out and there was the most awful sound she had ever heard, a guttural moaning, a primal scream. It was only when the woman beside her wrapped a heavy arm around her shoulders and stayed her back-and-forth rocking with a strong maternal hug that Jessica realised the sound was coming from her own mouth. The hug tightened. Jessica finally wept.

She had calmed a little. Her head throbbed. Her nose felt rubbed raw. In the darkness they sat in the rank stench of their own bodies, their anxiety seeping out through their skin. These women who barely washed, it seemed clear—bathed constantly, as they were, in their own grief.

Maude opened a scrapbook on the table in front of Jessica and pointed to a photograph pasted inside. A furred body crumpled to the dirt of the road. White stripes across its scrawny side like moonlight through fence posts, its dead jaw a wide-toothed grin. She flicked through the pages. Newspaper articles, photographs letters. These scraps of evidence. These small fragments of lost men.

Melaleuca, Ida Bay, Lune River, Dover, Low Rocky Point, Glendevie, Cockle Creek, Southport. All the little towns and roads and the forests pressing against them. There was a map on a corkboard mounted on one of the walls. Maude swept her hand across the little bristle of coloured flags. She was speaking but Jessica couldn't make sense of the words. Was she having a stroke? She could hear the pounding of the blood in her head. Something in the tea. Some flavourless drug. She was reminded of her first time with LSD, that odd disconnection. The ability to focus on the movements of a person's lips but not hear the words. The police had asked about drugs. Did Matthew take drugs. She was having another panic attack. She knew it. She felt incapable of doing anything about it at all.

Maude lifted her by the elbow and she allowed herself to be led. She imagined this was some kind of initiation and thought instantly of her mother. A sudden clear memory of being held down on a table by her mother—this was after they'd found her by the river, throwing rocks into it with a boy—the hands of the other women pulling her legs wide, the shame as they checked her, the little finger inserted to be sure she was intact, her face flushing with blood even now.

Maude closed Jessica's fingers around—what? She looked down to see she was holding a little green flag at the end of a pin. She had been led towards the map. The flag had a word written on it: Matthew.

Don't consort with boys. Not till you are married. Married in the eyes of God.

The other flags on the board all had names on them: Peter, Charles, Albert, Don. Twelve flags. She didn't need to count them. Jessica forced her eyes to focus on the map, the scattered roads, the solid area of green without any tracks or towns. She put her finger on Southport, traced the road back to Dover. Placed her pin at the halfway point and pushed hard.

Matthew.

She turned to see the ring of their faces staring at her. Even the teenager, her eyes wet with unshed tears, and Jessica realised that the girl's baby must be fatherless.

A thick silence vibrating with unspoken loss. They sat and breathed in each other's stale exhalations. Breath like the grave. Jessica couldn't help thinking that they were rotting inside. And now she was one of them. She had started to decompose.

Then a voice, strident as a horn cutting through fog: 'They didn't believe in the Devil's Triangle and look what happened there.'

Jessica blinked.

'Ellen,' Maude warned.

'Well, look at the map. It's all just around here. Nothing up at St Helens or Devonport. It's *here*. Those things. They live in that forest here. It's the Devil's Triangle all over again. Perhaps it is tigers, but it could be anything. I told you about all the lights them people keep seeing, just around the south, Geeveston down to here, lights in the sky that no one can explain. I saw a thing on TV.'

'Tigers.' Maude picked up the teapot and tilted it towards her cup, *World's best lover* written on the side. A few dark drips fell into the cup and the air expelled from her lungs as she plumped back heavily into the overstuffed settee. 'We call a spade a spade here. Those are tigers, Ellen. We are not idiots or nutjobs or UFO chasers.'

'Although...' A large woman with small, dull-looking eyes. She brushed crumbs from her voluminous chest. 'Ellen might be right. We shouldn't be ruling out anything.'

'Just the scientific facts, Grace. Tasmanian tigers rise up and take people. Just the goddamned scientific facts.'

Jessica made her way back to her seat. There was no tea left in her cup and her mouth was dry. *Just the scientific facts.* Words stolen from her own mouth, the way she would chastise her own mother.

'We should watch your video, Jessica.' The old apple woman rested her cup back in her saucer, her hand a bundle of bones with skin pulled over like a thin glove. Her eyes were filmed. Cataracts.

Maude nodded. 'Marijam's right. I'll get you to send me a copy. We'll keep it with the scrapbook. Your man next to ours. Our evidence. But if you don't mind I'll show the others what was on your phone.'

'His phone.' It came out too loud, too strident. Jessica frowned. 'Matthew's phone.'

Maude was holding out her hand.

'I don't have the phone anymore.' She reached into her bag. 'The police took it.'

Maude glanced at the old woman, Marijam, something unspoken passing between them.

'I copied the footage onto my computer.'

Jessica slid the laptop out of her bag. She opened it, clicked the icon. Heard the hollow sound of wind through the speaker, watched as the women leaned forward, jostling for a better view of the tiny screen, a press of sallow flesh. She leaned away from the table where she had balanced her laptop on a copy of the *Sunday Tasmanian* and a pile of magazines. She wanted air, but the room was full of the stale breath of the women. She stared at the screen. It was impossible to look away.

Darkness, light, darkness.

Jessica felt suddenly guilty, as if it had been her in the car, risking the lives of wallabies and devils. She pursed her lips. The headlights blaring back on high beam. The animal rearing, the bones glowing pale in the light or the stripes standing out against its dark side, the too-wide mouth. Jessica knew that if you looked at the footage frame by frame it might be a mouth or a shadow or nothing at all, all of it hidden in the blur of movement. The women watched, nodded. Maude held her finger over the keyboard; moved it along the track pad, pressed start, setting the footage into motion again.

Jessica knew it by heart, of course, the terrible sequence of events. She felt it on the back of her neck. The cold of that stretch of road, the cold of her bed now he was gone, the cold of the ocean every morning when she launched the boat and dropped her net. The icy chill of the caves. She remembered sitting on the rock in the cave, watching the little lights above her like a universe of fixed planets. Each one a temptation. The insects flitting up towards the benevolent glow and their own death. She felt the chill spreading down her back as the creature reared up in the headlights, again and again and again.

When the women were finally done with the laptop they passed it back to her. Jessica cradled it in her lap like a child. It was hot, as if it had been snatched from a fireplace. She held it in her lap, and lay the flat of her hands gently on the top of it.

'Well,' the old apple lady said, her smile, unbelievably, wrinkling her face even more. 'We are glad you are with us, love.'

Jessica slowed the car to a complete stop and watched the trees loom bright in the car's headlights. She turned the headlights off and the trees disappeared. The tick of the engine cooling, a memory of movement. Full darkness.

There were others out there. Bodies dropped like litter on the side of the road, cold bloating bags of fur, alive now only with insect life. The flesh eaten back to bones. She could hear them now: foot scuffles, throat clicks, grunts and growlings.

She turned the lights back on. Perhaps it was this exact place—the police tape was gone but the trees looked similar. She opened the door and slipped out onto the verge. She had loaded the footage onto her own phone and she held it up now, trying to line up the trees to the frame of the photograph.

No. Impossible to tell one stretch of forest from another. What she needed was a crack in the surface, a fallen tree, an x to mark the spot. Instead, just the white bones of trees and not even a pool of blood to mark where Matthew was…taken. She was not a UFO chaser, did not believe in alien abduction, and yet the result was the same. A life taken from her.

She held the phone up again, pressed play. The lump of road-kill. The white stripes on its flanks. The rising-up into a blur of pixilation and yet there were the hips, the slight hang of a penis between withered thighs. White light from his headlights burning the detail from the scene. A human rising up, or an animal mimicking a human stance the way a bear might, or a dog rearing onto its hind legs, a whippet or a greyhound. Or a tiger, burning bright in the forest of the night.

She felt the skin of her neck tingle. Turned the phone off and slipped it into her pocket, and the cold pressed itself into her skin.

She found her way to the front of the car, touching the warm bonnet. It was so dark that if she stepped away from the vehicle and turned in any direction she might be lost.

Something in the trees. Something large and close. Not a wallaby, no thumping of a tail. She steadied her breath. In through the nose, out through the mouth. When she concentrated, she could smell something, a foetid smell of damp fur and earth. The rustle of leaves. Louder, and louder again. So loud that it must surely be right here at the edge of the road. A shaking of branches, a creaking of tree trunks bending, a breathing—she was certain that was a puff of breath—a snort. The thing, whatever it was, catching her scent. The creature rising up all white-ribbed fur and jaw and dark eyes, the odd transformation from animal to something almost human…Jessica peered out into the thick black for some glint of it, but there was none.

Silence now, beyond the edge of the tree line. On the road, too, only silence.

She listened for the sound of paws. Quiet as a cat. Of course. Now that it was close enough to smell she let herself know that this was true. This was a tiger. The tiger that took Matthew.

'Here,' she said, knowing that her tight throat had barely let out enough breath to make a sound. 'Here, kitty.'

She had come out scarfless, her neck exposed to the chill of the dark. Perhaps the tiger would leap at her throat, so soft and vulnerable. Or her groin. Animals aim for a person's groin—Jessica was certain she had read this somewhere. They catch and drag from the hipbone, the legs snapped back, the body disembowelled, the head dragging slack-jawed into the forest.

'Kitty,' she said, louder now. Needing to know what he knew, to leave this place of loneliness as he'd left it. Needing to find him, finally. 'Kitty, kitty, kitty.'

The light sliced a sudden white arc across the trees. For a moment she imagined this was her death arriving, the train-like roar of the end of her life. Then headlights swinging around a sharp bend of trees and a car was heading straight for her.

She looked not towards the oncoming car, but sideways, to the tree line, to where the tiger would be lurking.

Tiger, tiger in the headlights, eyes glinting, teeth bared. She felt a tightness in her chest, the sound of brakes engaging, squealing. She still did not look towards the car, too startled by what was before her: a hunch of muddied fur, red-reflected eyes, vicious teeth; but the jaw shorter than she expected and disfigured by a red lump.

Not a tiger at all. A devil. Squat and mean and grunting as it lumbered back towards the thickest part of the forest with its odd lopsided gait.

A devil is a dangerous creature but a devil didn't take her husband.

The car screeched to a stop so close to her legs that she could feel the cold rush of air it pushed ahead of its hulking body. A ute. Big metal roo bar that would have crushed her in another metre. She would have died, she had expected to die, no closer to knowing.

Jessica could not see the figure behind the wheel of the car. She could feel him watching her, trapped in his headlights. Swearing under his breath, stupid woman, dumb bitch.

She held her hand up, agreeing, with the kind of wave she might throw to a friend across a busy street. An idiot gesture from someone who had almost caused a fatal accident on a remote road out of phone range.

She climbed back into her car, started the ignition with trembling fingers and eased the vehicle over to the side of the road, pulling up right where the Tasmanian devil had disappeared into the bush. The ute driver revved his engine and gave the horn a good blast as he sped away, heading towards Southport, towards her home.

Jessica became aware of the beating of her heart in the silence that followed. She was alive. She had not been run over, or mauled by a diseased devil. She was here, safe in her car, unharmed. If only this had happened to Matthew: a close call with a devil, a near miss with a ute.

She turned the wheel hard and eased her car back onto the road, following the ute towards home.

'Cave life,' she said, pointing her torch towards the cricket that clung to the damp cave wall.

A little girl pushed to the front of the group and peered up with wide, dark eyes. 'Oh, *wow*.'

'Exactly.' Jessica felt herself beginning to smile. Curiosity killed the cat, her mother always said, but she had never managed to dampen her daughter's sense of wonder. Jessica had been a barrage of questions, slamming against the walls of her mother's church, shaking the bars.

'What does it eat?'

'The cave cricket? Well, there are tiny little insects in here, like fleas. You can't see them'—the kid was already beginning to scratch at her neck under the heavy woollen scarf—'and they don't live on blood like normal fleas, they live on little flecks of skin. When you scratch like that the flakes of skin fall to the ground and the little fleas hop onto them and eat them.'

'And what eats the crickets?'

Jessica trained her torch onto the darker corners of the cave. The lights were switched on but the spiders would be hiding from it.

'I'll show you if I find one, but there are cave spiders all around, hiding in the corners.'

'Oh, cool!' The little girl sidled towards the corner of the cave and peered up at the sharp arrow shafts of the speleothems.

Waves of pointlessness came and went, washing over her like shadows on her skin as she moved the group from cavern to cavern. It was a work day like any of her work days before. But when she took them all to the largest cavern and turned the lights off, she waited in the dark wondering if there was any point in turning the lights back on at all. What if she just left them all here in the dark. What would happen? They would eventually find their way out, she supposed. She would be reprimanded, maybe fired. She thought through these consequences with a dull curiosity, then switched on the light.

'Wow,' said the kid, blinking, pointing at the wall high up above her head. 'Cave spider. Wow.'

William was waiting on the wooden platform. She shut and locked the door. The next group would not gather for another fifteen minutes. She found herself grinning at him, happy to see his giant body there. The weight of sadness lifted for just a moment before she felt it settle comfortably on her shoulders again.

He held up a ticket. 'I thought I'd take the tour.'

'Seriously?'

'I had a day off. You know I've lived here all my life? Haven't taken a cave tour since Year 8.'

'I was going to have a coffee between tours. Do you want some?'

He nodded. She unlocked the storeroom and popped the top off her thermos. The coffee was pale and sweet. She let the steam warm her cheeks, holding the thermos lid close to her face.

The room was filled with the smell of fish. It was in his fingers. It would infuse his skin. She remembered the taste of Matthew, like she was biting down on fresh sushi.

'How's the first day back?'

She thought about it. 'I have no idea. I keep almost feeling something, but then it's gone, like when you remember something important and then you forget it again before you have a chance to say it aloud. Does that make sense?'

He nodded.

'You know, there's a whole network of caves here. They lead down to the river. Some people even feel like Newdegate links up to Mystery and Exit caves somehow, and my cave, the one I found, Winter Cave. It seems stupid that they haven't been explored properly; there might be other cave entrances all over the south. It's like a giant honeycomb under the ground. Not a honeycomb—something else…a neural network.'

'Like a brain?'

She laughed. 'Yes. A human brain. And we are nothing but tiny thoughts in someone's dreams.'

'Sounds like the science talking, Doctor Weir.'

The walkie talkie hissed to life. 'Jess?'

She held the handset to her mouth. 'I'm here, Donna.'

'We've sold eleven tickets to the next tour.'

'Thanks.'

'How are you coping?'

'I'm fine.'

''Cause if—'

'Fine, Donna.'

'Okay.'

Jessica holstered the mouthpiece. She frowned into her coffee. 'Everyone thinks I'm going to spontaneously combust or something.' She squinted up at William. 'Are you here to check up on me too?'

'Honestly? I just wanted an excuse to see you again.'

She felt the flush of blood flowing into her cheeks.

'Which,' he said, 'makes me sound like an arsehole. But I had a really nice night the other…I'm making it worse, aren't I?'

'No. No, I'm glad. I'm not made out of china or something. All this checking in, tiptoeing.'

'Well, if it makes you feel better, I'm not tiptoeing anywhere. Stalking, possibly…'

She laughed. 'Well, I suppose that could be flattering?'

They could hear a heavy thudding of footsteps. The first of the next group gathering on the deck. She heard the little running steps of a toddler and then a thump as the child tripped and tumbled to the floor. A second's pause before the wailing started, loud and constant.

'Welcome to the glamorous world of tourism,' she whispered. She tipped back the last of the coffee, raised an eyebrow, took a deep breath and opened the door.

Jessica lowered herself into the car. Two hundred and fifty stairs in the cave, and she had trudged up and down them dozens of times today. She was bone tired and cold enough to be shivering. She had been aware of William for the entire length of his tour. He was easily head and shoulders above the next tallest man in the group, towering quietly in the background, never interrupting, always smiling when she glanced in his direction. He had worked with Matthew. When he was close, she felt as if Matthew was in the cave.

When she had taken Matthew to Winter Cave to see her glow-worms, his laughter filled the cavern and the glowing larvae trembled on their fragile threads. He'd put his hand out to grab hold of a stalagmite, and she'd winced, knowing the damage the oils in his skin would cause. One touch and the whole future of that mineral formation would be changed, its growth arrested.

William touched nothing, said nothing. He was a quiet, solid presence in the group, listening, staring up at the formations. She had a sudden urge to take him to see her glow-worm caves, to see if they approved of him. He might be too big to press his way down some of the narrow corridors that led to the more spectacular caves.

At the end of the tour, when he shook her hand awkwardly and walked back along the forest path to his car, Jessica felt a pang of regret. A tiny version of the feeling of losing Matthew. She almost called out to him, surprised by her sudden wish for him to stay.

Now she reversed out of the carpark, the wheels skidding in fresh mud. They were creeping towards the solstice, the shortest day of the year. It was dark already and it wasn't even five o'clock. The shack would be freezing. There were the usual things to keep her busy—making a fire, trying to get the damp wood to burn, cooking a meal.

She stalled the car in the middle of the forestry road.

It wasn't enough. Making a fire, playing house. Why was she even going home? She sat, feeling the heater kick in and finally beginning to warm up. The shivering stopped but it was replaced by a thick, dull thudding in her head.

    She put the car back in gear and inched slowly down the road.

Jessica stood in the barren landscape of the carpark at the Southport pub. The campsite behind the pub had one tent in it now. Mid-winter, one single body shivering in a thick sleeping bag.

There was a storm coming, she had seen it on the weather report. A storm, and the tent was pitched too close to the creek. If it was a big storm the tent would be washed away.

She pulled open the pub door. A pop song battling with the blare from the television. Two tourists standing at the pool table, their goth-black hair and skinny jeans marking them clearly as outsiders. She was almost relieved to see the men at the bar glance at them suspiciously: perhaps she was less of an outsider with this couple in the room. When the man turned and she saw his face pale and powdered, his eyes lined in kohl, she almost cheered.

She walked past them and waited as the bartender poured a beer for a man with a roll of belly peeking out between his jeans and his shirt. Not the same bartender as before; this one was younger, her reddish hair streaked with highlights.

Jessica waited patiently. She smelled sweat and diesel and glanced over her shoulder at a tousled man, youngish, in a yellow down-filled vest. There were tobacco-coloured stains on the vest, oil or petrol, fish-gut fingerprints on the knees of his pants. Something glinted on the turned-up cuff of his trousers and she peered at it, wondering if he had been using glitter. A party, perhaps; helping a child with an art project. But it was a fish scale catching the light.

'What you having?'

Such a gruff, deep voice for a young blonde girl. Jessica was momentarily startled.

'Beer.' She didn't really like beer but she imagined the locals to be beer drinkers. She needed to fit in.

'What kind?'

Jessica hadn't thought that far ahead. She looked at the row of beer taps and chose the closest one. 'Cascade.' That was local, wasn't it?

'A ten or a schooner?'

Another unexpected question. 'Schooner,' she said, and her heart sank when she saw the size of the glass the woman took off the drying rack. Would she be right to drive after that? She pushed a ten-dollar note across the counter.

The beer was cold and mild. Not bitter like the stout that Matthew made. She sipped. She turned on her stool to face the man in the yellow vest. He was staring up at the television mounted above the bar. A game show with blank boxes, letters appearing one by one: e, n, o.

'Envelope,' she said, without meaning to.

The man beside her smiled thinly. 'You could have won a hundred bucks with that.'

'That was an easy one.'

'If you've got a PhD, I guess.'

She flinched. Was that how they all saw her? A smartarse snob?

'I'm Jessica,' she said.

'Yeah.' He raised his glass to his lips and sipped noisily. 'I know who you are.'

'You knew Matthew?'

'Ha,' he said, although she couldn't see why this would be at all funny. He gulped more beer and wiped his mouth with his sleeve. 'Did you?'

She was used to a lingering look of pity: a tiptoeing around her. Strained silences. She was glad of this brutal challenge. She shifted on the stool, straightening her back.

'Good question,' Jessica said, making lines in the fog on her glass. 'That's what I'm trying to figure out. Think you can help me with that?'

'Can I help you?' He lifted the glass to his lips and sculled a measure of the dark liquid. 'That's a pretty useless question. Will. *Will* I help you with that? Now that is a better way of putting it, isn't it? Doctor Masterton.'

He finished the beer and looked her up and down. She shifted uncomfortably, wondering if she should be pleased that he'd called her by Matthew's name.

'Your man,' he went on, 'he told us you still give head. My missus doesn't do that anymore. Two years in and no more blow jobs. What do you reckon about that?'

She opened her mouth. Closed it again.

'So, you know, if you want to hear a bit more about your boyfriend? Maybe we could have this conversation more comfortably in my ute.'

Jessica found her mouth open again. Could he be saying what she thought he was saying? It seemed impossible. She must have misunderstood him.

He ran a hand down the thigh of his stained trousers.

She looked at the dark crescents of his bitten-back fingernails. Closed her mouth. Slipped off her stool, half-turned towards the door, then turned back towards him. 'You didn't know him at all, did you? Matthew would never be friends with someone like you.'

'Someone like me?' He laughed. 'Someone who went to primary school with Matty? Someone who helped with his dad's roof when it caved in? Someone who didn't go off and get over-educated at a city university? Someone that's a real person? Have you even met a real person?'

'Matthew'—she felt the fury rising in her stomach like gas; felt her teeth grit together—'would never have associated with someone who would ask for a blow job in exchange for a conversation. You're not a "real person". You're just an arsehole.'

He shrugged. Finished his beer and licked the foam off his lips. 'I just assumed you'd be up for it. Matty's usual type…'

Jessica took a step towards the door. 'I don't care about the kind of girl Matthew dated in primary school.'

The man pulled her half-finished beer towards him. He licked the rim of the glass where there was a faint trace from her lips, and she shuddered.

She was already striding off towards the carpark but she could hear his voice clear and sharp behind her.

'Lady,' he said, 'you have no fucken idea.'

The storm came in. The shack shivered and groaned. Something clanged, a metallic sound. The chimney? If the cap blew off, she'd have to get someone in to fix it. People died in the cold without a fire. She had heard of a man who froze to death in a converted shipping container just north of there. The wind sounded human: a woman keening. The wind howling for her as she could never howl. Then a crack and a thud and the floor shook. A tree down, too close. It sounded like it had just missed the roof.

She hoped the man from the pub was out in this. She hoped he was on the road, drunk, cowering in his ute with trees coming down on either side. He hadn't told her his name. She was sure he was lying about the roof. She could not imagine Matthew so much as speaking to him. Matthew, with his sweet jokes and his good nature. He was a different species of man from that foul creature at the pub. Dogs, Glen had called them.

Another crack; she waited for the thud but it didn't come.

The phone buzzed in her pocket. She fished it out with trembling fingers. William.

'Hey.'

'Hey.'

'Are you copping this storm down there?'

'Yeah.'

'You okay? Thin walls on that shack.'

'I think a tree came down.'

'Do you want me to drive over?'

'No, no. There'll be trees down all over that road.'

'Nah, I've got a chainsaw in the back.'

She narrowed her eyes, wondering where the hell he would fit a chainsaw in the tiny Hyundai.

'No, I don't want you out in the rain chopping up trees on my account.'

'Okay, but if there's damage, call me. Promise.'

'All right, I promise.'

She jumped. 'Did you hear that?'

'No?'

'Thunder. Lightning. Right outside.'

'Just say the word and I'll be there in twenty minutes.'

'William…Thanks for calling.'

'I'll call again. In the morning. I'll call you on my break. Just to check. Is that all right?'

'Yeah,' she said. 'Thanks.'

She held the phone against her cheek. It was still warm. It felt like something living. And then the thump. A smaller one, a branch probably. The wind howled.

She gave in to the thought. What if Matthew is out in this? What if he's out there, in the storm, in the dark? She imagined him scared, panicked. She imagined him dressed in a wet shirt, shivering. Clothed in fur, his eyes peering out through the head of an animal. It was a night for panic and nightmare. It was a night to believe in ghosts.

Jessica heaped another log into the hearth and set the candles and the matches close enough for her to reach in the dark. Pressed her hands against the glass of the sliding door and felt the surface shiver in the cold. She peered out into the solid darkness. Stared until her eyes hurt. There was nothing to see. The ocean was in darkness. The rain filled the outside world with a dull roar.

Jessica put the last of her papers in a box and looked around at the other desks. Someone else would be at her desk soon. She had never really got to know any of the people at the university. She knew their projects by the books piled up at the edges of their desks. The person in the cube beside her had posters of ice shelves, penguins, the red hull of an ice-breaker. On the rare occasions when they were at their desks together she had sometimes stared at the back of his head: young; sharp haircut. She wondered if he had been to Antarctica, and felt vaguely envious. She would like the isolation. The cave-like solitude of a ship's berth, the barren sweep of ice fields. Perhaps she should have chosen a different specialisation.

She pulled her graph off her own carpeted pin board. It represented the variants in light emissions. Seven years of sitting quietly, letting her eyes adjust to the dark, documented here in one slowly declining line. When you looked directly at one of the little larval lights it disappeared, small enough to fall into a blind spot in the centre of the human eye. It seemed like a metaphor for her years of work. She thought of Matthew and wondered. Maybe she had been looking at him head on and had never seen him in a true light.

She folded the graph and placed it in the box, and just like that it was gone. All the work vanishing into nothing. She felt her heart race in her chest, her ribs tightening, crushing her lungs, her head dizzy. She wanted to run. She wanted the dark calm of Winter Cave: to perch on her familiar rock and peer up at the contained universe of embryonic lights.

Great. So now she was going to be plagued by regular panic attacks. Fantastic.

The dizziness ebbed and she checked her watch. Two hours till her shift. She wouldn't even have time to detour via the shack. She hefted the box up into her arms.

'Jessica?' Dr Ball, hovering in the corridor outside the postgrad door. 'I just finished your thesis.'

He was short, with damp patches of sweat at the armpits of his shirt. It was chilly in the building, but Dr Ball had a tendency to nervous perspiration.

'Oh?' Jessica lowered the box, resting it on the back of a chair.

'You make those little grubs seem pretty interesting.'

'Thanks.'

'It's lovely work—poetry. I'll be surprised if you're sent back for any changes at all.'

She tried to smile. She lifted her box back into her arms, struggling under the weight.

He turned, took a heavy step away and she remembered his interest in the thylacine. She had seen the life-sized model of a tiger crouching in the corner of his office. 'Doctor Ball.' She heard her voice, too sharp, urgent.

'Yes, Jessica?'

'I haven't read your book.'

He laughed. 'Different field, wouldn't you say?'

'I was wondering if you think the people who say they've seen the tiger are all crackpots? You probably say in your book but...'

'Oh. No, far from it. Some of us still hold out hope. There's plenty of wilderness out there, although I imagine the gene pool would be quite narrow. I wouldn't rule out a population of tigers riddled with some kind of disease, like the facial tumours the devils have. Actually a fellow down near Geeveston saw one recently. Murphy. Old logger from the good old days, so not easily spooked. There was a thing in the local paper about it.'

He paused, frowned. Then a gorgeous smile lit up his face and she remembered how engaging he had been in undergrad lectures. She found herself smiling with him.

'You thinking of jumping ship?' he said. 'Ditching those boring old entomologists for some stimulating marsupialia?'

'Might be fun,' said Jessica.

'We can always do with some fresh blood up in marsupials. Give me a call if you want to stow away on our ship of fools.'

'Well, I've finished one PhD now, might as well turn around and start another.'

'You will always be welcome.' He winked. 'And well done with that dissertation. Incremental light change. Who would have thought?'

And he trudged away down the corridor, his change jingling in his pocket.

Cockle Creek. Population: 3. Jessica peered through the streaks of water on the windscreen. Matthew loved that sign; he had made her take a photograph of it when they first came down this way. A perfect day. She had picked a shell out of the sand, thin as skin stretched tight, brittle, a warm cup of sunlight. Matthew had said you would come here if you needed to disappear. Murderers, wife-beaters, thieves. There had been a handful of tents clustered around the sign that said *No campers*—because who would move them on?—and Matthew made up brutal scenarios for each of the tent-dwellers.

The guy with the old-fashioned A-frame drowned his baby in the bath before fleeing. The high-tech dome belonged to an embezzler, and there was a million dollars in cash buried in the sand beneath the fly.

Now she pulled the car up in front of one of the three permanent dwellings, a neat wooden shack with paper daisies spreading out from the flowerbeds down the slope of the hill towards the sand. Jessica stepped over the gate, which was only knee high, and crunched up the gravel path. There was a blue rowboat dragged up on the sand. It would be a fair haul to get it down onto the water, flip it over, push it out over the gentle swell.

She knocked on the door. Waited. She could hear a clattering of crockery. Marijam, the wrinkly apple-faced woman from

Maude's house, had pulled Jessica aside before she left. Marijam seemed smarter than the others. Saner. *Come any time* she had said. She would always be home unless she was out for the nets. An evening away from the house every so often to meet with the other widows. Housebound or oceanbound the rest of the time. Pop around. She'd put the kettle on.

Marijam was home. Jessica heard the hacking rattle of an old hot water system wheezing out a tepid trickle. She knocked again, harder, and the rattle stopped, replaced by expectant silence. Footsteps—a shuffling, slippered sound.

When Marijam opened the door it was not slippers she was wearing but fat running shoes, fluorescent yellow and huge on such a tiny frame, making her look a little like a waterbird.

She smiled when she saw Jessica, a genuine pleasure lighting up her face.

'Oh, lovely,' she said, voice thin and tremulous. 'I hope you haven't been knocking for long. I'm almost deaf, you know.'

Marijam held out her hand and the tiny fingers disappeared inside Jessica's grip, thin as sticks. But there was power in her handshake, the strength to launch a boat and pull a net. Almost impossible to believe this woman was ninety. But then, Jessica's mother could easily end up as fit and wily as Marijam. This could be Jessica herself in sixty years if she kept launching her boat every morning.

Sixty years without Matthew. As the possibility began to spread out around her she leaned against the doorframe to get her balance, and Marijam offered her tiny shoulder in support. A sharp sweet smell of soap. Jessica allowed herself to be led inside.

'When Charles went missing I went about fainting all over the place for ages. Dropped like fruit in winter. You know when they wore corsets, my grandmother's time? Went down like skittles. Same thing. Short of breath when you lose someone.'

The house was dark, sparse, but neat and free of dust, the paint washed thin. The curtains were faded, with only a faint trace of the flowers that had once crowded the fabric. The wooden kitchen benchtop was scarred as if it had been hacked into.

'It gets better,' said Marijam, settling Jessica into a chair at the heavy wooden table.

She shuffled to the sink and there was that noisy rattle of pipes as she filled the kettle.

Everything about the place seemed oddly familiar: the anodised aluminium teapot, the angular modernist canister, the cracked floral plate—even the biscuits the old woman placed on it, salty sweet. All these things were the kind of details Jessica would have chosen for herself. The photographs fading in their frames depicted a line of fishermen in long rubber boots, a rowboat heading for a cloudy horizon, the tangle of ropes and coloured glass floats rubbing against the flyscreen above the sink. Jessica couldn't help feeling as if she had suddenly been transported into her own future, a spartan world of fishing and grief. Marijam was Jessica, refined by the years down to a bundle of bones held together by will.

When the tea was made Marijam sat opposite Jessica and reached over to pat her arm. The hug of those arms would be formidable.

'They're crazy, right?' Jessica said finally.

'Those women?'

Jessica nodded.

'Grief makes us crazy, don't you reckon?'

'But your own husband? What do you think happened to him?'

'I don't think. I know. He was taken by a tiger.'

'How do you know that? What makes you so sure?'

Marijam shifted on her chair. It creaked slightly under her bird-like frame. 'I saw it ten years ago. I was throwing a line in off Lune River. To be honest, I was taking some mussels free of charge off that farm down there. I was going to make spiced mussels with buttered polenta, I remember cutting the recipe from a magazine. Still have it somewhere.'

She shifted again as if she were about to get up and hunt around in her recipe books, but thought better of it. She took a sip from her cup.

'I looked over to the bank and I saw it. A dog, I thought. But remember I had just turned eighty and my eyes weren't to be trusted even then. Now? *Pffff.* If I saw the tiger now I might think it was a wallaby. But I let the boat drift closer. It was running laps on a small stretch of sand. Long tail, sluggish hindquarters, and when I got close enough I could see the stripes on it. It paused, like it knew me. I knew him too: my Charles, only those gentle eyes were filled with something else now, more like cunning. He took a step towards me and I got a look at the teeth on it. Froze my blood in my veins. I missed him so much. I should have stayed in the boat but I got out onto the sand. Held out my hand, almost like he should eat out of it. Stupid. He took another step towards me and his mouth opened, big mouthful of tiny teeth. The hair all at the back of my neck shot up and I pulled my hand away quick smart. Got the feeling he would bite it off if he could. Not Charles, the way he used to be, but this was something wild. I just stared, so focused on the beast I forgot to keep hold of the rope and the boat got dragged out on the next wave. I turned and waded out thigh-deep to get it back and when I hauled it to shore the tiger was gone. There were tracks, though. I looked at them long and hard.'

The old woman paused and tapped a spoon on the rim of her cup.

'That's how I know the tracks I found here not so long ago were his. Or one of them at least. This was a month back. You normally see them at night and I had seen it, something, skin in the moonlight. My eyes, I told you about them, but still I am sure it was a man, standing naked between my shack and the beach. He was just at the edge of the spill of light from the kitchen and his thingy hanging down for all to see.'

A sly, humorous glance at Jessica.

'My eyes are good enough to recognise a thingy when I see one, don't you worry about that. It was him, my Charles. But he was young still, like when he was taken. Then he dropped down to all fours and he ran off like a cat dragging his tail, that awkward gait like the first one on the beach, like his hips were heavy. It was Charles, I guarantee it.' She laughed. 'Unless it was a kangaroo. My eyes, you know. But in the morning, there was tracks just where he'd been, footprints coming in, paw prints leaving.'

She poured more tea into her cup and sucked it loudly. Jessica noticed the steam. Her own tea was still too hot to drink.

'Those women? They're mad all right, and most of them are stupid. But they're not wrong about this. A tiger took them all, one by one, picking them off. And they're still out there, somewhere. I'd swear blind—but I am almost blind, so I'd swear deaf, except I'm a bit hard of hearing too.' She cackled. 'I'll swear on my dinghy, because that's about all I've got that's still reliable. Your husband is alive.'

Jessica flinched, but didn't contradict the old woman. All the years between them added up to a kind of marriage anyway.

'And'—the old woman tapped the table to make sure she had Jessica's attention—'he's dangerous. Don't be fooled. Don't be a fool. He's changed into something wild and that's why he can't come back to you, not ever. It's why you mustn't let him.'

Jessica glanced away, out of the window. There in the garden, half-sand, half-grass. The sounds outside her shack. The scrambling in the darkness.

'The scientists I work with would say that's just paranoia.'

'But you know it's true.'

Jessica bit into a biscuit. Soft. Stale. If there was a tiger, if she found a tiger alive… She knew her little experiments with glow-worms, the tiny changes in light emissions, would not make a proper career. She was still working in Hastings caves, picking up rubbish, tutting at kids who tried to touch the stalagmites.

'You get any crays at the moment?' asked Marijam.

'What?' Jessica blinked. 'I—yes. A couple.'

'Commercial fishermen. I reckon they see my pot out and come out with seven or eight pots of their own. Put them in beside mine. It is like Amazon. You know Amazon?'

'Sorry? The river?'

'The bookshop. No, hang on. Not Amazon, that other one, the big one. Is it Amazon? Pick on a little bookstore, put a big megastore across the road. Discounts on all the prices till the little fella dies, then corner the market. I read about that on the internet.'

It was odd to hear someone so old talking about the internet. Jessica had assumed this woman would be cut off from a world of technology, living off the land, isolated.

'My pot goes in and then the damn commercial fishermen are all over it. You just watch out. Change your spot. Lead them astray. Bloody Amazons, the lot of them.'

'Okay.'

'Wily buggers.' She dunked her biscuit in the tea and ate it quickly as it began to crumble. 'And don't let that tiger anywhere near your house. Shoot the bastard. You have a gun?'

Jessica nodded.

'Good. Shoot it. It's a monster. I miss my husband every day but that thing he's become is a wild beast. A rabid one. Dangerous. Shoot him.'

Jessica stood. She didn't want to be here anymore. She saw the woman for what she was now, the shell of a person, kept alive by crazy rage. She looked into her sharp, clouded eyes and saw herself, turned sour.

'Thanks for the tea.'

The woman nodded, lips tight. Jessica had disappointed her. They had disappointed each other.

'I'll see you next week at the meeting.'

Jessica nodded, smiled as warmly as she could manage and walked quickly to the front door. When she stepped out into the chill of the air she felt as if she was escaping. She wasn't sure exactly what from.

There was a view. The house was tucked neatly up a steep concrete driveway with an aviary flanking the carport. A cockatoo arched its crest and screeched, stepping from foot to scaly foot. Jessica locked the car door out of habit and stood staring the cocky down. She had no desire to get closer to the bird but the front door was there beside it and she would have to eventually. She stood leaning against the car. She could see the sailing ships all moored along the Huon, the whole flotilla bobbing up and down on a gentle tide. The sun was out and it touched the water; made it seem viscous, like mercury poured out over the bay.

Murphy opened the door. 'That's Butch. He's harmless but don't put your finger in between the bars. Bites like a bastard.'

Murphy had a long balding head: a shining strip of skin flanked by thin grey hair on each side. He was dressed neatly in a pink shirt tucked into high-waisted trousers, and brown lace-up shoes. Everything about him clean and pressed and shining. Jessica walked over to shake his hand. His palm strong and dry.

'I hope I'm not intruding.'

'No, no. We're virtually neighbours. Come in.'

The cockatoo shrieked again and she flinched.

'Shush up, Butch.' The bird spread his wings and upped the volume.

Murphy bent to his laces and slipped his shoes off at the door.

She realised he must have put his shoes on to make the few steps out to the porch. Fastidious: not what she would have expected from a tiger hunter. She supposed she'd been expecting a cross between the rough types Matthew worked with at the fish farms and Indiana Jones. She stooped and pulled off her own boots.

The house was immaculate. Crocheted doilies on every wooden surface and neat watercolour landscapes. The couches were light brown leather. She perched on the edge of one, unable to shake the feeling that she was making the place untidy. She was wearing her clothes straight from the boat. Fish blood on her sleeve.

'So you're writing a story?' he asked, smiling. Sitting straight-backed with his hands folded neatly in his lap. He was well over seventy but he was fit. She could see all the wiry energy in his wrists. She could imagine him hacking his way through virgin bush. No Indiana Jones, but a thorough and hard worker.

'Researching. I'll write it up if there's anything in it.'

'Oh, there's something in it, all right. I've seen it with my own eyes.'

'The tiger.'

'Sure.'

'I read the interview in the paper.'

'I have that here.' He reached towards a manila envelope on the side table and opened it, and there were photographs and old letters and news clippings inside it.

'This is my father.' He tapped the fading photograph. A man, just as neatly dressed as Murphy, with his sleeves rolled up to his elbows, standing on a divot of wood that had been hammered into the gigantic trunk of a tree. It was the largest tree she had ever seen, the man dwarfed by it.

'That's how they climb up them. They put those sleepers into the trunk and climb that way.' She could feel her eyes glazing over. The room was hot, the fireplace blazing. She wanted to open a window but didn't dare ask. 'That would have been 1914 and that tree was up in the back of Geeveston. They used to take two teams in there, you know…'

There was no space for Jessica to interrupt. She sat, open-mouthed, as Murphy slipped one photo after another out of his folder. She had no idea what he wanted from her, except maybe a feature story on his entire family history from their arrival on the First Fleet. She listened and tried to focus on what he was saying but there was a fly slapping against the shut window and the sound of it clicking against the glass took up all her attention.

'That is an original clipping from the *Mercury*. I can get that copied for you if you like?'

At last, a break in the stream of logging and accidents and death and an industry in decline. She leapt in. 'I'm more interested in the tiger.'

'Father shot tigers. They took sheep, you know. There was a bounty.'

'Yes. I know all that.'

'But we were a little too good at shooting them, right?'

'But you've seen one.'

'Few times.'

'Geeveston?'

'Yes. Sure. Camping overnight at Geeveston. I do those walks, you see. For my eightieth my family hired a helicopter, dropped me down to the Southwest Cape. Best walk ever, I—'

'So, the tiger?'

'Oh, yes. That one, cheeky bugger, came right into camp and stole some of the beef I had out ready to put on the fire.'

'You got a good look at it?'

'Sure. It was like from here to the fireplace away. Stopped and looked at me and backed away with my dinner in its mouth.'

'Have you ever seen a tiger down my way?'

'Southport?'

'Or Ida Bay.'

'Saw one at Cockle Creek. Not down near the water but further inland. I strayed off the trail. You know, I was tired. It was hot. Summer. I was thirsty too, which is why I thought it was a person, walking just over the ridge. I was sure I saw him. Crazy, really, man with no clothes on. Why would you walk around in that forest with nothing on? Worst place for a nudist colony—all ticks and leeches and tiger snakes. Still, I could have sworn it was a man and I called out and I walked over to where he'd been. Saw him duck down on his haunches, like he'd dropped something. But I got closer and it wasn't a man. Couldn't ever have mistaken that for anything other than what it was. Tiger.'

'But you didn't have a camera.'

'No, didn't have a camera. I had a smart phone. My daughter bought it for me. I took a picture with that.'

'You have that?'

'Here.'

He searched through the papers in his file and pulled out an image printed in black and white. It looked as much like a tiger as her scrap of video footage. Eyes, long nose, teeth, the stripes on the flank half-hidden by the trunk of a tree. The thing was looking right at the camera. It was a blurry shot but it seemed clear enough to her. It might have been a dog. She squinted. A thin dog. Ribs, perhaps, not stripes.

'What did they say? The authorities?'

'They said what they're told to say. Tiger's extinct. Told me I had a skinny dog.'

'What do you mean, what they're told to say?'

'Preservation. If they find a tiger they don't want every hoon south of Hobart out there hunting it. They want to send teams in, covert. Scientists. They're looking for this one, all right.'

Jessica held the page in her hand. The eyes, looking up at her straight out of the page.

'Does that look like a skinny dog to you?'

She narrowed her eyes. Maybe. But that mouth, that elongated bite, the stretch of the jaw, the stripes or shadows or ribs. Not enough to convince her: conjecture, not science. But she took out her phone.

'Mind if I take a photo of your picture?'

'Sure. Go ahead.'

And the phone snapped, mimicking an old-fashioned camera with the sound of the shutter hissing down. Taking the image into its digital memory.

She fumbled the key in the lock; her hands were freezing. She tried again, blinking in the vague moonlight, and the keys fell. Dropped through a gap in the boards and were gone, plummeted to the storage room under the stairs.

It felt right. Nothing should be easy anymore. She wanted to wake up to sleet. She wanted to find a lump on her breast and know that it would be cancer. She wanted the car to slip on black ice and hurtle off the road.

For now, this small inconvenience, the key falling between the floorboards, would have to do. A tiny punishment for being alive and at home when Matthew was not.

Jessica pushed past the hibiscus growing flush against the wall, the spiked branches tearing at her coat. The under-house area was open—to the elements; to theft, if anyone fancied her tools or the smoker or the beer kit or the fishing lines. People rarely locked their doors here. Cars were left open. Boats hauled up and left unsecured on the strand. There was an ad for mooring nailed to a tree and, beside it, a dozen boats with their ropes looped casually around the trunk. Not like the city, where if you left a locked bicycle out there would be nothing left but the front wheel. That was one of the things Jessica liked about it here. People left you alone. They almost never stole your stuff.

As she felt around in the shadows for the light switch, there was a scuffling sound. Something hiding under here among the unopened boxes, a rustle of leaves. Not under the house. Beside it, among the trees and scrub of the sandy garden. Something big. She waited, listening for the thump-thump of a roo hopping off towards the waterline. Nothing. A dog? An old feeling, of being watched. Something was out there. It hadn't moved since the initial rustling. It was paused mid-step. Waiting.

A glint in the dirt. The key was there at her feet. She glanced down at it, kicked it with the toe of her boot. Took a deep breath and knelt to pick it up. Here, crouched like this under the house with nothing between her and the ocean, this is when it would pounce. She felt the hair on her neck rising. Goose bumps trickled down her back like melting ice.

Just take me now.

Had she said the words aloud? She stayed down, stooped over, the back of her neck exposed. She counted to ten, out loud this time. She wanted it to hear her. She was waiting too. A relief. The feeling of teeth sinking into the back of her neck, the weight of a tiger on her, the end of the ceaseless waking up and going to bed again, the day after day trudge of hours, constant as the sound of the sea.

Ten.

She curled her fingers around the key and stood. Then the sound again, a body large as a man, pushing through shrubbery just as she had pushed past the hibiscus a few minutes ago. She held her breath. It was close, she could feel it. Something watching her. One of her arms could feel the heat off it. Of course it was her imagination, the blood rushing to that part of her skin, pushed there by her wildly beating heart. *It will kill me.* Once the thought was there it couldn't be dismissed. Wild animal, rabid animal, kill or be killed. Here, crouched under the cottage, she was ready for it, the teeth of a shark, the sting of a manta ray, the claws of a tiger. *Kill me. Kill me. I'm ready. Kill me.*

The sound of a gunshot and she screamed, leapt back. Away from the bottle cap that rolled to rest at her feet and the hiss… the hissing sound of an exploded bottle. The ginger beer Matthew had put down just before he went missing, volatile as always, two bottles shattered and the beer fizzing to a puddle on the floor.

Jessica hesitated before turning the light off. In the dark she felt her fear return. There was something out in the garden at the side of the house. Devil again, perhaps. She wouldn't rule out that ugly cancerous face rooting though her neighbour's bins. A devil could snap her shinbone in two with one bite. A devil never let go of its prey: jaw locked, shaking, screaming to wake the dead. She was right to be afraid.

She took the stairs quickly, unable to lose the feeling of being watched. Tiger, she thought, tiger, knowing that she was going mad with her grief, knowing that there were no thylacine left. The animal was extinct, never mind that strange little man with his grainy photo of a dog.

She opened the door and when she was inside she leaned against it. The walls were so thin you could probably kick through them. The fire had died completely and it was as cold in here as outside. She stood in the corridor and listed the tasks ahead of her. Build the fire, light it, get the oven on, bake some fish, a potato to have with it, draw the curtains so she wouldn't feel so exposed, pull the doona up, get on the couch, turn the television on to dispel the demons of the evening.

Someone knocked. She hadn't even turned on the inside light; she was standing here in the dark. She looked to the peeling paint of the front door, her running shoes discarded beside it, the sand that had gathered there that she had failed to sweep outside. Through the thick wood of the door she saw the creature rising up, the haunches bowed, the jaw wide, the beast become man, or something like a man. She stepped towards the door, reached out to the handle. Took a breath, and opened it.

'William.'

'You got power problems? A fuse?'

He seemed taller than she remembered him. When had he visited? Three, four days ago? He was holding a saucepan between thick leather gloves. His fur-lined coat looked like the warmest item of clothing she had ever seen.

She snorted her relief, reached out and flicked the light switch.

'I just got home.'

'I brought some—' He held the pot out and even with the lid on she could smell how delicious it was.

She lifted the lid. 'Seafood mornay. Thank you so much. I was just trying to get up the energy to cook. You are a life saver. You'll stay?'

'No. I'd better get back. Shift in the morning.'

Jessica felt a stab of disappointment. She reached for the saucepan but he shook his head.

'Careful. It's hot.' He sidled past her and headed down the corridor towards the kitchen. She liked that he took up most of the space. He made the empty house seem less so. She shut the door firmly behind him and followed. He was standing nervously by the fireplace; he glanced towards her shyly.

'Is it being sexist if I offer to light the fire for you? I never know if that kind of thing is okay. Men and fire...' He beat his fists against his chest and she found herself smiling.

'It's fine.'

'Right. Sorry.'

'No. I mean it's fine if you want to help me light it. That was Matthew's job.' Men and fire indeed.

She watched as he built the fire and settled the logs on. The flame took easily—she could see the brightness of it light his face like a smile. It was nice to be looked after for a while. Someone else cooking her dinner, starting the fire.

He wiped his hands on his jeans and stood. 'You should call me,' he said, 'if you need to get something fixed. Or if you just want to hang out, I suppose.'

'I will,' she said, hoping he could hear in her voice that she meant it.

'Okay. Well, night.'

'Goodnight.'

And an awkward dance as he shuffled around her and into the corridor.

'I'm glad you came,' she told him. 'I was a bit...Something had me spooked.'

'What's wrong?'

'A devil in the bushes, I think. Nothing. Maybe a dog.'

'You see it?'

'No, but I heard it. Big. A dog, probably.'

'Lots of dogs in Southport.'

'Yeah.'

'You should think about getting yourself one now that—well, now.'

'Maybe. You're right. I should.'

'Labrador?'

'I like labradors.'

'Just 'cause there's a fellow with lab pups out my way. Can't give them away, they're a bit older now and they're headed for the pound if he can't find owners. And, you know, they're smart. Good guards.'

'Do you think I should?'

'Yeah, course. You shouldn't be alone out here. Not that it's unsafe but, I don't know. I get lonely myself. I might take a pup. Couldn't hurt.'

'Okay.'

He smiled and put out his hand, a strange gesture, but Jessica took it and shook it as if they had just finished a business meeting. She watched as Will folded his body into his tiny car.

'William?'

He paused, waiting, smiling at her.

'You could ask that guy with the puppies. I don't see why not, right? If he has one still.'

'I'm sure he does. I'll check.'

Will put the car in reverse, then nosed it into a three-point turn. She watched his tail-lights heading up the hill, and shivered. It was too cold. Inside the fire was roaring. She shut the door and threw the lock and spent a moment pulling all the curtains to. Unable to shake the feeling, still, that there was something out there.

She ate William's mornay straight from the pot. She had not

been at all hungry, but now she wiped the sides of the pan with a slice of bread and when the bread was gone she used her finger to get into the bottom of the pot, thinking she had never tasted anything so good. Probably it was just the cold and her bitter loneliness and all this held at bay by the fire that Will had stoked for her.

She left the light on and curled up on the couch. She conjured up a group of people talking about nothing on the television, laughing, joking with each other. She used to laugh so often.

Now she scowled and pulled the doona up around her shoulders and prepared herself to wait out yet another interminable night.

A sound. Tyres scraping on gravel. She stood, lowering her bare feet onto the cold floor. Lights swept over the curtain.

She padded over and peered out, holding the fabric so there was as slight a gap as possible. Headlights. The car was facing the window. It must have been parked across the narrow dirt road.

Who the hell would be blocking her driveway at this time of night? There were so few cars in winter, just a few tenacious residents. Fishermen, abalone men, loggers. The men she had seen at the pub; they knew where she lived. Jessica couldn't see past the headlights. She couldn't tell if it was a ute or a car or a truck, there was just this glare. She blinked. The lights flared: switched to high beam.

She squinted. The car revved and jumped forward; Jesus, it was going to hit her shack. It was going to burst through the window.

She dropped the curtain and leapt back. The sound of the engine rattled through the glass. The lights swung wild streaks through the curtain and across the walls. She held her breath.

Then the rattle of gravel as the tyres spun into reverse. And away. It was racing away. She pulled the curtain in time to see the taillights wave erratically from side to side. Too dark to see what kind of vehicle it was, and then it turned the corner and there was nothing left of it.

It felt like a warning. Like she had been warned.

Jessica picked up her phone, her hands shivering. She punched his name into her phone and heard the tone, imagining his phone ringing somewhere, too far away.

'William?'

Was he still in the car? Was he home yet?

'Hey.'

Her voice sounded calm. She didn't feel like her voice sounded. She felt rattled.

'I just… Will you ask him? That guy. About that dog?'

'Yes. Of course.'

'Would you ask him soon?'

'You okay? You want me to come back?'

She paused. She did. She really wanted him to come back. 'I just think a dog would be good company.'

'Boy? Or girl? If there's a choice?'

'I really don't mind. A feisty one. The one that barks the loudest. A brave dog.'

'Okay,' said William, 'I'll pick the bravest one.'

She felt her heart finally calming.

'Okay, great. Thanks.' The thud of blood in her ears seemed quieter now. 'Goodnight, William.'

'Goodnight, Jessica.'

The red welt tore down the back of the girl's calf, a long weeping gouge with a fainter one beside it. Claw marks. So she said.

'He called me.' Crystal clasped her hands protectively over the bulge of her stomach. She had a surprising little voice, high like a bird, like someone pretending to be a toddler. 'He called out "Crystal!" and I turned and I could see something behind the greenhouse and it was him. I know it was him. And I ran, and…' She lifted her skirt again and the big mark was inflamed, stitches lining it, dark crosshatching, and all of it red and swollen.

'I didn't stop,' she said. 'I kept on running because of what you all said. Like to not let them trick you. Not let them catch you.'

'What did the doctor say?' The women all turned to glare at Jessica.

'I told him I tripped and got caught on some lawyer vine.' She dropped her skirt, sat back down on the caved-in couch. 'I don't think he believed me but he stitched it up. I think he reckons someone's beating me up again.' She held the swell of her belly, stroking it as if to assure her unborn child that everything would be okay, but she was nervous, agitated. 'Do you think I'll turn into one of them now? What if I turn into one?'

'You should get a shot for it,' Jessica suggested.

'Can you get a shot for that? Like for rabies or something?'

'Tetanus.'

The girl snorted. 'This wasn't no rusty nail. He's been watching me. Following, I can feel him. Every time the sun goes down I can feel him.'

Jessica frowned. She felt watched, even now she felt like there was something out there in the dark. It had followed her from the car right up to Maude's door, she could smell it. It was that scent of a feral animal, that reek of the wild. It assaulted her, rising up from the darkness whenever she stepped out at night. She was going crazy. Letting these women get into her head.

'They stay close for a while.' Maude nodded. 'They still remember us. My husband followed me for a year. Now is the time we should be hunting it.'

And Jessica said: 'No.'

'Your man's been gone a matter of weeks. And Crystal's been widowed six months, the baby's not even come yet. So there's two of those creatures that still remember their human selves. We should hunt them down now.'

What? Jessica shook her head. A chill had caught her. She would be sitting here shivering if they weren't all staring at her.

'Soon. Tomorrow night.'

The television was showing the weather channel silently in the background. Two degrees overnight; a maximum of eight. All cloud. That ought to be enough to deter them, surely?

Maude shifted forward in the chair, a whiff of stale piss from her pale overblown skin. No one was looking after Maude. Even Maude had stopped looking after Maude. 'I'm bringing a rifle. You're coming with us.'

Jessica shook her head.

'Have you got a gun?' said Maude.

'She's got a gun.' Marijam, staring straight at her, those sharp, rheumy eyes. 'She's a hunter, this one.'

Jessica shook her head again. Why would she walk into the icy dark of the forest with a bunch of crazy women with guns?

But when she stepped out into the night, pulling the coat uselessly around her shoulders, feeling her teeth rattling together, she could smell him. She turned to see Crystal limping towards her ute, leaning heavily on Maude's arm and cradling her belly. It was mad to believe he was out there in the dark, watching her, running between trees, keeping pace with the car as it laboured over the badly maintained road.

When she pulled out onto the sealed road she stepped hard on the accelerator. She swung too fast and wide around the corners, driving like she was in a hurry, and she was. Trying to outrun it. Him. Wanting to get home before he did. She wanted to be safely inside with the door locked before she smelled that wild animal smell and felt the eyes staring deep into her.

Jessica sat in the car at the edge of one of the forestry tracks. Maude had given terrible directions and she had taken the wrong turn at first, juddering over potholes for ten minutes before realising she was in the wrong place. She was here now, though. Duck Hole Walk. An easy stroll, said the sign, glinting in the headlights. She slid herself out of the car and into a slurry of mud. They had all left at the same time but somehow, even with her wrong turn, she had arrived before them. Perhaps she had passed the other cars in a daze, worrying about her incredibly poor judgment in getting into this ridiculous adventure. Maybe they'd dipped their lights to pass her. The only thing she could concentrate on was the weight of the gun in the pocket of this strange, heavy jacket.

'You're going to catch cold without a coat,' the women had said to her back at Maude's house. Jessica shrugged. No point explaining the science, that you catch a virus, not a chill from the air. You hunt an animal not an imaginary beast, and no one seemed to care about the science behind that. The coat they lent her was too large, and smelled. Wood smoke and an underlying whiff of body that unsettled her. Whose was it? Too big for Maude. It must have belonged to her husband. Was it his sweat she was smelling? She shrugged it off and left it on the front seat of the car. Reached into the pocket and slipped her hand around the cold metal of the gun.

An arc of light swung up over the road, bouncing erratically across wild grabs of forest. It was the uneven road: potholes, fallen branches, boneshaking corrugations. Crystal's ute pulled up and she slipped down out of the cab, dwarfed by the huge vehicle. Just a child, really, her boots too big for her tiny ankles, even wrapped in thick woollen socks. Jessica wondered what it would be like to be carrying the baby of a dead father. Every kick a reminder.

Crystal reached into the back of the ute, stretched across the bulk of her own stomach and emerged carrying a rifle, semi-automatic, the gun almost as tall as she was. She swung it up over her shoulder looking comfortable, balanced.

Not the defenceless child Jessica had imagined.

'—kay.' Crystal's little-girl voice was at odds with the size of her rifle. 'Ready to hunt?'

No. Jessica knew that much. But she gripped her handgun firmly and nodded.

She turned on her torch—a ridiculous thing, a tiny cylinder

attached to her keys, made to find a keyhole in the dark—and led the way up to the start of the track. To one side of the path the bank reared up, heavy with old-growth trees, moss clinging to them. On the other side, the rocks tipped down to a creek. The wan torchlight glinted off white foam as if someone had tipped bubble bath into the little stream.

She trained the light on her shoes and moved forward. The forest seemed to settle around her, and for a moment she was her ten-year-old self, setting off in secret with the other kids from the compound into the hot scrub at the back of Toowoomba. Knowing they were both brave and wicked. The same sense of an illicit adventure beginning.

A tree had come down on the path. Jessica knew she couldn't climb over it; it was taller than she was, a trunk fat as two men pressed together and then a smaller branch stretching out above it. There was room to squeeze under, a little room. She looked back towards Crystal and shrugged.

'Bad start.' They had barely stepped into the forest, hunting in pairs, each couple taking a different track. She wondered how Marijam would manage, then remembered how much effort it took to haul the boat out every morning. She'd do just fine.

Crystal tutted. 'You're kidding, right?'

She pressed the butt of the rifle into the stony path and jumped easily, despite her bulk, up onto the log, then swung herself over like a child playing in the park. Jessica heard the easy thud of her boots hitting the ground.

Jessica turned the torch off and hitched her skirt up. She ducked down into a hunch, balancing on her palms while crab-shuffling sideways. She grunted to standing, feeling as old as her mother, tired to her bones. She should be in bed right now.

The light from the full moon disappeared into the thick forest canopy to their right, but the creek and the cleared path cut enough of a gap to let a little moonlight in, enough to see a few paces ahead. Jessica walked slowly behind Crystal. She slipped here and there but the path seemed solid enough. The damage must be recent, the fallen trees, the section of wooden boards that had lifted and skidded down towards the water. It would all be fixed by spring, when the tourists returned, but for now the path was unpredictable. When her feet plunged into icy water she turned her torch back on and sidestepped a little creek that burbled along the track.

Footsteps.

She turned her torch off and Crystal did too. They waited. The thud of her heart. She shivered. She would buy a winter coat. Tomorrow. She would go to the shops in Huonville, no, Hobart. She would drive to Hobart for a thick winter coat.

Somewhere out there the women were hunting. She should have stayed with them. They were insane, of course, but they were out there somewhere with guns. It was stupid to have split up into pairs. Disastrous.

Footsteps. No, the thump-thump-thump of a wallaby. Jessica turned her torch back on and lit up the muddied toes of her boots. Crystal had the rifle at the ready, but what was the point? They couldn't hit anything in the dark.

'Stay close,' Jessica said, loud enough for even the wallaby to hear. Speaking to Crystal but aiming the words out into the dark as if to warn him. Matthew was gone, dead. She knew that. She did. But there was this uneasy glimmer of hope in her, faint as the padding of soft paws in the leaf litter, pointless as the thin beams of moonlight that cut the canopy and highlighted scant edges of trees and undergrowth.

An uphill climb with every step a backslide. Treacherous here in the dark, despite the easy stroll the sign had promised.

Voices now. Distant. She crouched instinctively, but the sound was thin, miles off. Some of the other women? The sound of them carried on a faint breeze scented with unease.

Bye, baby Bunting, Crystal was humming. Her rifle pointed straight ahead, her torch gripped against the barrel. Jessica knew the words and her mind inserted them beside the tune. Daddy's gone a-hunting. Gone to get a rabbit skin to wrap the baby Bunting in.

Voices blown on the wind.

'Did you hear that?'

'No. Shhhh. Don't scare it.' That child's voice.

Thumping. A kangaroo. And rustling. Closer. Rustling. She hugged her shoulders. The walking hadn't warmed her, her bones were ice. Were they women's voices? Could be forestry workers out late, kids drinking in some clearing…surely there were no houses out here in the old-growth forest.

A woman's voice. Here for a second, clear as if she were standing just around the next bend—gone in an instant. Jessica continued to walk.

'I can hear it.'

Jessica stopped, listened. 'We can't kill it.'

'What do you mean?'

'Even if there was a tiger out here, how could I kill it? If it was my Matthew, your husband? Would you?'

'It isn't your man anymore. It's something else. Evil.'

'There is no such thing as evil.'

'The thing that stole your husband. The thing that took him. Devil dog.'

Jessica pressed her hand against her forehead and the little torch described great arcs of leaves and water and trunks. How long had they been walking? Ten minutes? Twenty? She turned and swung the beam around to where they had come from. A sliver of light swallowed up by dark space.

A crack like a branch falling or a small tree losing its foothold on the creek bank. A scuttling as something hurried away from the fall. Something large in the bush close by. Some breath from substantial lungs. She held her own breath to listen, heard a heavy tread and a yapping. Not a cry she recognised—but she wouldn't know a bettong from a bandicoot if it came to that. It was close, though. And it was loud and seemed tinged with anxiety. A warning call, perhaps; some large animal calling out to its mate. Hunters at large. Humans in the forest. No rest till they are gone.

Stay close. Even though he was dead and gone and she would never see him in the flesh again: *stay close*. And the girl humming quietly, almost tunelessly. Daddy's gone a-hunting.

The beast broke cover.

Jessica scrambled back, the ground dipped, her foot slipped on mud, her hands stretched out to catch anything, twigs snapping between her fingers, her balance gone, her body pitched off-centre and beginning to fall, a handful of leaves sharp and cutting, a sapling gripped and bending, holding as her feet slipped and scrambled on the steep slope, holding the sapling one-handed, swinging her other hand to grab a branch.

The torch was gone. Still in the clumsy moment of falling, she saw it. Something, pale, the glint of eyes, too big for a devil, too hunched for a roo, too cat-like for a possum. A pale flank in the moonlight. And even as she fell she was looking for stripes. Moonlight through branches, saplings cutting her view, she saw them. Stripes, of course, but anything would be striped in this light, a feral cat grown to the size of a dog, a dog, lost and wandering the forest.

The glint of metal as Crystal flicked her torch on, swung her rifle up and it was there. Not where Crystal was pointing, but to the side of her, its long mouth pulled back, staring at her, grinning. The thing was focused on the girl, crouching, ears flat back. Angry, ready to pounce. Not a dog. Not even vaguely dog-like, maybe a cat, but no. It was something other. Short back legs, stretch of teeth, utterly alien.

Crystal spun around to find it in the dark, her belly seeming to swing round after. She lifted the awkward bulk of the rifle, but the thing was up and, in the air, and Jessica raised her gun and sighted and squeezed the trigger. The creature lurched to one side. A hit.

She remembered. The cans exploding on their log perches, her mother looking at her with narrowed eyes, a new respect. Sighting. Shooting. Killing. No cry, but a thud as the body hit the ground, a pale flash, kicking, a leg struggling for purchase in the soft ground and then the head flopping over. The eyes on her. And it was only now that she saw her mistake, the terrible mistake. She dropped her gun in the mud of leaf litter, the unthinkable error evoking her mother's voice. *Never drop your weapon. You will kill someone.* That seemed to matter less now that she really had killed someone.

He lay with his eyes open. Pale hair, thin as a whippet. The bullet had entered his forehead right in the centre. A clean shot, but she knew the exit wound would be a mess. She'd shot a lame horse once and she remembered the clean entry, the horror show of bone and brain exploding outward at the exit point.

His lips were parted as if he was about to speak. The eyes stared through her. He was young, with a full dark beard, but the chest below it smooth as a child's. His ribs protruding. Half-starved by the looks of it, hipbones jutting out over the genitals.

Crystal fell—for an instant Jessica thought she must have shot her too—crumpling like a puppet cut free. Her body fell onto itself, the big egg of her belly draped with lifeless arms, her mouth hanging open. But she wasn't dead. There was a high sound coming from her like a plane approaching, getting louder, and then her body began to rock back and forth in the dirt.

This was how Jessica came to know that the dead man was the father of the child: as Crystal crawled through sharp vines and mud and hard stones, dragging her knees through the muck to lie with him, completing the family portrait.

Jessica could not feel her feet. She lay in the cold wet but she wasn't shivering. She wasn't feeling anything. Maybe she'd broken her spine in the fall. Maybe this was the anaesthetic that fear shoots through a body. She had lost her arms, her legs, her sense of self and of time. Her world had shrunk down to the scene before her. A mother and a father and the child crushed between them. Just a pale edge of moonlight to give them substance; enough to burn the image into her mind. It would replay, she knew it. She would come back to this scene of loss and grief and love. The idea of devil dogs and evil had disappeared. There was only a family broken, a fatherless child.

She could see it now, the man living like an animal in the bush, naked, hungry, perhaps mad. Six months in the wilderness. It was not a dog she'd shot but the mad crouch of a man who had lost his mind.

She heard the women. A sound like cattle pushing their way through the scrub, a racket so loud that all eleven of them might have been pushing down old growth to get to her. But when they appeared, panting, limping down the cleared path there was only the two of them. Maude in the lead, Marijam not far behind, keeping a good pace on her strong old legs.

Their torchlight swung before them and settled on the scene. Jessica began to feel her fingers again. Her hands were empty. The torch was on her keyring; her keys must have fallen from her fingers. Would she find them in the dark? Had she locked the car anyway? Could she climb back into it and sleep safely in the dark? Could you sleep when you had killed a man? Would she ever be able to sleep again?

Jessica could smell Maude approaching in a fug of fear and sweat and urine, and then she rested a hand on Jessica's shoulder and the smell became overwhelming. Jessica scrambled away and retched. Nothing but bile stinging her throat, turning her mouth to acid as she heaved again and again, convinced all her organs would be expelled from her body, but of course they weren't.

When the urge to vomit passed her ribs felt bruised. She crawled to her feet, swaying.

'I lost my keys,' she said.

Maude raised her pistol: for a moment Jessica thought she was going to shoot her. Jessica, a murderer now, and the only thing to do would be to put her down humanely. Maude raised the gun above her head and shot twice into the air. It was the signal for the others to all gather: two shots for Duck Hole Walk. They would descend on her, closing ranks.

Maude shone her torch down at her feet where there was a glint of metal. Jessica stooped and picked up the pathetic little finger of torch. Clutched at her keys as if she'd fallen overboard and they were a line back to the solid hull of the world.

'I'm sorry,' Jessica said finally. Maude frowned. Marijam was standing close to, but not touching, the corpse. Leaving Crystal to her wild grief.

'Why would you be sorry? This is what we came here to do.'

'I killed a man.'

'You killed a tiger. A rabid beast. Shot it dead like you ought to. Rid the world of one piece of evil.'

'You're insane.' Jessica shook her head. 'That's the dead body of a man.'

'It's not a man. Not her man.' Maude was nodding over to the three of them, the nativity sketched out in shadow and moonlight, underlined by Crystal's sobs.

'Her child has lost its father.'

'Her child has lost a creature that would have stalked her and maybe killed her in the end. Or worse, taken her to become one of its own.'

There was no reasoning with them. Mad women. All of them mad women. Here were the facts, laid out in the mud and filth. The naked truth of the man. The terrible grief of the woman.

The loss. Why couldn't she see the loss?

'I'm going to jail for the rest of my life,' she said, the last of the numbness leaving her. She felt sharp now, alive to the truth of it all. One moment to change a whole life.

'No, you're not going to jail.'

'But—' Jessica stared towards the dead man, and found she had no more words.

'Leave him to us. There won't be repercussions, no one's looking for him anymore. He's already dead. No one's looking, and no one will find him.'

Jessica shook her head weakly. She couldn't be here, having done this.

'Go back to the car. Go home. Say nothing. Promise me you'll say nothing.'

She was shaking her head.

'Nothing has happened. And there'll be no consequences. We'll look after you, we'll protect you, but you have to keep your mouth shut. Promise me.'

She shook her head but her mouth was moving, forming words. She heard her voice, weak but clear. 'All right.'

The sound of the word shocked her. She would go to jail. No crazy old women could protect her. She should go to the police now. An accident. How many years would a confession, a plea of manslaughter, save her? How would she survive any amount of prison time at all?

She was nodding. 'I promise,' she said, and felt the ice of her words slip down over her shoulders and along the length of her spine.

Philip leans against the trunk of a tree, a big man, made bigger by the hopes and dreams of others. He is the chosen of God, which adds a few inches to his already considerable height. He walks with the Lord: his footfalls are strong and sure and without hesitation.

He has heard about Jessica, which is why he is here now. Jessica's mother is nervous. She tucks her hair behind her ear and smooths down her simple cotton smock, small signs of vanity. Why doesn't he see this? He is always talking about the evils of vanity, all the other sins of self-regard, and yet when the women primp and preen around him he seems to swell up with their attention.

Since he is the son of God on earth who will save them all if they follow him, he must take it as inevitable.

Jessica, however, has stopped believing.

Philip is a man and as such he is fallible. Every time he predicts a new date for the apocalypse—every time they all walk up the mountain with their crosses—Jessica goes with them, but she does so knowing they will all soon trudge back down again. She still joins the women in the cooking and preserving, putting food away for the End Times, but now she looks at it more as storing food for winter. There will be no End Times. Not soon, anyway. Certainly not in Philip's mortal lifetime.

He nods, and this is a sign that Jessica should raise her gun. Philip rarely bothers himself with women's business, but he has heard about her being a crack shot at the age of ten, and he has come to see for himself. Jessica knows she should be as nervous as her mother but, strangely, she isn't. She raises the rifle, braces it against her shoulder. It is all about breath. Breathe out. Sight. Squeeze.

The can leaps into the air, tumbles. The bullet will have pierced it at the centre of the label. It isn't hard. She wonders what all the fuss is about. She feels the pulse of her blood. Even this thudding will change the direction of the bullet. The shot must be timed to the breath and to the heart. She lines up the second can, sights, breathes out, pulse, shoot. Philip nods. Jessica raises the rifle and he holds up his hand to stop her.

The women are all lined up, waiting. They know what comes next. Her mother walks out onto the range. She replaces the next can with the bundle that she's been hiding under her smock. When she steps away from the log, Jessica can see she has placed a kitten there. It mews, stares at her, licks its black face with a rough pink tongue.

Another woman walks out and picks up the next can, and in its place there is a puppy. A labrador, sandy brown, velvety and wrinkled, with all its extra skin poised for a growth spurt.

The women step back, out of the line of fire. Philip lowers his hand: she is supposed to shoot.

They are waiting for her. She glances up towards her mother, who narrows her eyes. She wants Jessica to do this: she is angry at her for hesitating.

Jessica shakes her head. Jessica's mother raises her hand and there is a pistol in it. She is aiming the pistol at her daughter. Her aim has never been any good: she's pointing the gun at Jessica's shoulder. So, she'll be winged. Maimed but alive, bleeding out slowly.

Jessica raises her rifle. Philip's eyes are on her and her neck hairs are rising up. She breathes out. (No.) She waits for the pulse. (Please, no.) The kitten is all fluff and wide eyes. (No! No! No!) She fires.

The blood hits Jessica full-force, which is a surprise. It drips down her neck—she can taste the metallic edge of it on her lips—when it should should have sprayed back, away from the force of the bullet. This is a direct contradiction of the laws of physics and the betrayal of science feels worse, somehow, than her guilt from the kill.

Philip nods, satisfied. He has taken the basic principles of action and reaction and bent the physics against her, presumably in his role as the son of God on earth.

He nods to the other target, the puppy. She can't kill a puppy. But her mother's gun is still pointed at her, this time closer to her heart, her finger tight against the trigger. She has the puppy in her sights. It pounds its oversized paws playfully on the branch as if it wants her to throw a stick. She breathes out. Swings the rifle. She points it at her mother and her eyes widen.

With a small shift of the shoulders, Jessica swings the weapon wide of her mother and aims at Philip. The son of God, the saviour. He stares back at her, his lips moving. He is mouthing words but she has no time to make sense of them. The time is all for the bullet, slowing as she squeezes the trigger, feels the kick against her shoulder, sees the bullet travel and hit, all of this in slow motion, the hole drilling slowly through skin and bone, the rush of blood like a tidal wave approaching.

Jessica falls back as the blood crashes over her and there is nothing in the world except blood, gallons and gallons of blood; the sky is obliterated by a wall of it.

What was it he said? Her mind clutches at the last movement of his lips, the soundless words: *You're Dead. You're Dead*. And then his head exploded.

Jessica gasped. She had been holding her breath under all that blood. She woke and there was blood or perhaps no, not blood. Sweat. Damp on her forehead. She was panting; she was sitting up. She thought she might have screamed in her sleep. She woke to find herself alone in the bed and someone was dead.

Matthew. Yes. Matthew was dead. The grief hit her fresh and heavy. And then, after a moment, something new. Something terrible.

Duck Hole Walk. The sign was the normal kind, made for tourists in their thick ugly sandals and brand-new backpacks. Grade: easy. For Jessica, each step was another trudge up the mountain, barefooted bleeding, dragging a hunk of wood on a back full of splinters. Last night still a throbbing memory, dull and aching. She had slept. That was the first surprise. She had fallen into a long, disturbed slumber, waking from nightmare but falling back again into the deepest sleep. Waking to find her limbs unfamiliar, stretching them out as if this were the first day.

She ducked under the fallen tree, remembering. She slipped on mud, but in the light of day it was just mud. No threat, no supernatural soup of shadow and sound. Everything bleached normal by sunlight.

She was close. Here they'd paused; somewhere here. She searched the ground for some sign of her fall. Maybe here, where the leaves seemed fresh laid. Not random, dragged down the hill by a body in motion, but carefully dropped. A tracker might say: here. Something happened here and then was hidden.

But there would be no trackers. No dogs on chains to sniff and hunt out the scent of a wild creature crouching at the edge of the path. And where did he fall? The man. Not a dog, but a human, half-starved and taken down by her weapon. Where was it, the gun? She'd dropped it. Where? She had no memory of picking the gun up or taking it home. Maybe it was still here, under the freshly turned leaves. Or maybe this wasn't where he fell. She looked further up the path.

Nothing seemed obvious. The more she looked, the more crime scenes she saw. The only obvious thing was that there was no body. A tourist hefting their toddler along this track would find nothing amiss: no bloodstains, no bullet ricocheted off to lodge in a tree trunk. If you were to believe the forest's story, nothing had happened here except a storm, a few trees down.

She searched the path, the area beside the path, she climbed down over rotted-out logs, clung to moss-covered branches and lowered herself onto the slick rocks beside the stream. Maybe they had dragged the man down here, floated him deeper into the forest for burial. Or left him to drift into the complications of the river system where he would eventually snag on something—a branch, an outcropping of rock—and slowly come apart. Chewed away over time, food for devils and fish and ants, all the creatures of the forest conspiring with the women. The whole world protecting Jessica from prosecution.

She searched for an hour, maybe two. Her footprints were everywhere. New tracks to obliterate any sign of the old. She searched but found nothing. When she looked up it was darkening: storm coming. The changes in weather here were legendary: boats lost, bushwalkers missing. It was, unbelievably, colder still.

Jessica turned reluctantly and dragged herself back towards the forestry road. When the trees parted, the sky spat cold sleety flakes at her. Not snow, something wetter and dirtier. The Inuit would have a word for this frozen sludge. She picked her way carefully to her car. His car: she had taken the four-wheel drive. Even so, she felt it skate a little towards the opening to the track, the ghost of the dead man pulling her back. The wheels skidding, then catching and spinning forward, out of his grasp.

She made the sudden turn and pulled out onto the sealed road into the blaring horn of an oncoming truck, heavy with felled logs, angry from a long hard shift. Its tailwind buffeted her to the side, and she wrestled to keep the four-wheel drive on the road.

Then thought: why?

She could stop fighting the wheel. She could let the vehicle have its way and she would hit the trees at speed and it would be sudden and over. The relief of it being over.

She closed her eyes but the truck was past her now. She had the whole of the road and she exhaled into it. She was still here and she would have to live with herself and her actions. She felt a sudden urge to confess.

Philip used to demand confessions, each of them lined up on

a Sunday to spend an hour with him in a room alone. It was this cloistered horror that was the final deciding factor. She remembered the day, waiting her turn, her heart beating faster as one after another of them was whittled from the front of the queue. Almost her turn and then only one girl left and that girl about to stand and disappear into his room. She remembered standing, turning, walking and continuing to walk. Frightened, for the longest time, that they would come after her and drag her back. But she had just turned eighteen and she was free to make her own decisions and she walked till her feet burned with blisters and the sole of her left shoe was flapping. Standing in the town. All the people trying not to stare at the way she was dressed. Not knowing what to do next but the policeman approaching and that first terrorised response: fight or flight?

The police. Her confession to him back then, and his kind voice. 'Do you have any other relatives?'

Does she? If they gave her one phone call now who would it be to? Certainly not her mother. Not his mother either.

William? She would call William. It surprised her, but it was true.

She found herself home and could not remember getting there. She would make her confession later. Now she needed sleep. She locked the door behind her and collapsed in sudden finality on the bed.

Maude was leaning over her. Jessica woke, and she was there. She scrambled back but there was a wall behind her. She was in her own house. She had locked the door and yet here was the woman,

Maude, looming as if to strangle her.

Then Jessica noticed the cup in her hand and knew that she had made tea and was reaching over to place it at the side of the bed.

Jessica had locked the door. She remembered locking it. Maude had broken in somehow.

'Where's my gun?'

Maude's harmless-old-lady smile seemed to dissolve. 'You shouldn't be thinking about that.'

It was late afternoon. Jessica knew this because the light was leaning towards the bedroom door, shining directly onto the old woman.

'We've taken care of it.'

'It's my gun.'

'Sure. But we'll get you another. Just wait. This one is tainted now.' As if the gun itself was responsible: a weapon in disgrace.

'I brought you tea.'

Jessica looked at the cup but left it sitting there, cooling on the bedside table.

'I'm going to the police.'

'Are you?'

'Yes.'

'What about?'

The woman sat at the foot of her bed, the weight causing Jessica to roll uncomfortably towards her. Jessica shuffled away.

'How did you get in here?'

'You left the door open.'

'I didn't.'

'I came to check on you. For the group.'

'The group.'

'Crystal said to send her love.'

Last time she had seen Crystal she'd been clinging to her murdered husband, wailing.

'She's all right now. She just needed to grieve.'

'Because I killed her husband?'

'No. Her husband was dead months ago. You rescued him, if anything. Returned him to his loved ones. To the human world.'

Jessica shuffled towards the edge of the bed furthest away from Maude. She tried to swing her legs free of the covers but Maude reached out and gripped her knee.

'You won't go to the police,' Maude said. It was not a question; not even a gentle suggestion.

'What's stopping me?'

'Nothing, I suppose. They'll probably just send you home. Woman. Gone mad with grief. Imagining things, confessing to the death of a phantom.'

'There's a body.'

'Is there?'

'There was a body. It'll be somewhere. They'll find the blood.'

'Will they?' Maude indicated the window and Jessica looked out to a world covered in a thick layer of snow. Snow right down to the waterline. Magical.

'There wasn't anything to be found anyway, but they certainly won't find anything after this.'

'I killed a man. I shot him.'

'What with?'

'Give me back my gun.'

'You should drink your tea. Tea's good for shock.'

'I'm going to the police.'

'If you need to be punished, then go. They'll lock you up, but not in a jail. They don't put mad women in jail. If you need to be punished, to make your peace with your God, then let them lock you up. Take the meds and let them convince you that you've gone insane if you don't want to listen to us. But we are doing this for your own good. We're protecting you. We'll keep you safe. You'll see. You're angry now, but you'll come round. If not, go tell them that you shot a tiger and it turned into a man. Go tell them that.'

'I shot a man.'

'You saw the tiger?'

'There was no tiger. It was the man. He was crouched down. It was dark.'

'You tell yourself what you need to. You say whatever you like.'

'Why did you think you could let yourself into my house?'

'We were worried about you.'

'I think you should go.'

Jessica waited as Maude reluctantly eased herself off her bed.

'I'm sad you feel that way, but you might feel differently in the morning. We're meeting tomorrow night. To talk. You're welcome to join us.'

Jessica didn't answer.

'Good luck with the cops.' A smile playing at the edge of her mouth before she disappeared around the door. Jessica listened to Maude's heavy boots on the floorboards, creaking and groaning on her way to the front door.

Which she knew she had locked.

Jessica heard the door close behind Maude, the sound of the

engine coughing to life. She watched her drive through the snow. Snow down to sea level. This was the first time in all the years they had lived here that the snow had come down this far. Plenty of it in the mountains, but never right down to the ocean. It was oddly mild, as if the snow was insulation against the cold. She got out of bed, and she felt rested and warm. For the first time in weeks she was not even close to shivering.

Paranoia. No one was watching her. No one knew yet. But all eyes were on her, the fresh widow. She was no longer the anonymous figure that ghosted through the shop a few times a week, picking up her mail, buying bread and butter and rice.

She reached for a rye loaf, heavy and already stale. Country life. Everything old before it reached her. A blonde woman, her hair dark at the roots, was pretending to read the ingredients on a packet of corn chips. She had tied her T-shirt in front so that it pulled tight across her breasts.

She was scowling at Jessica. Was she? For a terrible moment Jessica thought this woman knew. But of course she couldn't. Still, Jessica took the loaf and hurried to the checkout. The blonde woman moved to stand behind her, too close. She could smell the woman's perfume, oddly familiar. She had smelled this before, what was it? Jasmine? Sickly sweet. Where had she smelled this before?

The girl at the till took her money and she pulled her hood up and hurried outside. She stopped suddenly. A police car. She saw it next to her…to Matthew's car and it meant so many things at once. She forced herself forward. To hesitate would be a sign of guilt, but she was, of course, guilty. This was the opportunity for confession. All she had to do was walk up to the officer and tell him.

Crazy woman, lunatic, confessing to crimes that had never happened, murdering a man who had been dead for months. She walked towards him and he turned. He half-smiled. It was the same one, the man who had brought Matthew's car home. His young, slightly pudgy face, his smile was his own admission of guilt.

'Hey,' he said. He looked embarrassed.

'Hey.'

'Look, I'm sorry we didn't find him.' For a moment she thought he was referring to the dead man, the father of Crystal's child. 'That forest is so dense. There are only so many tracks and—'

'I know.'

'I saw his car, your car, and I just wanted to—'

'Yeah. No worries.'

'Well, my wife has been meaning to drop some food down. It's hard, you know, to know what's right.'

'Thank you.'

He retreated into his car. Window open. She could lean in: *I'm sorry too. I'm sorry I just killed a man. I am a monster. Arrest me.* But she smiled and nodded and he pulled out of the carpark, and now she was withholding information. Obstructing police. Now she was committing one crime to cover up another. Digging in deep enough to bury herself.

She opened the passenger door by accident, as if Matthew was about to get in and drive his own car, Jessica riding shotgun.

Shotgun.

She walked back around to the driver's side, heart pounding. Hauled herself into the cab and sat, trying to calm herself. The blonde woman was standing outside the shop, just standing there, holding a single packet of corn chips and staring at her.

Something in her eyes. Jessica remembered her dream from last night, the sudden shock of nightmare. She reversed out of the carpark, almost into the path of an oncoming logging truck that slammed down on the horn as she slammed on the brake. A second near miss. She was cracking up.

She looked up. The woman was still there, staring. Jessica eased back and out onto the road.

Paws thumped against the door of the four-wheel drive. A labrador, not a newborn puppy like the one in her dream, but a young dog. The animal let its tongue loll, claws scrabbling on his paintwork. Matthew would be angry. Matthew loved that car.

'Hey. Brutus. Hey.'

The sight of William filled her with a sense of relief.

'Meet your trusty hound.'

'What?'

She slipped out of the car and the dog was on her. She laughed. The sound felt odd, unfamiliar. How long had it been since she laughed? The puppy stomped sandy paw prints onto her stomach, her thighs.

'Brutus, down boy, down.'

She dropped to her haunches and took the soft dog head in between her palms and felt the wet tongue catch her neck and the smell of the animal's terrible breath and she buried her face in one of its ears and she was crying. Tears spilling onto her cheeks and a sob coming, dragged up from the depths of her, loud and full and interminable. Once she had begun to cry it seemed she could never stop.

'Oh, hey, Jess, hey,' he said, stooping to rest a hand on her heaving shoulder, but she couldn't stop.

She spoke to him through gasps. 'I don't know why I'm crying. I don't feel anything. I honestly don't feel sad.'

But she was howling now, no possibility of explanation, and the dog hopping up to rest its front paws in her lap and licking away her tears, loving the salt, and snuffling at her ear and burying its soft muzzle in her neck. William pushed the dog away and eased Jessica towards the front door of the shack.

'Got the key?'

And she heard him but could do nothing to respond. He lowered her down onto the step and the dog was on her once more, the relief of a warm body hopping up into her lap. She wrapped her arms around it and buried her head in the soft fur. William went back to the car and got the keys from the ignition. She let herself be picked up, manoeuvred into her own house, half-dragged, half-carried, with the comforting thump of the dog's tail against her thighs.

She found herself in bed and a cup of tea beside her and the warm weight of a dog on her feet. It was getting dark. She must have slept. She had a story to file. Jessica swung her feet over and onto the icy floor. Her head hurt. She reached over and pulled a jumper over her head. She was still wearing her day clothes, which was a relief.

'Will? William?'

She could hear him in the kitchen. She struggled into her shoes, feeling hungover, unbalanced and stumbling as she got out of bed. The dog stuck fast to her side—what was his name?

'Hi.'

'Sorry.'

'I made dinner.'

'I have to file a story.'

'A story… When?'

She looked at her watch. 'Fuck. An hour ago.'

'Do it. I'll keep the dinner warm.'

'It's almost done. Just have to do the conclusion.'

'Okay.'

She sat at the table and pulled the laptop towards her. The dog placed his warm muzzle in her lap. 'What's his name again? Your dog?'

'Brutus. Your dog.'

'Serious?'

'You said you wanted one. I got his sister.'

'He is beautiful.' She ruffled his ears. 'Brutus. I'll welcome you later. Giant cuttlefish come first. Environmental disaster or natural rhythm of the ocean? What do you think, Brutus?' The dog settled onto her feet and started licking the toe of her boot.

She had lost a lover, she had killed a man. She owned a dog. The whole world had changed in a handful of weeks, but the giant cuttlefish were still absent from the western waters, a new dinosaur had been identified from fossils, a new species of microbe had been discovered in a spacecraft clean-room in Florida.

Science remained an ever-ticking clock. The secrets of the universe revealing themselves day by day, and there is no magic, only things that we do not yet understand.

The dog liked the boat. At first he ran from one side of it to the other, setting it to rocking as if on a bad sea, snapping and barking at gulls. The net was a challenge, unravelling it without exciting him. He stood and shifted his weight from one paw to another as if he were expecting a game.

'Brutus, no,' and he pleaded, whining, a high excited sound at the back of his throat.

But he settled in time, turning a slow circle to curl up awkwardly on the wooden bench. He added a feeling of weight and stability that the boat had been missing.

Approaching shore, he became excited once more and jumped out before she could catch hold of his lead. He swam for the beach and ran back and forth at the tideline waiting for the boat to slide in and settle. She dragged the boat up higher, tied it to the tree and picked up his lead. The road ran close to the front of the shack and she didn't want him racing out in front of a car. As they climbed the rock wall he began to bark and the sound of it changed from play to fury.

'Quiet, Brutus, quiet.'

But nothing would silence him. She saw him drag his lips back and bare his teeth in a vicious snarl. At the base of the stairs he was straining at the lead, choking on the chain collar, and then she smelled it too. That wild animal reek.

'He's been here.' This to Brutus, but the dog was not listening. She clipped his lead onto the rail. If she let Brutus go, if he were to meet the thing, the tiger, Matthew, if he were to aim himself at her lover with so much fury. Not Matthew. Of course it couldn't be Matthew. But standing here with the smell of the wild strong in the air she remembered the hunt. A clear image of the thing she saw, more cat than man, the smell, the gun in her hand...

She was losing her mind. Just like the women. She was becoming just like them.

She left the dog chained up at the base of the stairs. The sliding door to the porch was open. A tiger could never open a sliding door. Something else then, someone else. Maude, who had let herself in through a locked door. Maude, who had offered to protect her, made veiled threats when she wouldn't accept the kindness.

'Hello?'

No sound. The curtains brushing her arm in a gentle breeze. She stepped inside and the scent of it was stronger. The lounge room looked untouched. Papers spilled over the table, her copies of *New Scientist*, still in their plastic, piling up beside the couch. Her laptop listing at a gentle angle on top of it all.

The kitchen empty, the smell stronger in the corridor. He was in their room. That was where the smell was coming from. What if she opened the bedroom door and he was there on her bed. She remembered the pleasure of finding him each morning, the soft pale skin smelling of sleep, the pale pink kiss of one nipple peeking out from under the sheet, his skin prickling to goose bumps as he woke and realised suddenly that he was cold, pulling her warm body towards his chest.

How fiercely she had loved him. She felt it now, a bolt of pure desire.

She swung open the door, and it smelled like a den full of devil cubs. The scent of the wild so strong that she coughed, held her hand up to her mouth. The smell was in her bed, on her sheets. She bent and sniffed her way towards the strong heart of it, his pillow. An indent in his pillow, the book he had been reading no longer poised on the side table, but splayed out on the floor, his place lost forever. She bent, her hand trembling; held the edge of the sheet and exhaled as if she were taking aim. She pulled at the covers and they slithered off the empty mattress. She bent slowly in the soft mess of linen and blankets and peered under. Nothing. Dust. Nothing. She stood and moved to the clothes basket at the end of the bed, untouched since he was lost. His clothes were still tangled with hers. She picked out a shirt, blue, stained at the armpits. Held the fabric to her face and breathed in.

Matthew. This was what Matthew smelled like, not the terrible stench of whatever had been lying on her bed. She clutched a jumper and breathed him in, flooded with a bitter sadness. She felt a lump forming in her throat, her grief reaching up to choke her.

She picked up a T-shirt, green, with a picture of a monkey printed on the front. She had bought him this shirt, ordered it on the internet. She held it to her face. The smell of Matthew, and… Something else.

She pulled her face away and stared at the shirt. Pressed her face against it once more and breathed in. Something not quite familiar; she struggled to place it. Sickly sweet, like a soft drink, or a…

Jasmine. It was the smell of jasmine.

She dropped the shirt back into the basket. Took a step backwards.

Jessica turned and ran down the stairs to where Brutus was growling, straining at the lead. She unclipped it and watched him scramble up the stairs, hurling himself inside. He had found his way to the bedroom and started tearing at the mattress, eviscerating it, the stuffing coming free in great clumps. Growling, snarling, barking between bites. If the mattress had been an animal it would have been disembowelled. Then, when the mattress was hollowed out, the dog started ripping and tearing at the sheets. Jessica picked up the green T-shirt. She pulled the dog away from the mess of torn cloth and pressed his muzzle into the T-shirt.

'Smell it?' she asked. 'Smell her? Have you smelled her before?'

But of course she had not had the dog when she stood at the Dover shop waiting to be served, with the blonde woman standing too close, staring angrily at her shoulders, stinking of this same perfume.

The dog pulled away from her, turned back to the bedclothes and continued to tear them till they were unrecognisable.

She would have to sleep on the couch. It pulled out into a bed—uncomfortable, the mattress thin and worn, but it was always warm there by the fire. She would sleep by the fire.

Brutus started barking at 7 p.m. William wasn't due till nine. His shift finished at eight and it would take him an hour to navigate the dark and winding roads. *What if he doesn't arrive? What if he texts—leaving now—and then, like a recurring nightmare, there is no sign of him? The dinner cold, a police car pulling in to her drive.*

She was making paella for the first time and had started early.

All the ingredients weighed, sliced, separated—Jesus, do you really need to wash the rice?—then the dog barking, furiously; snapping at his own reflection in the glass. Salivating. Why would a dog begin to salivate? She remembered the way he'd torn her bed apart, as if he were searching for a deadly enemy in there and would eat them whole.

She checked her watch. Seven o'clock was the time of the gathering. The women would be at Maude's place, waiting for her to arrive. Maybe they knew she wouldn't be coming; maybe they'd decided to arrive on her doorstep instead? She felt grateful for Brutus, but that was illusory—those frail old women had guns.

Past eight, and the barking persisted. The dog's snapping and snarling had made her nervous. She had locked every window, bolted the front door. She pulled the curtain and slid a lounge chair in front of the glass, which was no protection at all, but which lent a vague sense of cover. She opened the oven and slipped the cooked paella inside to crisp the top, unconcerned about overcooking, making the mussels tough. She was thinking about the moment William would arrive. The body of the man dwarfing her, making her laugh, forcing her to relax.

Surely the dog was getting hoarse by now, its mouth frothy, its eyes stretched wide so the whites showed. Surely it would run out of anger at some point.

'Good boy,' she muttered. 'Good puppy.'

He was early. Jessica was surprised by the relief she felt at the sound of his car pulling up beside hers, running to the door, unbolting it, close to weeping with the release of tension. She stopped. Breathed. Tried to calm herself. She smiled as she opened the door, but he frowned, looked past her.

'Is that Brutus?'

'Yes.'

'What's up?'

'He's been doing that for almost two hours.'

'Seriously?'

'Brutus? Here, boy.'

And the dog paused reluctantly and ran up for a pat before placing himself back at the sliding doors, barking, barking, barking.

'Is someone out there?'

And the cold shuddering down her shoulders, worming its way along her back and settling sour and heavy in her stomach.

'Want me to have a look?' William put his hands against the glass, shielding his eyes from the glare of the inside light. 'Is there a porch light?'

She flicked the switch and there was movement, something, gone now. William stepped away from the window. Rested his hand on Brutus' head. 'Shhhh, boy. Shhhh. It's just a stray, I think.'

'A dog?'

'I think. Or a bloody big feral cat. But I think it was a dog. Skinny dog.'

Brutus lay down as if he'd thought about it and decided William was right. Nothing to worry about. But there was a low percolation deep in the back of his throat and she noticed his ears twitching.

'Smells good.'

Jessica had forgotten the paella. She slid it out of the oven and tapped an open mussel shell with the edge of a spatula.

'That'll be tough now.'

'But tasty.'

She scraped some of the rice onto the plates, the bottom crisp as a pie crust, and it smelled good. She sat opposite William, the dog close to her feet, and thought: there were things that could distress her if she dwelt on them, the dog out there in the dark, the women meeting to discuss that other thing, the thing she absolutely wouldn't let herself remember. But Jessica wanted to carve out this tiny moment for herself. She let herself smile when he made a joke, enjoy the food despite the overcooked mussels, warm herself in the glow of fire and the company.

At some point they moved on to the couch and it seemed easy enough to lean into his shoulder. The sheer physicality of the man made her feel safer than she had since Matthew disappeared.

'Look at your hand.' She touched his hand, tentative. He could rest his thumb on her hipbone and his little finger just near her knee: a hand as long as her thighbone. She measured it out in flesh and inches and held it there when she was done.

The mood shifted. There was a pause, a moment for decisions. She needed to think…and yet thinking led her down a terrible path. The mess she was in; what had happened to her and what she had done. A decision would mean an acknowledgment of cause and effect.

'I don't want to think about it. Is that okay?'

He nodded.

'If I try to make a decision about all this I'll explode.'

'I don't want you to explode.' His voice rough suddenly, deep and husky.

She stretched her own small hand out, thumb to little finger, and it was a tiny span across the top of his thigh. She would need four hands to mark out the length of it.

'Hah,' she said. 'Too small.'

'Really?'

And when he moved her hand up and over slightly, it was clear her outstretched fingers were the perfect measure after all.

She was obliterated. She was dwarfed by his body. Sitting astride him on the couch she was a child taming a great beast, hanging on to his shoulders hoping she would not be thrown. He picked her up and she held her place with her legs, stretched as wide as they could be, wrapped around his hips. Not a single piece of clothing removed, but as she sat, cradled and lifted by the man, she knew the clothes were no protection. Half of her understanding this was one more complication, another disaster like a landmine in her life, the other half wanting to crawl out of her clothes, her skin, her memories and emerge naked as an earthworm. Blind and blinking into a new world.

She unbuttoned her shirt and the dog growled, then William's mouth was on her breast and there was nothing but this. Sex like the ocean, obliterating everything but the immediate sensation. His tongue, the pulling of his lips, a line cast out from his mouth, hooking her there and falling down through her stomach and down again, curling around the hard anchor of his cock which rubbed against her with an exquisite pressure.

The jeans had to go: this thought so urgent and immediate that she didn't care if she fell. She let go of his back and unclasped the fly and unzipped, held up and against him by his huge, solid arms. Somehow he held her and cradled her body in one arm and tugged the jeans off her with the other. All this while she was cut loose, unmoored and unmuddied, and when he pressed her against his body once more she was so wet already it was as if this was no more than swimming. Just a kick of her legs and her hips tipped with the waves and she felt the size of him, too big, she thought, too big and too naked, but it didn't matter now. All the hurt had been done to her already.

She shut her eyes and rocked down and the pain split her in two, and she wanted the pain because of the dead man, because of the loss and the fear, but this wasn't pain. This was just a feeling of gluttony, of taking too much inside. She held still. Let her muscles relax around his cock and when the pain had been observed and reinterpreted, she nestled her hips down on him for more purchase. Tipped them back again to press her clitoris onto his pubic bone. She looked up. His eyes were closed and his expression…Grateful. Joyous, like a child on Christmas morning.

It was too soon, but she felt herself climb, rising up as he rose up into her. His eyes locked to hers, his pupils dilated, the strangeness of his body, so alive, and the pulse of their movements massaging her back to life. She was breathing quickly now. His skin flushed, she could see that her pleasure excited him, a feedback loop escalating her own joy.

'I can't…' she said, but there was no time to warn him how close she was, her muscles tensed, her head leaned back, her hips bucked and she was coming. And he clamped his arms tight around her and stumbled a step forward before righting himself. She felt the heat and the pulse and the dampness like her heart restarting, hidden as it was in the depths of her body. She felt him buck hard up into her and she arched her hips towards him, every thrust a gasp of breath.

She laughed, but he was still lost to the last of the pleasure, rocking up and back and she clung to his shoulders and found herself grinning into his neck.

And then he was still except for the thrumming of his heart against her chest.

She let him lift her off him and lay her on the couch and spread her legs out so that he could look at her all swollen and sticky.

She liked him looking at her like this. She liked that his eyes were wide as if she had given him some rare gift. Then he bent his head over, sweat dripping from his forehead, and he placed his lips on her cunt and he kissed her and this was how it ended. Lips wet and smiling when he pulled away.

'I want more of that,' she told him. Her voice was strange to her, thin and breathless.

'I want that too. And…after. More nights like this.'

She nodded. And then she breathed out, smiling.

The dog started to bark again.

William pulled away. 'What's wrong, boy?'

It was over. That was the end of everything: Jessica knew this even as he pressed a hand against her stomach and urged her to stay where she was while he moved to the window, naked, hard again, as if searching for her in the cold empty dark.

Dog or cat or tiger. Tiger, tiger burning bright.

She was putting her shirt back on, strangely embarrassed now. 'You should go.'

She wanted him to put his clothes on. She wanted him to step away from the window.

'There's nothing out there.'

She wanted to turn back the clock and undo what they had done. She wanted to do it again.

'I think you should go.'

'There's no one out there. It's a dog or a cat.'

'Please go.'

And he turned towards her then, deflated. 'Okay.'

Matthew would never have left. Matthew would have talked her into letting him stay. Maybe she wanted him to stay. But it was too late now.

She watched him pick up his clothes. He looked so chastened, Jessica wanted to reach out and hug him, but she couldn't. He shut the door of the bathroom and when he came out, dressed, cowed, she took his huge hand in hers.

'I—thanks—more than…' She lifted his hand to her face and pressed her lips into the centre of his palm. 'I'm sorry. Just the barking and…it's maybe too…' She gestured to the cold emptiness of the cabin. 'It was so good. Honestly. I haven't felt like that in—'

He nodded. 'I would like to see you again.'

Jessica nodded. Yes, she knew he wanted to see her again. And yes.

Brutus barking and they both looked towards the window.

'I don't feel good leaving you. Not if there is the possibility that someone…'

'I'll be fine.'

'I'll call you tomorrow.'

'Will you?'

'Yes. I promise.'

'Okay.'

He kissed her. It made her uncomfortable to be kissed like this with some dog or cat or tiger out there in the dark. The world had been banished for a moment; now it was back. She kissed him and then pressed her hands against his chest and moved him away from her gently.

As he left he glanced around nervously. Nothing. Nothing out there but the dog barking and barking and sometimes howling as if someone, something was lurking out there in the dark. She closed the door quickly behind him and leaned against it. The world was back and all the things in it and all the things that she had done or had done to her. She walked back down the corridor to stand beside Brutus, growling and barking by her knee.

And the blood hit her like a wave. She was drowning in it. She was gasping, sitting up in bed. No, not bed. The couch, because the dog had destroyed her bed. Brutus and his constant barking, and eventually the falling falling falling into dream. The rifle in her hands, aiming, each time something different in her sights. She didn't want to remember but she was remembering now. That last dream, the one where she could line up her sight, picking out her mother, no, Philip, no...

William. Such a surprise to see William in the sights.

Squeezing the trigger.

'William?'

No. He wasn't here; she had sent him away.

The blood knocking her back.

'Will?'

And only the sound of Brutus barking barking barking. No stopping that dog. No moving him from his vigil by the sliding door.

It was almost light. The dog was silhouetted by the coming morning. Little glints of sun on the shifting tide. She should be up and dragging the boat out. She longed for the habit of casting out a net, pulling in a pot crawling with the insect legs of crayfish. She stood tentatively. She felt sore, as if she had been running, and then she remembered the overwhelming pleasure of last night.

The sense of safety, the wonderful freedom of letting go. Safe in those huge hands. Except...

They hadn't used a condom. Before Matthew, at uni, she would never have slept with a man or even a woman without protection. She was a scientist. She knew the risks. And here she was now, running blind and headlong into consequences. Infection, pregnancy, the damning judgment of the people in town. What if someone really had been out there in the dark, watching them? Grieving widow turned suddenly into treacherous slut.

Brutus was still barking.

She picked up her phone and brought up William's contact. *Hey. Thanks for last night. I can't stop thinking about it. I would like to see you soon.* Her thumb hovered over send.

Would she? Would she like to see him soon?

Bark. Bark. Bark.

'For fuck's sake!'

She was fully dressed. She hadn't even changed into her pyjamas. She opened the sliding door and Brutus bolted, down the stairs, out into the tiny garden, leaping over the rocks and landing in the damp sand. She saw him kick up sand as he ran. She called out to him, too slow coming down the stairs to see where he had gone.

'Brutus?'

And just the sound of the waves coming back to her.

'Fuck's sake,' she said again, climbing down onto the beach. The tide had left a line of jellyfish almost at the rocks, glistening in the reluctant grey light. Her boat had been moved, shifted to one side by the rising water. It lay sideways, still tied to the tree where she always moored it, but blocking her usual climb down from the rocks. She followed the dog's tracks, the only footprints on the beach. They raced past three other shacks then left the sand and disappeared into the grassy climb at the verge.

'Brutus!'

Nothing. Not a sound. Not a trace of his footsteps. Jessica began to walk along the road. Some of the houses had lights on. Some had smoke pouring from their chimneys, some were cold and sleeping, abandoned till the tiny window of summer opened again.

'Brutus!'

And the few occupied windows lighting up now, one after the other. She was calling them out of dreams and she didn't care. She had lost her boyfriend. She wasn't going to lose her damn dog as well.

There wasn't enough petrol in either car. Christ. She swore as she searched the boxes under the house. There was a hose. She cut a length of it. How could a person be such a fucking idiot? She sucked, tasted the bitter petrol just in time and slipped the end of the hose into the bucket. Spat onto the grass. She held the hose until the petrol trickled and stopped. Add it to what was left in the other tank…maybe enough to get her to Dover, to a petrol station. She poured it carefully into the Mazda. Piece of Shit: her name for the car with its dodgy lights and terrible turning circle and the doors that needed to be slammed or they wouldn't shut, and yet it was a fuel-efficient piece of shit. At least compared to Matthew's four-wheel drive.

She checked her phone. No message from William. She tried to call. Waited till it rang out before climbing into the car.

As she navigated the precarious turns around the cliffs, she looked down to the water. She turned the wheel hard, correcting a drift towards the precipice, and the flyers slipped off the passenger seat. *Missing dog.* She had used the same template as the posters for her missing husband. Same font, same position of the photograph—not a photo of Brutus but a similar labrador that she'd found on the internet.

It made her look bad, she supposed. This apparent inability to keep track of her loved ones.

If you don't find the lost relative in the first forty-eight hours then it is unlikely that you will find him at all. She pressed redial and let the phone sit on the passenger seat, shouting out into the abyss.

It was her, the blonde girl. Perhaps she had always worked at the petrol station. Jessica rarely filled the tank herself. Matthew liked to drive; she liked to stay close to home. He would take the car out for supplies, bring it home with a full tank. She had been here a few times, of course, but she had barely noticed the blonde woman. Just another local yokel with her T-shirt knotted to show off her spray tan, her nails too long for someone who works a petrol pump.

The smell of the perfume hit her like a slap. Jasmine. She almost choked on it. She wished Brutus was in the back seat. She wanted him to recognise the smell, to reassure her that this really was the same scent, the smell she had found on Matthew's shirt. She wanted the dog to bark at this woman.

She remembered last night. That little flip in her guts. No dog to bark now. No message from William on her phone.

The woman frowned when she saw her standing there, second in line to pay. The man in front of her hitched his trousers up with his thumb, zipped his padded coat and stepped out into the cold. Jessica shuffled up to the counter.

'Seventy-four fifty.'

'I...' She shut her mouth, drew breath. This was ridiculous. Matthew was gone. Whatever was done was done. There could be no recriminations now. So what if he'd been fucking this girl, what good would it do to find out the details? And maybe—a tiny maybe—she was just a friend. A goodbye hug, the sweet smear of jasmine on a collar.

'I need some two-stroke.'

The woman stood staring, her lips bright red and slightly parted. Her eyes cold and narrow. The perfume. Jessica struggled with a surge of hatred. If something had happened between her and Matthew it was on Matthew, not this woman. Jessica watched and hated the cartoonish sway of the woman's hips. Heels, high heels working in a servo. Bleached blonde hair. How could Matthew fall for a cliché? She felt her mouth tightening as the woman bent for a small container of two-stroke oil; bent further for a five-litre can.

She handed them both to Jessica. 'Go crazy, lady.'

Jessica filled the can, squeezing all her hatred into her clenched hand on the nozzle of the petrol pump. She wanted to throw it all into the car and drive off without paying. She tried to remain calm, almost pleasant. She handed over her credit card. The woman waited for the payment to go through, looked over her shoulder, nodded with her chin. 'Nice car.'

'Have you got a problem?'

'Sorry?'

'Have you got a problem with me?'

'Do you want a receipt?'

'No.' Jessica took her card back. 'Thank you.'

She sat in the car, her chest tight. Turned the ignition on and the car lurched forward. She'd left it in gear.

'Fuck.' She tried again. Successfully starting the car seemed like an achievement. Her hands were shaking. 'Fuck.'

She leaned forward and her palm hit the horn and it beeped. It felt good. She slammed her fist into it again. Very good. She leaned on the horn. She thumped it again and again. People were staring at her. Crazy lady, crazy with grief. She held her hands to her face and screamed into them. *Fuck. Fuck. Fuck.*

She had her petrol and her two-stroke. She had put up posters for her missing dog and missing boyfriend; a lover also missing, or avoiding her. She eased the car out of the servo and back onto the road. She wanted to be on the water. She wanted Brutus in the front of the boat and the icy chill of the wind off a gentle tide and the fish below. She hadn't realised how much she needed that dog. Only a few days and the loss of him would destroy her. She wanted William back on her couch, she wanted him inside her. She pressed redial and glanced down at her phone as the call rang and rang and rang out unanswered.

Fuck.

But then the phone buzzed and she flinched. She pulled over to the soft leaf litter on the verge.

It wasn't William's number. She picked the phone up warily.

'Hello?'

'Hi.'

And the disappointment was like the water in the bath running out, gravity suddenly pulling at her, all the weight of the world returning.

'You didn't come.'

And only now recognising the voice as Maude's.

'No.'

'We just wanted to make sure you haven't been speaking to anyone.'

'No.'

'Because we'll know, sooner or later. Probably sooner. Fucking town.'

'I haven't.'

'Because grief sends you crazy. Crazy enough to sit in a car beeping the horn over and over again for no reason. Don't worry. I've been there.'

Jessica glanced over her shoulder back to the empty road. The water was still draining out of the bath. She felt heavier and heavier. She had never weighed so much.

'Anyway. We are just checking in to see if you're okay.'

'Right.'

'Let you know we're looking out for you. Day and night. Just say the word. You don't even have to say the word. We'll be there. Do you understand?'

'I think you've made it clear.'

'Benefits of country living. All this neighbourliness.'

'Okay.'

She stopped the call. Dialled William one more time. *Come on. Come on!* And something was wrong. Brutus was gone. William wasn't answering. Perhaps she had made it all up. Perhaps it was all an extended hallucination: the coven of women, the hunting, the dog, the man, the sex. How could any of it be real? She was losing her mind.

She drove home on a familiar road but everything around her seemed less solid. It was insane; all that had happened was insane. She would wake up knowing it was a nightmare or she would find herself locked up. She pulled up outside her shack and there was Matthew's car, still dented in the front fender. So it had happened. It was all true, or some of it anyway.

And if it was all true—had she killed a man? Had she slept with a man? Had there ever been a dog to lose?

Jessica woke up on the couch, disoriented. Where had the day gone? She had checked her phone about a thousand times. She remembered defrosting some smoked salmon. She did not remember eating it, but maybe she had. She certainly wasn't hungry now.

The fire was out. She reached through the icy dark to open the door and put another log on the last embers. There was that animal smell again. It was so strong that she turned, expecting to see it—the dog, the tiger, the devil—standing close behind her. She felt the prickle of warning up her back. She wanted Brutus. She wanted William. She should call him again. One last time. She had offended him somehow, something she had said. He just needed a day to recover.

She shouldn't pester him now. Matthew always said she fussed too much. She never gave a man his space. Men needed their space. And she could be bossy, too. She should never have sent William away like that.

Maybe she should call him one more time. Apologise for bossing him around. She reached for her phone and felt the house shake. Footfalls.

'Brutus?'

Human steps. On the back stairs, the ones that came up from the beach.

Who could be walking up those stairs? Maude? William?

She remembered the police arriving at the beginning of things.

If she hadn't opened the door that first night, if she had let them knock and knock, she would not know that Matthew was lost. She could have stayed hidden inside. She'd had enough food for weeks, maybe months. She should never have opened the door.

There was a scrabbling sound there now. Scratching, dragging sounds, and then, at last, a knocking. Whoever it was knew she had heard him. He was waiting just beyond that curtain, ready to deliver the news. Of course it would be bad news; there could be no other kind.

Jessica dragged herself towards the door. There were things in her way, a shopping bag with cans in it, still not unpacked. When had she bought these supplies? Not today, surely. She stepped over her handbag, dropped where she had been standing, a pile of newspapers spilling out across the lino.

Was there a story to file? What day was it?

She put her hand out to touch the curtain. When she saw the police officer's face, she would know. A body had been found. Some new clue. The promise of sadness set like black ice on the road.

She gripped the curtain and eased it open.

There was a moon. Without it she would not have been able to see him, his face. As it was…

Unmistakable.

'Matthew…' A catch in her throat.

Why didn't she fling the sliding glass door open? *Where have you been?* she should be saying. *You scared me half to death.* Just enough light to see that it was him, but something in his eyes, a wildness. Something new, or had it always been there? Had she forgotten him, so quickly?

He wasn't wearing anything at all and he was thin. So thin, with the light playing on the ribs, painting stripes on his pale flesh. He had never been thin. He was a shadow of the man she loved.

Jessica put her hand up to the glass. Matthew mirrored her gesture, his skin against hers. His mouth was not touched by even a hint of a smile. His eyes were flat, but smart. Curious.

And she knew. Realised with a flood of relief that she didn't need to wonder anymore. This was what happened to Matthew. This.

Slowly, Jessica slid the door open.

There was blood on his thigh. Leaves in his hair, which had grown longer, clumping in thick strands of mud. He stepped into the shack and she could smell him. He was ripe in the way that homeless people are ripe. Old sweat, unwashed. Not quite the same smell as the animal reek she had smelled on her mattress, but similar. Wild human instead of wild beast. There were scratches on his arms and his back. His ribs stuck out rudely.

She stepped back as he entered. She left room for him and he took it, his skinny thighs trembling. He stared at her.

Matthew.

They are not human anymore. They are the devil.

But his eyes were the same. Confused; perhaps a little afraid, but the same deep brown. His lips parted—she thought he was going to speak to her, but he closed his mouth and walked to the kitchen. His back a mess of red welts, as if he had been whipped.

Perhaps he'd been abducted, or…if he'd been running on all fours, his chest protected, maybe his back would have caught the twigs and branches.

He opened the fridge, the interior light spilling on his skin. He must be freezing. How had he kept himself warm? His face. Matthew's sweet face, only the cheeks sunken, emaciated. She felt as if she could pick him up in her arms, carry him to the couch. She needed to cover him in some way, but she couldn't move.

She watched him pick a cryovac packet of salmon from the fridge, tear it open with his teeth and squeeze the whole slab of fish into his mouth. He chewed noisily. Reached in for the bowl of leftover paella and scooped it into his mouth with his fingers.

She remembered William. She felt the blood return to her face. A tightening in her stomach. She turned, walked to the bedroom, aware of each cold step, one after another. She was shivering. For him: she wasn't cold at all. She didn't feel anything at all. His coat was still in the cupboard where he had left it. She wrenched it free—the smell of him, similar but different. She held the coat to her face and the grief rose in her. Matthew was gone, but Matthew was here. She was walking towards him. There was food on his chin and his hands and mud in his face and something, a bug, crawling in the thick locks of his hair.

She forced herself forward, holding up the jacket: denim, fleece-lined. He hadn't worn it for a year, but she remembered him leaning on the rail at the dock, watching her fishing, laughing at her for coming up empty-handed: that jacket, the collar turned up against the cold.

She wanted him back. She wanted him so much it hurt. And he was. It was not a real thing yet, it was a dream of him or a nightmare. She didn't know if she would wake, drowning in blood, unable to breathe, killing somebody. Oh God. She *had* killed. He was dead and how could anything go back to what it was?

She put the coat on his shoulders. He turned, mouth twitching.

The bowl dropped and shattered.

She stepped back as Matthew lunged towards her. Her eyes closed and the stink of him making her gag. His skin cold against hers, trembling, both of them, and his arms, and the crawling horror of his hair against her neck as she stood like a stone in his embrace. She felt bile rising in her throat, the burn of it all the way up to her mouth. His mouth on her throat. If he were to bite down now she would deserve it: that man in the forest, the gun; William.

But he didn't bite. He let her go, and she was shivering.

'I'm sorry.'

He was staring at her. His mouth opening, closing.

'You…You just smell so bad.'

Jessica held her hand to her mouth. The stink on her skin.

'Where—'

And then he laughed, doubled over, snorting. The laughter made his shoulders shake.

Matthew.

Matthew always laughed at her. Matthew would slap his knees and laugh till he could barely breathe. She loved this about him. She loved that she could make him laugh. She loved him.

She thought she was laughing herself, but when she tried to breathe, it was all snot and tears and she found she was crying. Sobs that shook her as much as the laughing shook him. He stopped, stood, sighed and wiped his eyes with the back of a mud-crusted hand.

Jessica continued to weep. It seemed she would never stop. Her head ached, she could feel it pounding. She forced herself to breathe.

'I've been gone,' he said.

Strange. She hadn't expected him to speak. He was an apparition, she'd assumed, or he was an animal creeping in for food. Words made him human again.

The tears stopped. She stared at him. This was her boyfriend, Matthew. Naked, starved and bruised under his old denim jacket.

'Where was I?' he said. Almost as if she'd interrupted a story he was telling.

She shook her head. It was the question she should have been asking.

Later, all this could happen later. He needed a bath first. He needed to be warm. He needed hot food.

She felt him following her to the bathroom. Smelled him behind her and it was unsettling, but she put the plug in the tub and let the water run hot, as hot as she thought he could take. She poured bubble bath in, although it would take more than bubbles to shift the filth. The curtains were open just a little. Anyone outside would be able to see him standing naked. They would see it was him, Matthew. Returned.

She shut them firmly. 'Get in.'

Then all the curtains, checking them, pulling them tight, locking the doors. Locking the windows. Suddenly terrified that someone might see him—see him and take him from her.

Jessica sidestepped the broken crockery and opened the fridge.

There was fish. She could make fish chowder, then, something hot and hearty. And scotch. Is that what they gave people for shock? She didn't have any brandy. Scotch or vodka or cooking sherry.

She put stock on the stove to heat and poured a nip of scotch; made it a double. Poured one for herself and drank it quickly in one hit before filling the glass up again.

He was in the bath. He had turned the tap off. The jacket was abandoned on the tiles, fleece up, like the pelt of a dead sheep. She dragged the stool up and perched by the tub. He took the scotch from her and gulped it; she sipped hers slowly, watching him, the bubbles obscuring his body. What she could see was all skin hanging loosely on bones.

'Where have you been?'

He looked past her. His eyes unfocused. '…Outside?'

'You can't have been outside for the whole time. You'd have died; it's winter.'

'I don't know…'

'There's scratches on your back. Have you been hit?'

He sat up suddenly, the water slopped over the edge of the bath. She picked up the jacket, but it already stank and she let it drop back down in the wet.

'Did someone take you?'

Matthew held his palms to his eyes. It was obvious that he couldn't remember but she pushed on anyway. 'You were in the car. You were coming home. There was an animal, something dead in the road, you stopped the car. You took your phone? You filmed it? An animal. Something unusual?'

He pulled his hands slowly away from his face and opened his eyes. He stared at her and there was something, some menace in his eyes. Flat dark brown.

Something moved in his hair. She shuddered, drank the rest of her scotch quickly, wished she had brought the bottle in. Then he blinked, and it had been nothing. This was Matthew.

'You've got to put your head under. There's…Fuck. Where have you been?'

He held his nose and slipped down under the surface of the water. He opened his eyes, staring up at her through an uneven landscape of bubbles and dark water.

If she reached down now she could hold him under. He was so thin. She could put her weight on his chest and he would not be able to fight her.

Jessica was horrified by the thought, this scrap of nightmare chasing her out into her waking hours. This was the woman who had put a bullet in the chamber and squeezed the trigger: some other self.

A dark shape floated out of Matthew's hair and scrambled at the surface of the water. She scooped it out onto the floor, paused, wondering what would be best, and finally brought the base of her shot glass down on it. Hard enough to hear the crack of its carapace; not hard enough to shatter the glass.

His face broke the surface, slopping more water onto the tiles.

'We're going to have to cut your hair.'

'Jessica.'

She loved the way he said her name, using the whole of it, making it some sweet, flowery thing, making more of her.

'I don't remember anything. I remember driving. I don't remember anything after that. But…'

'Matthew?'

He shook his head. Drops of muddy water flew off his hair and splashed the wall.

'I think...' He squinted. 'There's someone chasing me.'

'Who?'

'I don't know.'

'Men?' Then: 'Women?'

'You have to hide me.'

The fear was back, his fear. Hers too.

'I can't go outside. You have to protect me.'

Those big dark eyes. She felt all her care sucked into them. She gritted her teeth, reached out and placed her hand on the horror of his hair. She stroked it. Matthew. Her Matthew. She hadn't even hugged him back yet. She had to stop before she was overwhelmed by the memory of her love for him and all the sadness, all the emptiness, a pit that she would not let herself collapse into.

'We have to let your family know you're home. The police. Your mother. She's so upset...'

'Please don't.'

She heard the lid of the pot rattling. She stood.

'I'm going to make you something to eat.'

'Did you close the curtains?'

'Yes.'

'They're going to kill me.'

She nodded. She remembered the weight of the gun in her hands. Saw Crystal felled by her grief, holding, sobbing, screaming into the dead man's chest.

'We'll have to cut that hair off,' she said. 'Then I'll make some chowder.'

*

Her hands were against his back, holding him at arm's length. His flesh clean now against her palms. They dragged the pillows off the lounge back into the bedroom, lay them down on the empty frame.

'The dog…' she said, beginning to explain, and then gave up. The dog would lead to a conversation about William, the smell of a feral animal on the mattress, the smell of jasmine on his shirt. They were both exhausted. 'Tomorrow. We'll have to talk tomorrow.' She stretched out her hands to touch him. He was here with her and she was almost content.

He curled himself up into a foetal position with his wounded back facing her and in a minute his breathing had deepened.

Jessica checked her watch: 3 a.m. She sighed. Breath was hard to find, as if there was something pressing down on her chest. She turned away from him, shifted to the edge of the cushions and closed her eyes.

A knock at the door.

She gasped. She was alone. Panic rising. Maybe she had dreamed him. She was still dressed. She always seemed to go to sleep with her clothes on, she wasn't even sure where she had left her nightdress, a pile of abandoned clothes desperate for washing in the corner of the room.

He was gone. The sliding door was open.

He had been here.

He had left her.

Another knock, and Jessica opened the door.

Marijam.

'Oh. I didn't hear a car.'

The old woman looked frail. She had a beanie pulled down low over her forehead, her jacket zipped up high against the cold.

'I brought the boat.' She nodded down towards the beach. It was a long way from Cockle Creek to Southport. Jessica had never tried the trip herself, but it would take over an hour. You would have to carry extra petrol with a small motor like the one Marijam had on her little dinghy.

Tough old bird, thought Jessica. 'From Cockle Creek? That's a good way.'

'Gone further.'

'I imagine so.'

She should invite the old woman in. That would be the polite thing to do. Jessica glanced over her shoulder, wondering what evidence of Matthew there was. Matted hair shaved and fallen onto the bathroom floor, the bowl of paella still smashed on the floor in front of the fridge. Clothes, perhaps. His jacket, the smell of him still strong on the couch.

'I'm sorry I missed the meeting,' she said instead.

'You were missed. That's for sure. That's why I'm here. Checking up. I'm the delegate.'

'I haven't told anyone.'

'We know. We would hear. Eyes and ears everywhere. Maude would have warned you about that.'

'Yes.'

'Where's your dog gone?'

'I don't know. You tell me where my dog has gone, if you have all those eyes and ears.'

'I hear he was taken by a tiger. Your tiger, I suspect. That one that's stalking you like my husband stalked me.'

'Look, I just want to be left alone.'

'By us? Or by him? That thing.'

'Everyone. I just want to get on with it, okay?'

'No. Probably not okay. You know about us. We know about you. Best to stick close, right?'

'I won't tell anyone about the hunt.'

'Good to know. Because they found a shirt.'

'What?'

'Man's shirt. Some blood around the collar.'

'What?'

'No one knows whose shirt it is but if they get to ask Crystal she'll tell them she recognises it.'

'But he didn't have a shirt on. Didn't have clothes at all.'

'Who? You see something, did you?'

'No, but—'

'No body. No gun. But if they find a gun I wonder if there'll be prints on it. I wonder if the weapon's traceable?'

'Marijam—'

'But they haven't found a gun yet. Just a shirt. Nameless man's shirt. Maybe they'll be asking if it is your husband's shirt. Last man down and all that.'

'Marijam, please.'

'I'm just the messenger, young lady. Don't shoot the messenger. Well, you can't, can you? You don't have a gun. Did you? Did you ever have a gun?'

'Get off my property now.'

'I'm going.' She held on to the rail and stepped down a little stiffly, turned back and grinned. 'Oh, that wouldn't be your net down around by Blubber Point, would it? Hope it isn't. Someone's gone and cut a hole clear through it. Vandals, most likely. Damn kids.'

She was more sprightly on the sand. She almost skipped down to her boat and pushed it out; jumped in, the waves washing up over her gumboots and onto her tracksuit pants. Small engine. Several cans of two-stroke resting in the back.

Jessica didn't wait to see her putter away. She closed the door and leaned her back against it. Her phone was in her pocket. She fished it out. No calls. She dialled and waited but William still wasn't answering. She wanted him here. She wanted his huge arms around her, protecting her. The ring tone stopped.

She opened the back door, stood on the balcony. Her net was somewhere out there, slashed, hours of work. And her dog lost, somewhere; she had only had him for a handful of days. And then her boyfriend.

'I'm leaving the door open,' she said to the rising tide.

Food on the floor. The house leaning in on itself. Jessica took some more fish out of the freezer. She would need to go fishing again. She would have to find her nets, if Marijam really had slashed them on her way past. There might be fish in them even now, dead in the nets. She needed to put the boat out soon.

She defrosted a chicken breast in the microwave.

She felt the shake of the floor as someone came up the stairs. Oh.

She closed her eyes, heard the door slide open, closed. The curtain drawn.

Matthew stood behind her. She smelled him. Wild musk. She

felt the weight of his hands warm on her shoulders. Just weeks ago she would have turned and put her arms around him. Now she breathed in the smell of him. Strangely altered, strong, like sweat and earth and leaf mould. Maybe this was the way he had smelled before the salmon farm turned his skin to acrid salt and brine.

She turned the stove on, pressing the clicker till the flame leapt up under the pan.

Matthew. Back. He was back and he was hungry. She dropped the chicken breast into the spitting butter and pressed it down flat.

He couldn't settle. He had paced, staring out through the curtains of first one room, then the next. He had eaten almost constantly, still hungry regardless of what food she gave him. He let her feed him, run another bath for him. There was still a whiff of the wild trapped in his hair.

She sat in the lounge room listening to the slap of water as he moved, restless even in the tub. She looked at the piles of paper arranged carelessly on the table, the clothing strewn over the floor. It had been his job to nag her to pick up her things. He was the one who preferred a clean table.

A bag for the used clothes. She folded the ones that smelled all right. She had left them bundled in the washing basket after taking them out of the dryer. Now it was almost impossible to tell the used clothes from the fresh ones. Still, it felt good to find some kind of order in the chaos of the last few weeks.

Here were the clothes she had been wearing the night William was over. She held the shirt to her face. She remembered sex. She remembered those scant hours as a sweet relief from the continuing nightmare. She dropped them into the garbage bag. When she washed them those hours would disappear. Not a word from William since.

She heard the rush of water, Matthew stepping out of the tub, as she emptied the bag of clothes into the machine, then he was behind her. His face at the nape of her neck, sniffing: for a moment she was afraid he could smell William on her. But that was days ago. She had showered three times since then.

He lifted her skirt. His mouth still on her neck, open now, hungry. She tried to turn towards him but he was on her, leaning against her, the weight of him forcing her head to the clear plastic. She could see a red striped sock turning in the front loader. She shut her eyes.

Smaller than William. His hips at the same height as hers, the hands grabbing at her breasts through her shirt so much smaller; everything smaller. She closed her eyes, but all she felt was the comparisons. The memory of being lifted and held safe. She had relaxed; now she was struggling.

When she opened her eyes there was the red striped sock turning round and round, caught up with a pair of jeans. Her skin prickled.

This was Matthew, returned to her. His thighs, thinner now, the bones sharp against her rump. She prised his hand off her breast and he pressed his fingers between her legs. She felt the rise and sudden fall as she clamped his hand against her. She struggled to push away from him, and turned.

Matthew. His eyes staring at her, hungry as he had been hungry ever since he returned. She held his head between her hands and kissed him. His tongue lapping at the underside of her teeth, his hands finding her buttocks and clinging there. His penis, smaller than William's (impossible to not compare), pressing against her and she pushed her skirt up over her hips and stepped onto him. He stumbled back, finding balance with his back to the wall, more earthbound than before. More immediate. She pushed him down till he was sitting on the floor and climbed onto his lap. Until this moment he had not seemed real to her, not quite. He was inside her now, thrusting up into her, and now, finally, she knew that he was back.

But it was a struggle. Him wrestling with her, turning her, flipping her body over and mounting her. Her push and shift to roll beneath him, thrusting up at him, dominant in her position beneath. They shifted and turned, rolled, found their feet, tore into each other. Afterwards she would find three large scratches on her thigh that he must have made. He would be similarly marked: her teeth on his shoulder. In his diminished state they were physically matched.

Again, the difference between one man and the other, this gnashing, threatening pleasure. She rolled on top of him one last time and held him there with one hand, pleasuring herself with the other. She came, her back snapping to a taut curve, her eyes squeezing shut. Then, before the contractions had finished, he had lifted and turned her and pushed inside her from behind, coming to his own climax, shuddering and grunting, and that smell, turned earth and wild places, exuding from his skin as he collapsed onto her sweating back.

He was up and off her in a second and she stayed for a while, facedown on the cold tiled floor, beginning to shiver as the moisture turned chill on her skin. She stood shakily and stripped off her shirt; wiped the damp floor with it. Towelled herself down and threw everything into the washing basket. Another load to do now. More mess to clean. She felt sore and bruised. She sat on the toilet and watched the machine pause, change direction, turn anti-clockwise. The same red sock, still going around. She heard the sliding door open, no sound of it closing. Matthew would be gone.

She wanted to talk to William. A terrible need eating at her, a betrayal. She checked her phone. A dozen unanswered calls to him. No point in calling again.

She lay down on the couch by the fire and closed her eyes.

Blood. She was drowning in blood. She couldn't breathe—

Then she opened her eyes and it was dark and there was someone on her and she still couldn't breathe. There was an arm pushing her neck down. She tried to shrug it off, but she couldn't. She felt her underpants tugged down. She felt him enter her like that. Again. Too soon, and without warning.

Matthew. She closed her eyes. He was grunting above her. Not sex, this humping, not like anything else she had experienced. She was dry and it hurt and for some reason all she could think of was that time he took his plate and threw it at the wall, the green smear of pesto on the white paint. Then the other time, the grit of sand as she wiped her fingers across the laptop screen, the night she would not let herself go back to, she couldn't go there, she couldn't think about any of it, and as the nausea came she tried to breathe through the pressure on her chest. She made herself go slack-limbed. She endured. He humped.

And then he grunted and came and slipped off her and there were footsteps and the sound of the screen door opening and the rattle of the stairs. Was this how it would be now?

She rolled over. The fire was still alight. It was warm but there was an icy chill coming in from the beach. She stood. Her knees threatened to buckle, but she remained upright although her legs shook. She took a few tentative steps towards the door; shut it. Locked it.

She would keep it locked. It was terrible, but he would have to knock now, begging to be let into his own house. She was horrible. What kind of a girlfriend would do this?

She hesitated, but she left the door latched.

There was still just the faintest discolouration on the wall. Jessica remembered how vivid the green had been, the violence of the shade.

She sat at her desk. Touched the laptop screen: the metal was slightly warm. Her fingers rubbed at a spot on the screen, recalling the grit of sand. She let herself remember. She had pushed the memory down so hard she thought it had been erased. But it was all still there. She felt the action of pressing save, that most familiar of repeated gestures.

She'd been hitting save as she heard his car pull up in front of the shack that night.

She'd been so sick of it, she remembered. She'd spent all day changing commas to semicolons, then she misread the formatting for her reference section and it was all over the damn place. She'd stood, leaving the laptop open at the offending page, and gone to the stove to put the kettle on.

Matthew.

Matthew was home from work and he would want a cup of

tea, hot and sweet. It was still early but it was almost dark already. Winter on the way.

'Heya.' His usual welcoming call.

'Hi, love.' Her habitual response. 'You want a slice of date loaf with your tea?'

'Oh, yeah.' His voice was muffled. He was out front, in the toilet. Coldest room in the shack. In the lounge room the fire was roaring. Pea and ham-hock soup bubbling on the stove. He had cooked the soup, of course, but at least she had thought to defrost it in good time.

She took the date loaf out of the fridge. He'd baked it on the weekend. A man who baked and cooked all her meals, and cleaned the house. Only a couple of slices left. She would learn to make date loaf, save him some time. He did so much for her and what did she ever do for him? Or banana bread, that was easy; she had made it once at university. Although you couldn't always get bananas down here.

She heard him in the lounge room, his big sandy boots, the shuffling of papers as he made a place for himself to sit down. Her papers were all over the couch, too late to race in and tidy them away now. Her mother definitely would not approve, but it wasn't for long—only a few weeks till her deadline for submission. And this time she wouldn't hesitate.

Are you really ready to submit? Is it the best it can be?

Matthew always asked her this. Four years past the end of her scholarship, and every time she thought the thesis was ready to submit he would touch her shoulder with a gentle hand and gaze at her with soft puppy eyes and ask: *Are you sure? Is it the best it can be?*

It would never be right, though. It would never be the best. She just wasn't that good. Time to admit it and give in. Her supervisor said it was now or never; she had run out of last chances. It was time.

And she would clean up when it was over. She would bake and make dinners and freeze them and clean the lounge room and make the bed...

The kettle whistled so she lifted it onto the bench and turned the stove off. The stove was from the sixties, a relic. She had repeatedly asked Matthew's mother if she could replace it and was always met with silence. Maybe when she had finished her studies she would just do it: order a new one and move the old one under the shack. She'd ask Matthew about it next week.

Everything on hold now till she pressed send.

She poured the tea, turned, spilled a little, startled by his body blocking the entry to the kitchen. Looming, still and silent. He was staring at her.

'Jesus. Matthew,' she said, feeling her heart pounding in her chest.

'What were you doing this Saturday, again?' His voice was quiet and low. She didn't like the sound of it.

She squinted. What had she done? Something. She had done something wrong.

The hot cup was burning her fingers; she shifted her grip. She needed to put it down on the table but here he was, blocking her path.

Saturday. She had no idea what he meant. What was happening Saturday? What had she done this time? She was hopeless, distracted. Did she have a supervision meeting booked in? Surely not—not this close to submitting.

She could smell the sudden sweat pooling in her armpits. Her cheeks were pinking. She looked guilty. She *was* guilty but she wasn't sure exactly what of. Whatever it was, she was sorry already. She was ready to apologise as soon as she remembered what she had done.

'What are you doing on Saturday, Jessica?'

She hesitated. She couldn't meet his gaze. 'Ah…referencing?'

'No,' he said, 'try again.'

'Re-reading my literature review?'

'Saturday night, Jessica. Saturday night.'

Her fingers were burning, the tea was too hot. She turned and dropped the cup in the sink. She shook her hands out.

'I burned my fingers, Matthew.'

'Someone's birthday, maybe?'

'What?'

Then she remembered. She tried to push past him, but he stood his ground. She had to turn side on and press her back against the doorframe. Her computer was open. When she moved to look at the screen she saw a rain of multicoloured balloons bursting. *You're Invited!* Then Gus's name and address.

'You opened my emails? You checked my emails?'

'It was already open, babe.'

But it wasn't. She had just then stood up from her referencing. She clearly remembered placing a semicolon on the screen, deleting a comma, rubbing her eyes and hearing the car pull up in the drive. She hadn't checked her emails for hours. In fact she had been running that program, Freedom, to block the internet. Matthew would have had to disable Freedom, turn the hotspot on from his phone, open her email and then the email from Gus.

He had only just got home. He'd gone to the bathroom...

She hadn't heard him flush. Perhaps he'd had a few minutes alone with her computer.

'That's insane.' She could hear the anger in her own voice. She could feel the rise of it, tight in her chest. 'You went through my emails.'

'Gus.'

'You're fucking insane!'

He moved closer to her, too close. She could feel herself shrinking down to nothing.

'Who's Gus?'

'You know who.' But her voice—such a nothing thing, taking up no space at all.

'What's Gus to you?'

'A friend. A work friend.' But already her voice was more sob than sound.

'Happy birthday to Gus.'

'I'm not going.'

'You're not going, now?'

'I never was! I'm not—'

'Oh, *now* you're not.'

'I'm not.'

''Cause you should go.'

'I don't...'

'You should go to Gus. You should go now.'

She saw his hand stretch out towards her laptop. She saw his fingers curl to grab it. Her thesis! She snatched at her thesis. That's how she saw the laptop now, it was her thesis, nothing much else. She got her shifts emailed to her. She got some junk mail. She got her online subscriptions, *Nature* and *New Scientist* and *Nautilus*. She filed her own *Science Weekly* stories. She kept some research in a file for that, but mostly it was just her thesis. The only complete copy of her thesis.

He had hold of it now and her fingers snatched but they slipped and then her thesis was in his hands. He snapped the laptop shut roughly and flicked his hand back, as if to keep it away, out of her reach.

And then it slipped from his fingers—or he flung it or it flew of its own accord away from him—but whatever the reason it was airborne briefly and then the crack of it against the fibro wall and the shiver of the whole shack at the impact, the curl of her spine as she folded down over her womb. As if her thesis was an infant, protected inside her belly, and the sound of it cracking against the wall was a kick to her guts.

All the air spilled out of her in a sharp hiss. She was suffocating as surely as if he had wrapped both his hands around her neck.

She rushed to the child, the spilled baby, but he was there first and he held the laptop so easily above his head and out of her reach. She threw herself at him. She punched his chest with her fists and he laughed at her as if she were tapping him with her fingertips. She punched with all the force of her clenched fists and he moved then, grabbing her wrist tightly with one hand then turning and flinging, and the sliding back door was open—had she left it open? Was this her fault?—and the beach was in darkness beyond the back stairs and there was her laptop cartwheeling away from the light. A balletic arc of silver disappearing on the way to the water's edge.

A sound.

Maybe it had come from her throat or maybe it was the sound of the hot water system finally exploding. She was on the stairs before she knew it, slipping, falling, pushing herself out of the acacia bush, slipping over the wall of rocks and lying facedown in the damp sand. She saw the glint of it and rolled towards it and snapped it up into her lap and only then knew that her ankle was twisted.

A sharp pain shooting up her leg but she stood with the laptop clutched to her chest and limped away down the beach, past the summer shacks, all dark and shuttered. Past the boat tied to the tree trunk, past the pile of cray pots and the floats hanging from the neighbouring eaves. A shooting pain in her leg and she wasn't wearing a coat at all. The cold was a thing she was pushing through like a field of sugarcane, like her childhood fears every time she ran away from the compound, determined that this time she'd make a break for it. She was aware of the cold as an obstacle: she leaned against it. She moved quickly through it over the damp sand and up towards the road.

The road curved up a steep hill. She was halfway up it before she realised that she was on foot, walking away from the shack. Walking away, not walking towards. There was nothing to go towards at all. She reached the top of the hill and looked out over the ocean, the blink of the lighthouse on Bruny Island and beyond that…Nothing till you hit Antarctica.

She thought about the ice melting. She thought about the sea level rising. She had filed a story about that just last week, but she couldn't remember the stats. All she could think about was her thesis, the beautifully rendered tables, the lines of light generation, the circadian rising and falling as the glow-worms woke and slept again, setting up a rhythm that breathed steadily across the eight long years of her research.

She was walking downhill, almost running. Her leg didn't hurt so much now, just a bruise, not a sprain or a fracture. She walked on, past the jetty then away from it. There was someone on the jetty, someone fishing, probably. She didn't stop to look. She walked away from it.

The low, long building of the pub and local store was in front of her but she wasn't walking towards that either. Then it was behind her. So she'd been walking for forty-five minutes: that was how long it took to walk to the shop for milk.

Time was only relative to mass. The road disappearing behind her marked the hour. It was late. The lights of the pub shone brightly out towards five cars parked beside it. Slow night. The cars meant it was a weeknight.

Time really is relative. She thought about how you might travel away from Earth at almost the speed of light and no time at all would pass as your loved ones aged and eventually died. She wondered if Matthew was still her loved one. But if not Matthew, who? There was only him, and if she loved no one then she might as well be out in space, shooting off at light speed, suspended in her haste to leave him behind.

She hugged her laptop closer. Did she really love the thesis? Was it really like a child to her?

She stopped. The pub was behind her now. She was at the turn: left to Ida Bay, four hours' walk, and beyond that the caves where she worked. To her right was the cold, dense forest where even an SOS call could not penetrate the canopy.

She had left her phone behind at the shack—with Matthew,

her only loved one. She dropped to her knees at the crossroads, placed her laptop on the ground and hunched over to open it. The light spilled up onto her face. She held her breath for a moment and only exhaled when the screen reassembled itself into an image of falling balloons. *Come to my party!* She looked at Gus's name; felt a wave of hatred. She hadn't realised how much she hated him till now. She should have said that to Matthew. She could have avoided all of this if she had just told him how visceral her hatred for Gus really was.

She clicked out of the invitation, out of her email program. There was her thesis. It was still there safely on her screen. She hit save: multiple times, just in case. Scrolled back through the document, checking that everything was there, everything working, the beating heart of her life down here at the southernmost place in the country.

She heard footsteps, and turned. It was a man. A thin, crooked man. There was some moon and in that light his face looked sallow. Sunlight reflected, she reminded herself. Weak reflected light from the sun. It made his face into a landscape of craters. It made him seem mean and threatening. She held her laptop close. To protect it, but also to hide her breasts.

'You right?'

'Yes, thank you.'

'You're Matthew's woman.'

Not a question, but it seemed like he was waiting for her to reply.

'I'm just walking,' she said.

He looked at her laptop. He looked at her bare arms. He looked at her hidden breasts and at her legs in the cling of denim.

He looked at her puffy red eyes and her bruised, slightly swollen lips. Had she fallen on her face? She couldn't remember. Probably. She was so clumsy.

He looked at her face for what seemed like a long time and then he reached for her. She flinched. He was holding her arm.

'Come inside. You can use my phone.'

Why would she want to use his phone? She noticed his house then. She had stopped right beside his gate. His lights were on. His door open. There was an axe in a log by the front door. There was a woodpile and a broken-down car, just a skeleton of rusted panels and spilled tyres. She could see his bare walls inside. No curtains, no paintings, nothing feminine. A house that belonged to a man alone.

'No, thank you,' she managed.

'You can't be out in this cold, sweetie,' he said and his grip on her arm tightened. She yanked her arm away and shouted at him. 'No! Thank you.' And then she ran, turning to the right, to the dark woods, but he was behind her. Walking fast, keeping close.

'You can't go that way. There's nothing there. Don't be scared. I'm just...'

She kept running, walking, running, and he was behind her. He was matching her step for step. She felt her heart beating; too fast. She was frightened now. What if he dragged her into the forest? There was no one to save her, no one to hear if she screamed.

She heard a car engine, tyres scattering dirt as a car pulled up at the side of the road and the man stopped, turned. Jessica stopped too, looked back into Matthew's headlights. Matthew's body beside her, Matthew's arm around her waist, pulling her towards the car, and she was grateful. She let herself be led.

'Any trouble?' the stranger asked.

'Nah.' Matthew stopped, shook the man's hand. 'All good now.'

All good. The relief of his arm around her. This one sure thing.

'That right? All good?' He was speaking to her. Jessica nodded. She let Matthew lead her. Let Matthew ease her into the passenger seat. When he shut the door she felt safe inside. Matthew climbed in. Turned the car around, waved to the stranger as men do, one finger raised.

'I'm sorry,' said Jessica. She was shaking, but she was not sure if it was anger or relief. 'It's just…'

Then she saw Matthew's face, the tears streaming down it.

'I'm such a shit,' Matthew said.

She hesitated. The way he'd hurled the laptop. But he was crying. He was so vulnerable, so scared.

'No. No, baby, no, you're not.'

'I'm a fuckhead.'

'No—'

'You should hate me.'

'I love you.' She put her hand on his thigh as he geared down for the turn.

'No wonder you want to leave me.' He was weeping openly now and her heart was breaking. She reached out to stroke his cheek, wiped the tears away, but more came to replace them.

'Leave? I love you. I'm not going anywhere.'

'Leave me for Gus.'

'Gus? Gus is an idiot.'

Matthew raised a hand and slapped at the side of his head. He tugged his hair—hard—and she winced, reached out, stilled his hand.

'I hate Gus,' she said, remembering that she'd felt this to be true. 'I'll never leave. I hate him. I do.'

'You don't.'

'I swear.'

They had stopped outside the shack now, such a short drive. Such a long walk.

'Honey, honey.' She turned his face towards her. 'I love you. I love you. Gus is an idiot. I love you.'

His eyes flooded with relief, and she kissed him.

He clung to her awkwardly, turning his body to press up against her. She spread her fingers through his hair, smoothing down the place he had just slapped. She stroked his scalp. He let his tongue stray into her mouth. Then her jeans were undone and he was tugging them down. She was pressed against the seat. It was awkward, her hip hurt. It was cold. He was on top of her. She started to push him away, but she loved him. She made herself relax. He prised the laptop from her fingers and it was okay. It really didn't matter. Matthew was the loved one. Her studies were just something she had done. Something that was almost over. This was what was real, and he was still weeping when he pushed himself into her. He lifted her awkwardly and then it felt right. The comfort of him rocking against her.

'There, there,' she said; a whisper. 'I love you. See? I love you.' She checked up and down the street but the road was empty, the windows blind.

'So much,' he said and then he touched her in the way that only he knew, and she closed her eyes. She didn't care who was walking along their street. She couldn't think anything, couldn't say anything, and the sky was ripe with stars and she opened her mouth to them and they were inside her.

Jessica startled awake. The sun was so bright. She blinked, shaded her eyes. Her body ached but that was just how she felt after sex. Always.

Not always.

Why hadn't William called her back? He had told her he wanted to see her again. He had said it right here, on this couch. She looked out to the bright sun reflected off the sand, painting stripes and squares on the couch. A view of the water.

And from the strand? A view of the couch. Her heart started to thump wildly in her chest. She knew where William lived. She had the address in her phone, although she had never visited.

She backed out carefully on the slick road and turned the car in his direction. And drove.

Old logging track. Cluster of houses. There was nothing unusual about William's place. There were a thousand houses like this one, prefabs, nothing to distinguish one from another. There were a few letters in the mailbox, their damp ends curling out into the weather. No car in the drive. Jessica pulled up on the street outside and checked the address in her phone. Number twelve. And even as she stepped towards the gate she could hear the dog barking, claws scratching against the door. Jessica hurried up to the front door. Her knocking was obliterated by the barking and scrambling. She backed away and peered in through a side window.

A dog, a young labrador similar to her missing puppy. She had forgotten that William had another dog from Brutus' litter. The poor abandoned thing leapt at the window, frantic, scratching at the glass. Jessica turned around and looked helplessly out at the houses next door. The one on the right had a for sale sign. The one on the left had not seen a lawnmower for some months. Across the road a woman stood at her open front door, staring at Jessica. She was dressed in a long quilted jacket with the flannel legs of her pyjamas hanging down to her ugg boots.

Jessica hurried across the road. 'Do you know how long William's been away?'

'No, I don't, but you can tell him if he doesn't shut that dog up someone'll shoot it.' She paused, looked Jessica rudely up and down. 'Round here people like some peace and quiet.'

'How long has it been barking?'

'Two days. Straight.'

'William hasn't been home for two days?'

'If you can't look after a pet you shouldn't have one.' She turned and shuffled inside, slamming the door.

Two days. Two days ago William had left her place and had since failed to answer his phone. She ran across the road and pushed through the shrubbery at the side of the house. Most of the windows were closed. She rattled each one and the dog followed her, scrambling from one room to the next. A window at the back was ajar. She opened it; the dog jumped up, scratching at the wire screen. It was easy enough to push the screen in. Jessica hauled herself up over the sill. The puppy jumped and licked and whined.

The place smelled terrible and when Jessica walked into the corridor, sidestepping puddles of urine and lumps of dog shit, she could see why. In the kitchen a big bag of kibble had been torn open, the remnants of it scattered about the floor. The fridge was open and anything within reach torn, eaten, spread onto the linoleum. No water, but it was clear from water splashed around the little bathroom that the dog had been drinking from the toilet bowl. In the lounge room it had torn all the cushions and strewn the stuffing around.

Jessica filled the empty bowl with water and the dog, a female pup a little bigger than Brutus, divided her attention between drinking and turning to Jessica for a pat. Starved of water and attention in equal measure.

The puppy finished the water in the bowl and then there was the scrabbling of claws on the lino as she ran, tripping and falling, to what must be the bedroom door. The puppy sniffed at it, jumped up onto it. There were already gouges in the paint, so it wasn't the first time the dog had thrown herself at the door.

Jessica turned the handle and pushed the door with her shoulder. It didn't move. She bent low and tried again, putting her back into it. It shifted minutely—there was something blocking it. Jessica felt her heart skip.

'William?' She pushed again. The door inched forward, the gap big enough for the puppy to slip through, sweet little tail disappearing. Jessica heard her snuffling and whimpering, and pushed harder. She squeezed through the gap.

But for his size, William would have been unrecognisable. His huge hands, the massive spread of his body—but his face was a swollen ball of dried blood. And there were no eyes. That was what struck her: his eyes had disappeared into a mask of doughy skin.

Matthew alive.

William dead.

She shook her head. It was all upside down.

She stepped away from his body. She had wished Matthew back to life, but this wasn't fair. This trade, one man for another.

'Please, God. Take Matthew back. Leave William.' She heard her mother in her voice, betraying herself. Praying to a God she did not believe in.

The puppy was standing on the lifeless chest, nuzzling there. And then, as if it really was a miracle, William's hand moved towards the dog's head.

He was alive. Barely. She should have checked before begging for divine intervention.

The puppy was licking the dried blood on what had once been his nose. Jessica pulled her away and reached for her phone. Dialled triple zero.

Then: 'Ambulance,' she said, before the woman had time to ask. 'And police. Everyone. You've got to send everyone you have right now.'

She stayed on the line as they told her to. She spoke to William when they said she should and he made a sound. When he opened his mouth she could see his bloodied, broken teeth.

How can you fix something like that? How do you treat a man with no face?

'You've got to come quickly,' she said.

They told her to wet a cloth and she had to leave him, the puppy tucked under one arm, the phone tucked up under her chin. She found a tea towel and filled a glass and when she approached the bedroom again she knew he would be dead now. She dripped water near his mouth and he opened his lips and licked at it. She let the drops fall into him and he began to shift and move and she shushed him.

'You have to lie still.'

He made a sound that might have been her name.

'Yeah. It's Jessica. I'm here. I'm here.'

He took more water, sucking it off the cloth.

'Hey, after this,' she said, 'if you scrub up okay…do you want to go out with me?' It sounded ridiculous, like something you would say in primary school, but she said it again anyway. 'Do you want to go on a date or something?'

He began to laugh. His lips shifted into a swollen smile and his chest rose and fell and he grunted and hissed in pain. Broken ribs, she supposed. She hugged the puppy closer so she couldn't jump on him again.

'Well? Do you?'

He opened his toothless mouth. 'Yeah, all right.'

'They're approaching the house now, ma'am. Can you hear a siren?'

They had heard her flirting with him. She felt a little embarrassed. The siren was there in the distance.

'I hear them.'

'Stay on the line, ma'am. Is the door open?'

'I think so.'

She felt something on her leg. His big hand, squeezing. She tried to look into his eyes but they were eclipsed by dark swollen flesh.

She heard the ambos in the house.

'They're here,' she said, standing.

'The police won't be far behind,' said the voice on the phone.

She moved his hand off her leg and shuffled back, making way for the three people in blue uniforms. Nodding to their backs because they were all around him, touching him, helping him, saving him.

'Jesus,' said the woman ambo, short and stocky and practical. 'You've been in the wars, mate. What's the other guy look like?'

Jessica frowned. She was pretty sure she knew.

Portia shivered in the bow of the boat. Jessica had thought about changing the dog's name to something less Shakespearian but somehow it had stuck. The dog liked it too: looked up and seemed to grin whenever she heard the name.

She wasn't grinning now. Jessica had thrown an old blanket over her, but it wasn't the cold. The dog was afraid of the rise and fall.

Brutus had been such great company on the boat. She remembered the comfort of him sitting like a figurehead at the prow, panting happily and staring out at the horizon. She missed him. Portia was not as brave, but Jessica thought she would get used to the listless back and forth of a morning tide.

The ocean looked like liquid silver. Light touched the crest of each swell; the surface thick as it undulated, a great beast breathing. She missed the weight of the gun in her pocket.

She had stepped down from the stairs at the back of the shack cautiously, as if trying not to wake a sleeping lion. She had always felt safe on her way out to the boat but if he came at her she would not be able to defend herself. Jessica had checked to see that none of the neighbours were watching. She knew how it looked. Frightened, beaten girlfriend, glancing nervously around, clinging to the dog's lead. She supposed that was exactly what she was. Frightened, beaten. Not physically, but she felt cowed. She wondered when she had become this unrecognisable self. She had felt invincible when she first came to Tasmania, but Matthew had somehow slowly worn that bright, fierce young woman away.

It will be okay, she had said to William when she visited him in Hobart hospital, but she couldn't be sure of anything anymore. She couldn't protect William. She hadn't even been able to protect herself.

The boat rose and fell on the tide. Something flashed in the distance. She kept her eyes softly focused on the horizon and was rewarded by the sight of a flipper.

'Seal!' She pointed, and Portia raised her nose to sniff the end of her pointed finger. 'No, there.' But the dog didn't understand pointing. She settled back down, whimpering.

'Seals used to get into the fish farms,' Jessica said to the dog. Something to talk to now. Not a crazy monologue, but an odd, not quite one-sided conversation. 'Matthew used to make it sound so comic and so awful all at the same time.' The seals, jumping and biting, ripping the livers out of the fish and leaving them uneaten, a feeding frenzy, the water turning red; and yet the seals looking like acrobats, turning somersaults, clapping, gawping, clowns of the sea. He would be doubled over, describing it. It only occurred to her now that he'd been laughing at a scene of slaughter.

They motored on. There was quite a way to go, but first the nets.

'Look there!' And the dog, stupid dog, licking her pointing finger. Sweet, stupid dog. She patted the dog's nose and Portia began to shiver as she shifted over to pant against Jessica's feet. 'Don't you get sick.'

Jessica could see her nets in the distance, two in a row. The brightly coloured floats bobbing at the place where the nets ended. She pulled the boat closer and cut the engine.

The dog stood too quickly and the boat listed, and then she whined and shook as Jessica hushed her and petted her until she finally settled. Jessica stood, cautiously, and reached over for the grappling hook. She swung it out, catching the rope first go. She pulled the float towards the boat, hauled the rope in. The weight, an old milk bottle filled with sand, thumped into the bottom of the boat and she pulled at the net. She didn't realise the damage at first, just a tangle in the net from the weather, but she had left the nets out too long. She should have brought them in the night before last, only there'd been William and the hospital and the long drive to and from Hobart. She pulled more of the net in. Dead fish, half-eaten, their skeletons sticking out of the wasted flesh. A red roughy, a cod. The tear in the nylon.

The next haul untangled the corpse of a young wobbegong shark, ugly tendrils dripping from an equally ugly mouth.

Oh God. So sorry.

And something else, something big. At first she thought it might be a seal. It was definitely the body of something, and huge. She pulled at the net till her fingers felt raw and swollen and the boat rocked as she tugged at it. As it came closer she could see weed clinging to the bulk of its body, only it wasn't weed, and eventually she could see that it was hair.

Matthew.

What if it was Matthew?

No, it was fur. She held her breath as she hauled. She searched for the pale stripes that she had seen on his phone, glimpsed in the forest when they went hunting. She pushed at the corpse with the grappling hook, turning it over.

'Oh, fuck.' The soft nose. The dead eyes, open and trusting, the guts eaten away.

Brutus.

Something had attacked the dog, but it was impossible to know if it was before or after he was caught in the net. Here was a second shark, a sandpaper of skin flicking over, still twitching, but too late to save it. Maybe the dog had drowned, floated on the tide towards her nets, caught there, belly exposed to the sharks and crabs and flatheads. Maybe the corpse had washed out on the tide, snagged in the net.

Matthew, starving: staring into the open refrigerator for more meat. She remembered him inside her, pushing into her, hurting her, taking what he wanted.

Jessica dropped the net. She was suddenly worried that Portia might see and become distressed. Dogs grieved, she knew they did. And this was her litter-mate, her brother.

Jessica needed to get him out of the net but his muzzle was caught, his teeth tangled. She pulled and prised until the head fell away from the net and the body began to sink. She watched it disappear, falling down though the clear water, dissolving into darkness. It would be welcomed down there. His body would not go to waste.

She pulled the net in. No more fish, alive or dead. She huddled beside Portia, hugged her close, buried her face in the warm fur. Portia whimpered and tried to climb into her lap.

'Good girl.' Patting her till she settled at her feet again.

★

She moored the boat to a tree. Marijam's house was turned towards the ocean, Jessica could see that now, approaching it from the tide line. There was a garden bed on either side of the path, which was swept clean of sand. Four steps down and the ocean had carved a fifth step, a gouging. The water taking the beach, wresting it from the shore, leaving a net of weed in its place; a fish head, where Marijam had cleaned her catch and left the scraps for the gulls.

Marijam looked small and hunched as she heaved herself slowly down the steps, a mythic crone. She reached into her pocket and pulled something out. A gun: Jessica's gun. The old woman weighed it in her hand as if trying to work out if it was the real thing or just a toy.

'Maude's on her way to Hobart,' she said, holding the gun up as if to shoot the horizon, sighting along the barrel. She checked that the safety was on, then she threw it towards Jessica, who lunged to catch the weapon as Portia tensed to jump for it.

'Down, girl.' The heft of it, the comfort in her hand.

Portia yipped and bounced as if expecting Jessica to throw the gun for her to chase.

'Down, sweet.'

'Good dog you got there,' said Marijam. 'Needs some training.'

'You think?'

'She'll come good. I've seen her mother. Good loyal dog.'

Jessica put the gun into the pocket of her jacket and buttoned it away tightly. The dog whined and ran to the slope where the stairs began. She sat quietly, looking up towards the old woman, who reached into her pocket again. She pulled something out and Portia snapped it out of the air and settled down to chew.

'We baked scones. For your William.'

Your William.

'Got him some flowers. A big old bunch picked from our gardens.'

Jessica nodded. 'He'll like that.'

'No, he won't,' she snapped. 'Men don't go in for flowers around here. And he can't eat, I hear. Not solids, anyways.'

Jessica nodded again.

'But it's the thought. And he'll remember it. More to the point, you'll remember it. They're for you as much as for him.'

'Thank you,' she said. 'I suppose.'

'It's what we do.' Sounding just like Maude. She turned and stepped off the stairs, sinking into the soft sand, somehow maintaining her balance; seeming younger on the strand. More in her element. She bent to ruffle Portia's ears.

'Marijam,' Jessica said, squaring her shoulders, squeezing the cold solidity of the gun through her jacket pocket.

The old woman lifted her chin, waiting to hear what she had to say.

'I want to go hunting.'

'Good,' said Marijam. She nodded, walking quickly through the soft sand to take Jessica by the elbow. She could feel the strength in the old woman's hands, the daily ritual of putting out the boat and bringing in the net. Again she felt dizzy, seeing her future staring into her eyes. And it wasn't so bad really. Tough, solitary, self-sufficient. Wise? Maybe.

'We thought you might. Meet us at that same place, tonight, just on sunset.'

'I'll be there,' said Jessica.

'Never doubted it,' said Marijam. 'I was going to run that gun over to you this afternoon. You saved me a trip. You're a good shot. A fighter.' And then she turned quickly, dropping another scrap of food which the dog leapt for, and scaled the bank to the steps leading to her house. Jessica's future self, retreating.

Not so bad.

Back on the water the ocean was spread out for her like butter, like a path she was set on. The clean wake arrowing out from the back of the boat, the nose of it pointed in the only direction possible.

'Want to go hunting, girl? Want to go get him? Catch him? Hey?'

Portia sat up. The boat rocked. She barked, excited. Jessica shushed her.

'Good girl. There's my good girl.'

And the ocean parting before her like a scene from her mother's Bible. She felt the gun in her pocket.

'Come at me,' she said, quietly. 'Just come at me now.'

Jessica knelt down in the damp leaf litter and held the fragment of shirt out for Portia to sniff. The dog snuffled at the fabric then licked her hand. Would this work? You had to train dogs to do this kind of thing. The puppy whined, perhaps remembering Matthew's scent from the attack on William. Then she jumped up to put her paws on Jessica's shoulders and lick her face.

It was stupid to think this tiny baby dog would lead Jessica anywhere. But she felt safer.

'You've got me, I'm afraid,' said Marijam. 'I'm slowing down these days. Run ahead if you need to. I'm good on my own anyway. You okay with that arrangement?'

Jessica nodded. The others paired up and set out. She let Marijam lead the way. She was quick for an old lady, using a walking stick like a third leg. Jessica found her feet slipping in the mud where Marijam was sure-footed. When Portia pulled, Jessica slipped and landed heavily on her bottom. She began to wish she had brought her own walking stick.

'My father used to be a logger around here,' said Marijam. A quiet sure voice. Jessica hurried forward to hear.

'I used to go with him sometimes. Tough work. Took a day or two to get a tree out of here. They'd only pick the big old ones. Roll them out on wooden tracks, float them down the river up to Geeveston. Not like now. Come in and clear-fell a patch in an hour.' She shone her torch up towards the treetops and laughed. 'There! Look it.'

Jessica looked up to the canopy but saw nothing but leaves bathed in torchlight.

'No, lower, down...there, there where the light...'

Jessica saw it. A bit of something sticking out of the side of a sturdy trunk. A peg of some sort, wood or metal.

'Used those to climb up the trees. Take one at a time. Big old trees they were, not like now. And all the things we'd see, quolls and devils and wallaby. He'd talk about the tigers. Shooting them. Everyone shot them. He wasn't so sure they took the sheep like the authorities said. He thought it was something else, something fiercer. Tigers were pretty docile. But he needed the bounty so he shot them anyway.'

Portia stopped; sniffed. Jessica tried to pull her on, but she growled deep in her throat.

'There you go,' said Marijam, stopping, turning back to stand, hands on hips, staring at the dog. 'She's a good dog you got there. I told you so. She's got him.'

'William's,' said Jessica.

'Huh?'

'She's William's dog.'

'Ah. Well, she's got a score to settle there. Looks like she might be yours now, though...She's bonded. You might have to apply for custody. Or co-parent.' Marijam smiled.

Jessica could see the little girl who used to play in these forests. The wicked humour, the naughty grin.

'Oop! Mind where she takes us,' said Marijam.

The dog was pulling Jessica off the track, into the frightening clumping of trees. Into the thick dark. Jessica held fast to her gun and let the dog lead her. They were travelling fast now, pushing between tree trunks and over thorny bushes. And for a while, miraculously, Marijam kept pace with her, until she stopped and shrugged.

'Just take the lead,' Marijam said. 'I'll catch you. I know all this area round here.'

Jessica didn't know the forest at all, but she trusted Portia, held fast to her lead.

When the trees eased out into rocky ground she began to feel like she had been here before. Then the dog stopped at the rock face, at an overhang, an entrance, and she knew exactly where they were.

Her cave, Winter Cave. Not the main entrance, but a hidden side passage that she had been down only once or twice. She stepped into the cave and looked up. A few little lights here and there. And when she looked at any one of them directly, it disappeared.

'Hello, my friends,' she whispered to the glow-worms of Winter Cave.

Jessica used the torch on her phone, wishing she had red cellophane to protect the glow-worms from the glare. Portia sniffed, tail hanging seriously, pointing down at the floor of the cave. She zigzagged her way towards the cave wall, picked a turn and then another. There were so many networked paths and Jessica was being led away from her familiar routes. At every turn she looked up; the lights blinked above her, waving her forward. She held tight to the lead and let the dog drag her along. She tried to remember the complicated twists and turns but it was impossible to keep track.

The dog stopped; Jessica waited. She was disoriented. She looked up but the ceiling was dark. What? Every passageway had its own little colony of *Arachnocampa tasmaniensis*. You rarely found a part of the cave networks without a few of the little lights.

The dog made her mind up and turned towards an entrance, and Jessica followed. The passageway twisted for a bit, then opened out into a large cavern.

Someone had made a house here.

That was Jessica's first thought. There were wooden pallets stacked up in neat formations, platforms for shelving and benches; then she noticed the bottles.

Home brewing. She was used to the bottles that Matthew kept under their shack. This looked just like that, only the bottles were bigger and there were tubes feeding into them, tubes and funnels. She took a sharp breath in and the air in here burned her lungs. A sharp smell. Unpleasant. She wasn't sure what she was looking at, but it couldn't be home brew.

She turned her phone off and looked up. The roof of the cave here was dark, desolate. She aimed her phone upwards and switched the torch back on. The webs that must have held the worms were all empty now. On a low overhang nearby she saw the shrivelled body of a dead worm still hanging from its silken thread.

Something had happened, a glow-worm apocalypse.

And with that thought she felt a tightness in her chest. She tried to breathe in but there was something stopping her. The air was poison, was it going to kill her? She heard her pulse throbbing in her temple, let go of Portia's lead and pressed her palms against her too-quick heart.

Jesus, a full-on panic attack—not poison at all. The dog was sniffing around the buckets and bottles and…She had seen this kind of set-up in movies, Friday night crime shows. A drug lab. Meth, that's what it looked like. Cooking meth in a glow-worm cave in a national park…why…?

But Portia was growling low and deep in her throat. Then she turned, stared straight at Jessica and barked. Picking up on the panic? Jessica forced herself to breathe again. Tried to calm the stupid heartbeat.

'Hey, girl,' she said, holding her hands in front of her, trying to ease the dog's stress too, but Portia barked again and her lips curled back in a sharp-toothed snarl.

Jessica backed away, but the dog stalked towards her, growling, a constant low threat, her back legs tensed. She leapt, and Jessica brought the gun up quickly, stumbled to one side, followed the arc of the dog's body with the barrel of the gun. Her finger tensed on the trigger but when the dog landed, snapping and snarling, she could see there was something on the ground there. She fumbled with the phone, almost dropped it, aimed the light towards the crouching figure.

The phone was in her left hand, the gun in her right. She saw a leg kick out, connect with the dog's ribs, send her rolling and yelping towards the nearest pallet. There was a rattle of glass, something falling, smashing, the dog barking, claws scrabbling on rock.

Matthew curled up to standing. His body glistened in the light from the phone. He was naked and when he unfurled his spine she could see the pale flesh shadowed between his legs. She remembered that footage on his phone, the slow curl from beast to man.

Not just a man.

Jessica kept her finger steady on the trigger.

Portia leapt. Matthew swung his hands like a club and Jessica felt the blow as if it had connected with her own chest. She stilled her breath. Sighted along the barrel of the gun.

'Jessica!'

She squeezed the trigger, but the sound of his voice had been enough to twitch her hand and the bullet thudded into the rock wall behind him.

It *was* Matthew. His voice hurt and small, a damaged thing. The voice of never-meant-to-hurt-you. Every time the apology, the excuse, this tiny voice. This damaged little boy–man.

And she had missed. She never missed. Matthew had made her doubt herself yet again.

He was running. Jessica saw the shine on the floor where he had been, a little pool of blood, a trail of blood. She hadn't missed. She had wounded him.

She called after him but he was gone. She looked down to where Portia was cowering, whimpering.

And William back in the hospital in Hobart.

'*Fuck*,' she said, and to the dog, 'Stay, girl. Stay. I'll be back. Just stay.'

She held the gun high and straight. She felt each step, sure and firm, slow at first and then faster as she turned and turned again through the snaking corridors. The ground was slippery but she was used to it here. She turned a corner, gun first, felt herself climbing as the floor sloped upwards. There were lights here, little lights glowing steadily above her. They were like a chorus, urging her on with their glow. Her colony. Undefeated.

She heard a sound ahead; picked up pace. The passageway crouched down around her and she kept moving forward, on her knees now. And when it fanned out into three large entryways she paused; listened. Swung the light down and found a spot of blood. She took the middle path.

She was gaining on him. She could feel it. Each sure step one step closer and her hands were raised. She was ready. A sound behind her.

She turned. Something…a shuffling sound, getting closer. She stood her ground. She could hear her heartbeat, the blood thundering through her body, trembling her hand. She took a breath to still it.

At the Olympics they have an event where you have to run, jump, shoot. Jessica had stumbled on it one day back in Toowoomba, before Matthew. She watched, imagining how fast your heart would beat after running up to the target, how skilfully the competitors drew breath, steadied, aimed, fired. She felt the pulse in her wrist. Her gun was ticking up, down. She took a breath, held it. She rested her finger on the trigger, ready to squeeze.

Marijam.

She exhaled.

The woman stopped, frowned at the gun. 'You shoot it?'

Jessica shook her head. She turned back towards the mess of corridors. She listened.

'Heard your shot. Thought you'd got it.'

'Winged him.'

'Good.'

There was a sound, a distant scrambling. Jessica ran, quick and steady, winding her way through the labyrinth, faster, leaving Marijam shuffling slowly behind.

Gun first around each corner—like a cop on a late-night TV show, she thought, camera light down till she swung around. She used to practise this in the compound when she was a kid. Playing End Times, the sinners coming at her like zombies through the corridors of the old church. She was transported back now to that simple game. Goodies, baddies, the sinners, the saved. Jessica, Matthew.

She had no doubt now. She would pull the trigger.

The mountain was honeycomb. The soft curve of intersecting paths. She looked up and saw the vaults open above her. Sidestepped chasms that spiralled down to darkness. She felt the damp rock wall and knew she was home. The shack wasn't home. The shack was Matthew's place, his family's place. The shack was a trap he had made for her, and like a lame animal she had sat in the snare waiting for him to come home each day. *I'm all you have*, he had told her and, like an idiot, she had made it true.

She held the gun up: straight and steady. Running towards her target. Fast, accurate. Monitoring her heart rate, controlling her breath.

These turns were familiar now. She looked up, saw the glow. Her colony. The corridor branched up ahead; she knew it before she saw it: three caverns at the end of three twisting paths.

She stopped and listened.

He was in her territory now. She knew these caves intimately. The centre path was a dead end, the cave to the right had an exit but it involved a climb. She turned left, walking slowly now. She swung the light ahead and the cave opened up around her. Damp teeth glittering up from the mineral ground, a curving curtain from above and then the drips that had gathered over thousands of years. His eyes were bright in the light, just his eyes visible as he crouched behind the outcrop of stalagmites. She stepped forward. Her finger was careful and sure on the trigger.

'I've got you, Matthew,' she said, surprised by the calm of her voice. 'Give up now.'

There was something wrong with his movement. Crawling, dragging, a little hop in his step. She moved closer.

It wasn't Matthew. The head turned and she saw the long muzzle, the mouth opening, deep and full of tiny teeth. She had never seen anything like this: nothing like a dog or a cat; something other. Something rare. It darted forward, found the rock wall and paced back again, sensing it was trapped, trying to the left, then to the right, then back again. Its haunches were oddly heavy, as if it were dragging its hips. Its tail was long and bushed out slightly towards the end. Its ears were pricked and its eyes were small and flinty. The stripes were almost luminous in the light from her phone. And it was small. Too small for the word *tiger*.

'Shoot it!'

Marijam, standing at the entry to the cave behind her, and the sound of her voice startled the tiger. She saw it crouch, then hop, balancing on its curved back legs, its feet delicately touching the stalagmites before it started its pacing once more.

Marijam went to push past but Jessica sidestepped to block her path. The creature sniffed around the rock formations; Jessica watched it. Each flinch of fur, each tic of an ear; the turn of head and gape of jaw. She watched as the creature turned and locked eyes with her, and it was extraordinary. She felt a strange looseness in her chest just looking at the animal. As if she had been transported into some wilder past, communing with something ancient. She stared and the animal stared back. If it was him, Matthew, she would know.

There was nothing of Matthew in its eyes. She wasn't scared of it. It was a thing of wonder.

Marijam reached for her hand, for the gun. Jessica flinched, holding her hand high, but Marijam was wiry and strong. The old woman curled her hand around Jessica's fingers and clenched her hand on the trigger and the sound of the shot filled the cave, her cave.

The glow-worms shivered in their tiny webs. The tiger yipped and yowled. It was the sound of a baby in distress, an alien baby. She watched it turn and push past a pillar at the back of the cave. There would be an exit there. She knew where it was: too small for a man to walk upright, perfect for someone crawling or something running on all fours. The passage led down to the underground stream. She knew it. She had tracked it once: thrown luminous glow-sticks into a trickle and followed them down. Through the honeycomb to the stream under Winter Cave, out at Exit Cave.

A hard climb, but a clear and even path. She noticed the creature limping: some pain in a back leg.

'You let him go,' Marijam hissed.

'It wasn't him.' She sounded sure. But that limping—she had shot Matthew in the leg. It wasn't him. It couldn't be him.

'It was the tiger,' said Marijam.

'A tiger.' Jessica nodded. She lowered her gun. 'A thylacine,' she said, relieved that she could hear certainty in her own voice. 'Just think about that.' She stepped forward, towards the place where the tiger had disappeared, and shone the light on the ground. Little drops of blood.

Jessica breathed out. She felt light-headed, as if something fragile and heavy had finally fallen away, a shell she had been hauling around with her without even knowing.

'I know where it's going.'

She didn't need to hurry now. There was an easy way, a shorter way. She turned a corner, Marijam fast on her heels, and there was the sound of water and the clear stream at their feet. She stepped into it, felt it lapping at her ankles. The tunnel came out behind a curtain of flowstone. Jessica raised her gun, just in case. Just in case. She heard a scramble, felt a surge of wanting: she wanted to see it again, a thing so rare, a creature of myth.

A shuffling sound, an awkward drag, a body moving into view. Matthew.

Jessica frowned. Above her a thousand larvae glowed. They were awake now. This was the peak time, hunting time. They were on their highest alert.

She kept her gun steady.

'Don't move.'

But he did move. Into a crouch. His lips dragged back into a snarl.

There was a sound behind her, a scrabbling on the slippery stone. She felt Portia push against her legs, race ahead, heard the deafening bark rattle the walls of the cave.

'Stop,' Jessica called; then, ridiculously: 'Heel!'

The dog didn't stop. Matthew ignored the rush of fur and

teeth, was staring straight at Jessica as his muscles tensed in the crouch and he leapt at her, his arms outstretched, his fingers bent into claws, teeth bared. She felt a shiver of horror along her arms. He was coming for her, suspended in air, aimed like a bullet in her direction, and Portia leaping towards him. Two beasts of flesh and fur and hair on an inevitable trajectory.

She breathed out. Pulled the trigger. Matthew fell.

Portia landed on his chest and shuddered there, growling, trembling, snapping.

In Jessica's dreams there had been a wave of wet, a hot sluice of blood, and she felt it now. Not his blood, but her own, flooding to her face, her hands, her shoulders. A rush of adrenaline. She felt awake, alive.

Portia turned and ran towards her, barking. Jessica dropped to her knees and there was the dog, licking her face in an ecstasy of relief. Marijam's hand on her shoulder, warm and solid. Jessica felt the calm, steady breath.

Matthew lay in the river. A trail of blood seeping out of him and flowing out with the clear mountain stream. Jessica could see something twitch in the torchlight, a tiny pale fish, nibbling at his neck, his chin.

'I've been asleep,' she said. 'I've been fast asleep.'

Marijam laughed harshly. 'Well, this racket would wake the dead, I reckon.'

The dog looked up before they heard the footsteps. A single yip; not angry this time.

Maude had her gun raised. She lowered it as she approached. 'Heard the shots. Thought you might need some help here.'

Marijam shook her head.

Crystal pushed towards Jessica, stared at the body on the ground then opened her arms. The tight drum of the belly between them, the kick of the child. Only a matter of weeks now before it would be out in the world. She hugged and let herself be hugged and felt a tickle of breath on her neck.

'See?' It was a whisper in the high-pitched little voice. 'It's going to be all right now. You just do what you have to do, then get on with it. We're good like that. Tough as nails.'

They stepped out into the stone cathedral. There were still signs. All these weeks later and there were traces of what had happened here. A scrap of police tape, heavy boot prints in the silt, a filter from a cigarette, a nail. She bent and picked up the nail and slipped it into her pocket.

'You okay?' William stepped towards her, took her hand. He still had a limp, but it bothered her more than it seemed to bother him. *Six months off work*, he had said, raising his arm to high-five her, but she had only frowned, feeling the guilt settle heavy on her shoulders.

Jessica looked around the cave now. Just small traces. All the blood cleaned off, all the drug paraphernalia taken in as evidence.

It was self-defence. Of course it was, how could it not be? And yet Jessica had hesitated before her plea. She was guilty. She still woke up from her recurring nightmares bathed in sweat, wondering where she was in the world.

Here. She was here. With William, and Portia, doubled in size now, sleeping quietly at home in Hobart, a good girl, such a good girl.

'You okay?'

She took a shuddering breath in. 'Yeah,' she said. 'Yeah. I'm okay.'

'You ready for this?'

Jessica felt tears pricking her eyes. She wasn't ready for this. She would never be ready for this. But she nodded. She had come all the way back down here. What else was there to do?

Tomorrow she would start work at the university.

If not today, then when?

'Come,' he said. 'I need to sit down for a bit.'

They sat on the cave floor. It was cold, but warmer than it had been back then in the dead of winter. She remembered the cold that night. She remembered.

She held her breath. She reached out and took William's hand.

'One,' said William, he squeezed her fingers gently and she liked him; she might even love him. He was a good man. There were good men, and this was one of them.

'Two,' said William, and before he could take a breath she said it.

'Three.'

She turned the torch off. She kept her eyes shut. She tilted her head towards the sky. On the next in-breath she opened them.

Darkness. And in the darkness a glimmer. A little light; two of them, three. A few more just at the mouth of the cave.

'They're coming back!' she said, breathless. 'They're resilient little buggers, aren't they?'

He squeezed her hand again but remained silent.

'Look at them shine.' She felt something on her cheek, water, a drip from a stalactite, but then another and another, and she knew she was crying.

'Turn the torch on,' said William.

But she said, 'No. Not yet.'

And she cried quietly, and she held his big warm hand and she looked up to the cave roof which was the sky and one by one the stars blinked on and there was her universe, coming good, getting on with it: hunting, waking, living.

'Are you looking?' she said to William. 'What do you see?'

'Stars,' he said. 'What do you see?'

'Everything,' said Jessica. She let go of his hand in the dark. 'It's beautiful.'

ACKNOWLEDGMENTS

Thank you first and always to Text Publishing, such a brilliant publisher. I am a massive fan of your list. And in particular to my editor, Mandy Brett, midwife to this and many of my books. And to Jane Novak, my agent and my friend, who plucked this book out of my 'maybe it won't ever see the light of day' pile and made me take a second look at it. See what you have done? Text, Mandy, Jane, your belief keeps me upright and heading back to my desk. Your behind-the-scenes work is what keeps the world of literature turning.

This book would not have happened without Barry and Denise Elphick. Visiting you has been a wonderful excuse to explore Tasmania and to discover Southport and the caves. And to my dad, Barry in particular, who was never too busy to take me to the many locations described in this book. What marvellous adventures we have been on, on land and on the sea.

Thank you also to Emerald Roe, who generously provided me with a Southport shack which may or may not be featured in this book.

Thanks to Anthony Mullins, who braved the scary, wondrous forests alongside me and who adeptly pointed out the structural flaws in my story, working side by side with me on the screenplay version of this book to set us on the right path. You are my first and best collaborator. In particular I feel like you are a participant in the writing of this book. You certainly made it better and our filmic iteration of it may be even better still. May we create many beautiful things together for all the years that we have left.

Thanks also to the generous Lauren McGrow, who took me to Hastings (covertly) and Mystery caves and plied me with mulled wine, good food and even better stories.

To my sciency network, to Amanda Niehaus, Emily Purton, Nigel Beebee, Alicia Sometimes, Tamara Davis. And to the glow-worm scientists who were so generous with their knowledge and allowed me to mirror their research like a great big literary thief: Claire Baker, Arthur Clarke and David Merritt. You guys were my guiding lights in the darkness of the last days with this book.

This book is a shout out to the women in my life. I would like to single out my main crew here: Kristina Olsson, Katherine Lyall Watson, Ashley Hay, Ellen Van Neerven, Mirandi Riwoe (my first readers), Fiona Stager, Rebecca Harbison, Melissa Lucashenko, Kate Harrison, Michaela McGuire, Jackie Ryan, Carody Culver, Maureen Burns, Anita Heiss, Anna Krien, Susan Hornbeck, Bronte Coates, Suzie Miller, Claire Christian, Susan Johnson, Adele Pickvance, Kasia Janczewski, Rachel Edwards, Indy Medeiros, Linda Jaivin, Favel Parrett, Sally Piper, Cass Moriarty, Annie Te Whiu, Helen Bernhagen, Marieke Hardy, Greta Moon, Judy Horacek, Silvia Cosier, Léa Antigny, Jay Court, Sarah Lynch, Cora Roberts, Michelle Law, Tracey Chin, Jen Clark, Tania Christianson, Gillian Berthold, Fiona Macdonald—high five, sisters. Please keep teaching me stuff and challenging me.

And in memory of Cory Taylor and Narelle Oliver, who were both present and supportive during the writing of this book and who have carved out big holes in my life that can't be filled.

Also to the women who raised and made me: Lotty, Wendy, Sheila and Karen. I am you in my blood and in my bones. There is no separating us in art or in life.

To the men, trans and gender-queer folk who have my back, my gratitude, always. With particular mention of Trent Jamieson, Chris Somerville, Benjamin Law, Scotty Spark, Steven Amsterdam, Corey DeNeef, Ronnie Scott, Sam Cooney, David Stavanger, Jason Reed, Rae White, Ben Hackworth, Liam Pieper, Chris Currie, Colin Cosier, James Cosier, Martin Cosier, Ian Cosier, James Butler.

Thanks to my Avid Reader and Where the Wild Things Are family and in particular to Sarah Lynch, who I tortured with roster changes, going away every five minutes to write and edit this book.

This book was written while procrastinating—I was supposed to be writing a different manuscript with the support of the Australia Council for the Arts, so that funding was a two-for-one. Thanks, OzCo! See what a bit of financial support can do?

An early draft of a chapter from this novel was published in *Island* magazine.

And finally I would like to thank Gerard Donovan, who gave me my very first blurb for my very first book. Your novel *Julius Winsome* has been in my heart for the longest time and it kept resonating while I was working on this book. I have always wanted to write something as good as that, and it's a goal I continue to strive for.